# INTRODUCTION

*Strawberry Angel* by Pamela Griffin
Noelle accidentally dyes her hair a shocking strawberry pink, which is the catalyst that brings two adorable homeless children and their sick mother into her life. It also reunites her with Todd, her high school crush. With Christmas coming, Todd helps Noelle build a set and direct rehearsals for a play at the women's shelter where she volunteers. Can this "strawberry Christmas" be one to remember?

*Angel Charm* by Tamela Hancock Murray
Charm school owner Lydia Winters is known as one of the most engaging woman at her church. Yet despite her prayers, the Lord hasn't seen fit to send her a godly husband. But when her high school sweetheart Drake Kingston, now a widower with a rebellious daughter in tow, returns to town, can the flame reignite with the help of a child's crafted angel? Or will Lydia once again discover she shouldn't play with fire?

*Angel on the Doorstep* by Sandra Petit
Finding a stray crocheted angel gives Moira Sullivan the idea to make some angels of her own, which she delivers anonymously to every person on the hard working staff at First Christian Church. When Joe Corrigan discovers Moira is the secret gift giver, he coerces her into letting him help with the project. Will this forced togetherness bring them closer together or farther apart?

*An Angel for Everyone* by Gail Sattler
Kim is pleased with the beaded angel ornaments she's made as party favors for the church's annual Christmas party until Trent points out that there won't be 30 people attending, but 300. When the shock wears off and Trent offers to help make more, Kim doesn't know whether to be happy or terrified. She's tried to get Trent's attention for years, but he's never taken her seriously. Will his participation now make things better or worse?

# angels for christmas

Published by Barbour Publishing, Inc., P.O. Box 719, Uhrichsville, Ohio 44683
www.barbourbooks.com

*Our mission is to publish and distribute inspirational products offering exceptional value and biblical encouragement to the masses.*

ecpa Member of the
Evangelical Christian
Publishers Association

Printed in the United States of America.
5 4 3 2 1

# angels for christmas

*Crafty Little Angels Put Their Charm
Into Four Holiday Romances*

PAMELA GRIFFIN
TAMELA HANCOCK MURRAY
SANDRA PETIT
GAIL SATTLER

BARBOUR
PUBLISHING

# strawberry angel

## by Pamela Griffin

# Dedication

To all those who helped by critiquing this,
I extend a huge thank-you, especially to Mom
(who went above and beyond)!
A special note of appreciation goes to Sally Daniels
and shelter director Brenda Jackson (www.bwf1.com)
for their help regarding the subject of women's shelters.
And to my boys, Brandon and Joshua—
I sure enjoyed making the angel crafts with you for this book!
Thanks for being my two special guys.
As always, I dedicate this story to my patient Lord,
who's often worked through my foolish and embarrassing
blunders to the benefit of others—
revealing His glory in the process.

# Chapter 1

Noelle surmised that the addition of one more December birthday to lump with her previous twenty-two must have caused her brain to flip— or fry. After all, what idiot would take on a hair-dying job the day of a fund-raising banquet?

She would.

With only four hours to go until the big event, Noelle rushed to make it on time, but she wanted classy, dark auburn hair to go with the new bronze velvet evening dress she'd nabbed at a warehouse sale last week. Mousy brown just didn't cut it for her, and this had been the first opportunity she'd had to color her hair since she'd needed to work overtime at Odds & Ends Craft Supplies the past several days.

She groped for an oversized towel and threw it over her rinsed head. To avoid having any smelly fumes irritate her eyes, she kept them squeezed shut as she'd done throughout most of the process. Twisting the velour towel turban-style, she straightened from the sink. Steam still covered the mirror, so she couldn't see her image. She looked down at her hands and noticed the maroon polish on her nails had chipped. Great. One more thing for her to do.

Over the loud whir of the exhaust fan, a knock sounded at the front door of her duplex. She stopped rummaging through a shoe box of half-filled glass bottles containing a wide spectrum of nail polishes. What was that rule about being busy in the bathroom and the phone or doorbell ringing?

She slipped her glasses on and headed for the door, casting a glance at her baggy, gray, water-splotched sweat suit. It was probably just Shannon. Her neighbor had a habit of popping over unannounced. Noelle swung the door wide, expecting to see Shannon's elfin features.

Instead, rich cocoa-brown eyes in the handsome face of a deliveryman stared back. Impulsively, Noelle clapped a hand over the towel mound to keep it in place, her mind refusing to believe what her still burning eyes clearly showed her.

"Hi," he said, his voice smooth. "I have a package for you. I'll need you to sign for it."

Noelle's heart jumped. This could not be happening! Avoiding his curious stare, she accepted the stylus and poised her hand above the electronic keyboard where he pointed, putting her other hand to the bottom of the gadget he held to help keep it steady.

Her weighty towel began to topple backward. Trying to prevent its further downslide, she hunched her shoulders and scrunched her head lower, like a turtle retreating into its shell. But gravity was having its way.

"Sorry—I'll just be a second." She thrust the stylus and electronic keyboard at him, minus her signature, and partially closed the door, so he couldn't see her. She wished she could ooze into the tufts of sand-colored carpet and disappear.

Todd Brentley—the guy for whom she would have gladly given away all her teen idol magazines in tenth grade for just one date—stood on the other side of her door. And here she stood in matted, fuzzy blue slippers, with unmade face and wet hair hidden in a towel—and wearing her sloppiest clothes to boot!

She whipped the towel off and bent at the waist to retie it around her head. Vivid pink hair—not auburn—streamed down in wet clumps before her eyes.

"Agh!" She gave a strangled cry.

A tap sounded on the door. "Miss, you all right in there?"

Noelle shot to a standing position, wet hair slinging into her face. "Don't come in! I'm fine. I—I'll be right with you."

Gulping in a breath, she tried to think. She had no idea what had gone wrong, but she couldn't very well stand here and dwell on this latest calamity now, not with Todd perched on her doorstep. She swept the loathsome hair back, slapped the towel over her head like a hood, and clutched it under her chin. Determined to act as calm as possible under the circumstances, she swung the door open.

Todd turned from staring at the boxwoods that flanked the duplex. "Everything okay?"

"Terrific. Would you mind holding that thing steady while I sign?"

He gave a puzzled grin. "Sure. I always do. Sorry I caught you at a bad time."

"That's okay." She was surprised that she wrote her name legibly and the electronic signature didn't look too much like chicken scratch from the way her hand was shaking—though with these computer contraptions the delivery company used, her signature always managed to look like a second grader's who'd just started penmanship. Tacking on what she hoped passed for a smile, she handed the stylus back to him.

His gaze was plastered to her forehead, with something close to horrified fascination. "Thanks. Here's your package," he said, not looking away from that spot.

"Thank you." Noelle snatched the box from him.

He seemed to collect himself and gave her one of his dissolve-your-knees-into-puddles smiles, his teeth as white and even as always. "Have a nice holiday."

"You, too." Noelle backed into her apartment and shut the door, exhaling a relieved breath. Unable to resist, she hurried to the window and peeked through a chink in the cream-colored curtains, watching as Todd sauntered toward his brown delivery truck. Looking down at the electronic device in his hand, he suddenly stopped.

"Oh no," Noelle whispered as he turned, gave her door a probing glance, then strode back up the sidewalk, his long-legged gait quickly eating up the distance.

He remembered.

Noelle listened for the inevitable knock, praying she would make it through the rest of this afternoon without tearing her hair out.

On second thought, that might not be such a bad idea.

When the swift rap came, she stayed as still as a cardinal hiding from a curious cat, hoping he would just go away and think her busy in the back room. She should have remembered his stubborn streak. After his third knock, she tossed what she assumed to be her father's Christmas gift onto the sofa and crammed the errant strand that stuck to her forehead as far back as it would go beneath the towel. She inched open the door, putting her eye to the crack. "Yes?"

"Sorry to bother you," he said, his brow crinkling in a cute, boyish way, "but I was wondering if you're the same Noelle Sanders I went to Omega High with. The package said 'N. L. Sanders,' and you signed your name as Noelle. Not a very common name. At least, I don't think it is."

He rubbed a hand along the back of his neck, looking uncertain. It struck her as odd that the most popular guy in her graduating class could feel such a thing as embarrassment. Yet as much as she would prefer to remain anonymous, she couldn't lie.

"I went to Omega High," she admitted through the fraction of space between door and lintel.

A hundred-watt smile lit his face. "I thought you looked familiar! I'm Todd. Todd Brentley. You sat behind me in Art Appreciation during our sophomore and junior years. You helped me with my homework, too. Remember?"

How could she forget? Noelle nodded and reluctantly opened the door wider. She'd spent most of the time in class staring dreamily at his broad shoulders covered by his letter jacket and noticing how the fluorescent light picked out red highlights in his mahogany-dark hair—instead of concentrating on the teacher. Despite her eagerness to help by tutoring him with his English and aiding him in art, her own disappointing overall grade of a B-minus that semester had reflected her inattentiveness.

"So what are you doing back in Hartford Falls?" he asked, breaking into her thinking balloon. "I heard you'd come home."

"I found I prefer small-town life."

"Really? Maybe some afternoon we could get together and talk over old times."

"Sure." She politely smiled, doubting he would follow through.

"Well, I guess I'd better hit the road." Todd's gaze went to her toweled head. "You look busy, and I've got plenty of deliveries to make. Christmas rush, you know."

"Yeah. See you around."

After Todd drove off with a farewell wave, Noelle made a beeline for her bedroom to assess the damage. With the minutes growing scanter, she wasn't sure what to do.

Pulling off the towel, she glared at her pink-topped image in the dresser mirror. She grabbed the bottle of hair coloring standing next to a box with dark auburn curls pictured on front, and scanned the bottle's label. Nothing. She turned it over and saw a name printed on the bottom. PINK FUSION. *Not* Auburn Sunset. This bottle did not match that box. Someone had switched them.

Her first impulse to call the drugstore was eclipsed when she saw the time. Her complaint would have to wait until tomorrow. Less than three hours remained for her to figure out what to wear. She toyed with the idea of staying home, but she couldn't do that to her best friend, Cindy, who'd organized the event. But one thing was certain; bronze velvet did not go with Pink Fusion.

Todd thought about Noelle as he made the rest of his deliveries for the afternoon. When he'd transmitted the delivery information to the centralized database with his handheld DIAD while walking back to his truck, he had really looked at her signature on the screen for the first time—and realized then who she was.

He'd heard that she worked for a lucrative advertising firm in the Big Apple and wondered what had happened to cause her to return to their small town. According to his mom, the firm had planned to give Noelle a promotion, before she up and quit her job without explanation. Now she worked at a craft store and volunteered at the local women's shelter, which her friend Cindy directed. Seemed a step down for her to work retail, but he did admire her generosity in helping out at the shelter.

One thing about his mom, she was a wealth of information. Even if her news did border on gossip at times, Todd was grateful for the info he'd collected about Noelle. She still seemed a bit zany, but it was her zaniness that made him smile. Like when he didn't get the football scholarship his senior year because of an injury on the field that resulted in him never being able to play football again. Noelle had come alone to visit him at the hospital, holding a bouquet of helium balloons on which she'd drawn silly faces. The entire time, she'd cracked jokes and made her own silly faces to get him to laugh. And he had. Neither his family nor his other classmates and friends who'd visited had been able to extract more than a weak smile from him. But Noelle had made him laugh.

Todd glanced at his watch. Only one hour until curtain time and the role he'd promised Mom he would take on for the cause. He wondered if Noelle would be at the banquet and grinned at the thought of seeing her again. Too bad he hadn't thought to ask her earlier.

Exiting her car, Noelle was careful not to step on the hem of her rose-colored dress. Her brand-new dress still hung in her closet, waiting for an event when her hair didn't clash with the bronze velvet. She slammed the door shut, grimacing when her faint image reflected in the dark window. Well, there was nothing to do but grit her teeth, smile, and make the best of things. Because of the holiday season, both salons in town were booked solid through New Year's Eve. Even though she'd begged, no hair stylist had an opening to take her and try to fix the bad dye job, though a receptionist had taken her name in case a customer canceled. So she'd crammed her pink locks into a loose style atop her head and hoped for the best.

Noelle hurried through the crowded convention center parking lot and pulled open the heavy glass door. A glittery sign on a pedestal at the entrance pointed the way to the grand ballroom. Her heels sank into spongy blue carpet as she rushed through the double doors of the enormous area.

Spotting her mother near a table catty-cornered to the large stage, Noelle darted by the edge of the milling crowd, hoping to make herself as inconspicuous as possible on the way to greet her. This corner of the room was semi-dark, the high brass chandelier in the middle of the carved ceiling above the dance floor the only source of light. And that light was thankfully dimmed.

"Noelle! There you are. Wow, girl, what've you done to your hair?"

Obviously not dimmed enough.

Noelle faced her friend, Cindy, with a forced smile. "Interesting, isn't it?"

A short, blond man stood by Cindy's side. His gaze bounced up to Noelle's upswept hair, then down to her satin floor-length gown and up again.

"Hmm," Cindy murmured, "well you've outdone yourself this time, that's for sure. It's pretty, though. You look sort of. . .Christmasy."

"Thanks," Noelle said with a grimace.

Cindy grinned, her own ivory lace dress complementing her cocoa-dark skin and shining, straight black hair. "Let me take your coat. I'll put it with mine in the closet behind the stage. Oh, and you'd better let your mother know you're here. She was searching for you earlier."

Noelle shrugged out of her fake white fur and handed it to her friend. "It looks like a good turnout. You should raise a sizeable amount for the home with this crowd."

Cindy's smile turned into a full-fledged grin. "Yeah, I'm surprised at the number of people from out of town who showed up—like Diamond Jim in the Stetson over there. And your mother's idea should be the crowning touch."

Noelle looked away from the heavyset man with the diamonds flashing from his fingers, wristwatch, and tie tack. "What idea?"

"You mean she didn't tell you? Well, you'll see soon enough. I have to go show Paul, here, the ropes. He's agreed to be in charge of the dinner music and change out the CDs. You probably haven't heard, but Will fell off a ladder this morning. His leg's in a cast. The band had to cancel."

"You're kidding!"

"I wish I was. I don't know who's going to finish building that set for our play, what with Will laid up and Christmas coming in less than four weeks. You can still direct the kids, of course. You don't really need a stage for that. By the way, excuse my bad manners. This is Paul Reily. He's new in town. Paul, Noelle Sanders."

He gave a short nod, and Noelle managed a smile before Cindy whisked him away toward a sound system near the stage.

Bracing herself, Noelle joined her mother at the front. Her mom's soft peach cashmere dress was perfect for her slender build and blended beautifully with her ash-blond hair. She appeared professional yet elegant at the same time.

"Hi, Mom. Your daughter's here."

Her mother turned from talking with a tall, silver-haired gentleman. "Oh!" she exclaimed when she saw Noelle, her ready smile slipping into a stare of disbelief.

Excusing herself from the distinguished-looking man, she grabbed Noelle's elbow and led her to a long table covered with a cranberry red tablecloth and white lace overlay, one of many throughout the room. Out of hearing distance of the others, her mom lit right into her.

"You weren't kidding on the phone earlier. It really is Pink Fusion. What possessed you to dye your hair today of all days?"

Noelle felt as if her smile had frozen. She was surprised it hadn't cracked yet. "And a lovely evening to you, too, Mother."

Her mom gave an exasperated click of her tongue. "Your personal holiday makeovers almost always end in disaster—haven't you learned that yet? The colored contacts last year were bad enough when you lost one at the Christmas party and had to walk around with one green eye and one purple eye. But this! And wherever did you get that dress?" Her pained gaze scanned Noelle from head to toe.

"Oh, this old thing?" Noelle quipped. "Surely you remember when I was a bridesmaid in Lisa's wedding?"

"That was. . .four years ago. And in the spring, too." For a moment, her mother looked as if she might need to sit down. She eyed the short bell sleeves. "Aren't you cold?"

"It's crowded in here, and they do have central heating. This was all I could come up with on short notice. But I did wear my coat. I mean, I'm not completely loopy or anything." She gave a clipped laugh.

The look her mother sent questioned that statement. "At least the rose color does complement your hair," she amended. "And all that pink is pretty with your green eyes."

Noelle groaned. "Mother, please."

"Never mind. What's done is done. This is where you're to sit." Her mom gestured to one of the colorful place settings. A gilded name card sat propped near the silver-trimmed china with NOELLE SANDERS written in gold script. Her mother's was to her right.

"The decorating committee did a great job." Noelle hung her white satin pillbox purse over the back of her chair. "By the way, Cindy said you'd planned a surprise of some sort—"

"Oh, now what," her mother interrupted. "Mrs. Michaels is trying to get my attention. I hope another problem hasn't arisen. Sorry, dear. I'd better go see what's wrong." She hurried off, leaving a cloud of vanilla musk in her wake.

Noelle sank to the upholstered chair and eased out of her too-tight shoes. Four years they'd sat in a shoe box tucked away with this dress. Her feet must have grown. Rubbing one stocking foot over the other under the hidden covering of the floor-length tablecloth, she scanned the dressed-to-the-hilt crowd. Hopefully this banquet would begin soon so she could eat, donate her offering, and go home.

The lights grew brighter. A dark-haired woman in a glittering, red sequined dress took the stage and walked up to a standing microphone. "Good evening, ladies and gentlemen. Cindy Grafton, the director of the shelter, has asked me to emcee tonight. I'm Charla, and we're so pleased that you've come to help support our cause."

Settling back, Noelle listened as Charla outlined Haven of Hope ministries, describing it as a nonprofit organization with one hundred percent of its donations going to the shelter. With a sweet smile that would cause the world's worst miser to unzip his money belt, she thanked everyone for attending. "I do apologize for the delay with the meal," she added, "but due to van trouble, the catering service is running late. So we've decided to hold the auction first."

Noelle jerked to attention. *Auction? What auction?*

"Thanks to an ingenious suggestion from a member of the town council, we've added a twist to things this year, like nothing we've ever done before." Charla beamed at the crowd. "You ladies should be particularly interested. Especially those needing strenuous work done around your homes or places of business. The kind of work that requires heavy, manual labor. The kind of work that men do best."

Men in black tuxes walked from one of the wings backstage and filed into a single line behind the announcer. Each wore a red carnation on his lapel.

"Tonight, we're auctioning off the services of fourteen of Hartford Falls's very own. Men who've kindly volunteered their muscle to help us raise money to build a new wing for Haven of Hope. And what muscles they have, eh, ladies?"

Amid the snickers circulating the crowd, Noelle groaned. *This had to be Mother's idea. Only she would think up something as corny—and embarrassing—as this.*

"So ladies get out your checkbooks. And, men, don't feel you can't join in on the fun, too. I'm sure some of you could use another pair of hands to help paint that house or work on the roof. Oh—and for those who don't wish to participate but still want to make a donation, envelopes are provided at the back for your convenience, on the brochure table. Just nab one of the committee members afterward to give them your contribution. That said, let the games begin!" With these final words, the announcer swung her hand upward in a lighthearted gesture.

The last two men strode onstage and took a place beside their peers, turning to face the crowd. Noelle gasped and clutched the tablecloth.

Todd Brentley stood at the end of the line. And he seemed to be looking straight at her.

# Chapter 2

*W*hat's Todd doing here?

Noelle shook her head briskly, hoping the blood would flow back to her brain and she could think more clearly. Well, it was obvious what he was doing here, but why hadn't Mother told Noelle about this when she'd talked to her on the phone earlier? Surely she'd known.

Noelle compressed her lips. Oh, yes, she'd known. As chairwoman of the town council, her mother made it a point to be informed. And Noelle nurtured a sneaking suspicion of why her mother hadn't mentioned this tidbit to Noelle after her recounting of Todd's package delivery. She was trying to play matchmaker again. Anything to aid the cause of pairing off her daughter with a "nice boy" and get her married. On a hunch, Noelle glanced at the name card by the place setting to her left.

TODD BRENTLEY.

Noelle narrowed her eyes and sought her mother out in the crowd, while a woman exclaimed over winning the services of a landscaper to help with her garden. At last Noelle spotted the familiar peach dress. Her mother stood near the stage, watching the proceedings with rapt attention, a smile on her seemingly guileless face. Despairing of ever catching her mother's eye, Noelle swung her attention back to Todd.

A feast for the eyes was an understatement concerning this man. His black silk tux strained over broad shoulders. A crisp white shirt covered a lean but, she was certain, powerful chest. As if he'd just stepped in from outdoors, his dark hair had a sporty, windblown look. The stage lights picked up the twinkle in his eyes as he stared out over the crowd and gave them a good-natured grin.

*Mel, Brad, Antonio—eat your heart out.* Noelle vaguely listened as, one by one, the men were auctioned off—a grocer, a dentist, a construction worker, and more. But her attention never wavered from Todd.

Finally, it was his turn. Noelle watched as he took his place beside the announcer at the microphone, as the others had done. A sudden expression of interest shone on the emcee's face, and a cat's-got-the-cream smile formed on her red lips.

"I think I'll join in the bidding on this last round," Charla purred into the microphone. "I have chores needing done around the house. When a woman lives alone, the to-do list is constantly piling up." She let out a lilting laugh and lifted one scarlet nail into the air. "One hundred dollars."

Noelle bristled. Could she do that? Was the emcee even allowed to participate?

A chorus of frenzied bids rose around the room, increasing by twenty-five dollars each time. Heat flamed Noelle's cheeks. She was embarrassed for Todd, but mostly she was appalled by the behavior of her peers. Appalled and angry. Of the women who bid, Noelle recognized many as being single. They acted as if they'd never seen a man before.

Her focus swung back to Todd. Well, okay. Granted, they probably never had—not one like Todd Brentley anyway. Many men onstage were nice-looking, but Todd possessed charisma—always had. It probably had something to do with that breathtaking, boyish smile that could suddenly turn up to full power and light the room with a dazzling, melt-your-heart grin. Or maybe those velvety-brown eyes, full of mischief one moment, brimming with tenderness the next.

Charla bid again, topping the last offer of five hundred dollars.

Noelle shut her eyes. She couldn't watch any longer.

"One thousand dollars," a familiar, high-pitched voice sang out.

Noelle was going to die—then and there. If her heart beat any faster, it would jump out of her chest. Then again, that might be a blessing. At least death would remove her from this mortifying travesty.

Her mother wouldn't do this to her. She wouldn't. She may be responsible for a lot of things, but she wouldn't do this to her one and only daughter.

Noelle peeked one eye open to see her mother's peach cashmere sleeve lifted high in the air.

She would.

The exit sign over the fire escape door beckoned, only twenty or so feet away. Noelle could slip out of her chair and hurry to the door unnoticed. Right. Unnoticed—wielding a fluorescent beacon atop her head. Still it was worth a shot. This was worse than any measly fire. She considered it an emergency. By the time the alarms went off, she would be outside, racing away from this nightmare of a banquet. Of course, her coat was in a closet behind the stage, and the temperature had plummeted to the low twenties now that the sun was down.

"Congratulations, Mrs. Sanders," Charla said, voice resigned. "There doesn't seem to be any other bids. Todd Brentley is yours."

"And I have just the activity for him," Noelle's mother exclaimed. "One that will most certainly aid my daughter."

Noelle eyed the door again. What was a little cold air? Certainly no worse than being spotlighted in her mom's public matchmaking scheme. With her toes, she felt around for her satin pumps, found one, and quickly slid her foot inside, then searched for the other. Nothing but spongy carpet. She stretched her pointed toes further, holding on to the seat for balance, as her leg made a frantic sideways sweep for the missing shoe.

Nothing.

Desperate, Noelle dipped her head underneath the tablecloth and scanned the flowered expanse of carpet for the elusive rose satin slipper. Ah, there it was.

"Noelle, what are you doing?"

Startled by the suddenness of her mother's voice, Noelle shot up and bumped her head on the underside of the table.

"Ohhh," she groaned. Rubbing the sore spot, she awkwardly sat up—and gasped in shocked dismay.

Todd Brentley smiled down at her, obviously amused. "We meet again."

"Noelle," her mother's voice tinkled, as though the world had not just ended, "you remember Todd Brentley, don't you? Well, dear, he's all yours!"

Todd had never seen anyone whose face matched her hair. Noelle reminded him of his aunt's artificial Christmas tree. Bright pink all over.

Her rose-colored lips opened as if she would say something, then closed. A thick, pink curl fell from the top of her head, hitting her dark fringe of lashes and brushing against her cheek. She swept the tendril away with the back of one hand.

Strawberry soda pop mixed with a scoop of vanilla ice cream. That's what her hair reminded him of. The color of his favorite dessert when he was a boy.

"I'll be leaving you two now," Mrs. Sanders said.

Noelle's head whipped her way. "Oh, but—Mother. You're not actually leaving?" Her tense smile matched her voice, hinging on desperation.

"Not the banquet, of course. But I should mingle with the guests. It's expected of me. I'll return when the meal is served."

"But—we really should talk about this—"

"There's no need to thank me, dear. I'm always glad to help aid your cause in any way I can." Mrs. Sanders smiled benevolently, though Todd detected mischief in her expression before she glided away.

He pulled out the chair next to Noelle and sat down. "Great turnout."

"Yes." Her attention flicked to a nearby exit door.

"I had no idea there were so many wealthy people in our area. And I thought I knew just about everyone in town."

"Some live in Manhattan and other big cities," she said slowly after lengthy seconds elapsed. "I broadcasted news of the event through the local media—newspapers, radio—as well as fliers in the mail." Noelle turned impossibly green eyes his way—a vibrant holly green. But it was the anxious expression in them that arrested his attention.

"You okay?"

Half her mouth twisted up. "Let's just say that judging from the way my day has progressed, the events of this evening shouldn't really surprise me." She reached for her water glass, her hand noticeably shaking.

He tried to decipher that odd statement, then gave up and shrugged. "Your mother explained your situation. Just tell me when you want me. I'm always ready to aid a worthy cause."

Noelle choked. Pulling the glass from her mouth, she coughed and doubled over. Concerned, Todd directed a couple of swift slaps to her back. She wasn't choking on anything but water, so nothing would be stuck in her windpipe. He snatched a soft breadstick from a wicker basket nearby. "Here. This should help."

She shook her head, pushing away his offering. Her breathing returned to normal, but the narrowed, flashing eyes she shifted in his direction surprised him.

"Just to get things straight between us right from the start, let me tell you what I don't want, Todd Brentley." Her tone was quiet, seething with fire. "I don't want your pity. Just because she's my mother doesn't mean she always knows what's best for me. And in this case, she's sadly mistaken."

Baffled, Todd shook his head. "Sorry, but I'm at a loss as to how you think a thousand dollar contribution to the shelter could be a mistake." Actually he was at a loss about everything she'd said but didn't want to push his luck.

"That's not what I'm talking about."

"What else is there?"

"Nothing. Never mind. It's not important." She picked up

her water glass, changed her mind when it was halfway to her mouth, and set it back down. She snatched up a breadstick, tearing off the end with her teeth.

Todd eyed the breadstick he still held and tossed it on his plate. Noelle kept her attention fixed on the crowd, the breadstick disappearing in swift, angry bites.

Might as well give it another try. After all, that's why he was here.

Todd cleared his throat. "Saturday evenings work best for me. Just call when it's convenient. With time running out, I'm sure you'll want to make it soon."

"Look," she cut in, her gaze piercing him like the sharp needles of an evergreen, "I don't think I made myself clear. If and when I do decide to date, I don't need any favors from you in 'aiding a worthy cause.' So you're off the hook. You owe me nothing for this crazy auction. Zip. Zero. Zilch." She flicked her hand in a dismissing gesture with each Z word.

Todd's mouth twitched at the corners. "Date?"

The indignation blazing in her eyes gave way to mounting horror. "You know. What you and I've been discussing for the past few minutes. What you said about calling you on a Saturday evening when it's convenient. . . ." Her words trailed off, reminding him of a squeaky little mouse. A cute mouse, though.

He shook his head. "A thousand dollars is pretty expensive to buy a date, Noelle. I'm flattered you think I'm worth it, but. . ."

Noelle groaned and dropped her head into her hands. She briskly massaged her temples and two more pink strands fell from the top. "A fire is child's play compared to this. I could run out that exit door and get away before they caught me."

Confused by her strange mumbling, Todd clarified. "Your mother mentioned that the guy building the set for the Christmas play broke his leg. I'm supposed to take his place."

Noelle let out a short laugh. "Well, Cindy'll be relieved to hear that. I'm only in charge of advertising and directing the play. Cindy is the founder of the ministry, but then you probably already knew that. . .ohhh."

At her soft moan, Todd touched her shoulder. "You okay?"

"My pride is blown to smithereens, but what else is new?" She looked up. "I can't believe I thought—and said—what I did. You must think—well, I know what I'd think. You do, don't you?"

Surprised that he understood her garbled words, he took pity on her. "You want to know what I think?"

She shook her head no, then nodded yes, like an uncertain child who wants to please but is faced with a puzzling question. He hid a smile, putting his hand over hers. Her eyes widened, and his gut clenched.

"Well, here it is. I think you're the most interesting woman I've ever had the privilege of knowing, every pink inch of you. And I'm glad our paths crossed again."

His words made her feel better, as did his warm hand atop hers, but he could have left out the part about every pink inch of her. Also Noelle wondered about his definition of the word "interesting." She'd always heard the term used when one didn't want to hurt another's feelings: How do you like my new Mylar dress? Interesting. What did you think of your blind date? Interesting. Isn't this dribble-art wallpaper a scream? Interesting.

Then Todd's words hit full force. He was glad their paths had crossed again. Meaning—what? That he wanted to be with her?

*Yeah, right, Noelle. Why would the most handsome, alluring guy at the banquet want to be seen with the freaky pink lady—a combination of nineties punk rocker and Barbie doll reject?*

"Cat got your tongue?" He sounded amused.

"I think I've said too much already. I should save whatever face I have left."

"It's a nice face." Leaning back in his chair, he withdrew his hand from hers.

She missed the feel of it.

"Under the circumstances, your reaction is understandable, Noelle. Now that I think of it, I wouldn't welcome the idea of being bought as someone's date, like some sort of male escort. Seems cheap. I understand how you must have felt."

"Please, could we just drop the subject? There are apparently a number of things my mother chose not to reveal, such as her intention of bidding on you for building the Christmas set—which I'm grateful for, don't misunderstand me. But will you tell me something? Did she phone you about participating tonight and put you up to this?"

"No. My mom's a member of the committee, too. She's the one who talked me into it."

"Your mom's a member of the town council?" Another tidbit of information her mother had withheld.

"Yeah." Todd leaned close. "Listen. I'm starving and it doesn't appear as if the caterers are going to serve us any time soon." He picked up the breadstick from his plate. "I'm not all that crazy about a diet of bread and water, so how about we go grab a bite to eat and discuss the building project?"

"You mean just leave? Now?"

"The auction's ended, and I haven't eaten since lunch. I'm sure your mom wouldn't mind if you and I duck out for an hour or so."

*No, you're right. She'll probably do flips for joy.*

Todd grinned as though he could read her mind. "So how about it? Are you game?"

"Well..." Noelle studied the crowd, mingling again, though some were seated at their tables. Cindy faced Paul, with her hands upraised in obvious frustration. Noelle's mother laughed and talked with the mayor, who stood beside Diamond Jim. It seemed like a good time to escape. No one would miss her.

"Why not? I can spare an hour." Who was she kidding? His offer sounded like a touch of gold from Midas. That would explain why everything suddenly seemed to glitter.

Todd collected her coat from backstage and helped her into it. Somehow they slipped out of the grand ballroom, unseen—without the aid of the fire escape.

# Chapter 3

Noelle looked through the door of the all night mini-mart where Todd stood in line at the counter. He held a cardboard tray with what looked like two submarine sandwiches and paper cups of coffee. Her stomach turned over at the thought of food.

Feeling perspiration trickle down her sides and glad he'd left the keys in the ignition, she rolled down her car window a fraction. Most of the pins had slipped in her hair, so she plucked them out along with the huge clip, then pulled a brush through the Pink Fusion locks that now swept the top of her shoulders. She ignored the wide-eyed stare from a man who drove up beside Todd's car. In this laid-back town, one didn't see many like her, that was for certain.

"Can you help my mommy?" a soft voice said nearby.

Startled, Noelle looked out her window. A small girl of about six stood by the car, her short coat unbuttoned and with nothing covering her mussed blond hair. Several feet behind, a boy of about the same age stood, wearing mittens, a muffler, and a hat with his coat.

"Please, Miss Angel, can you help her?"

Noelle blinked at the woebegone expression on the girl's wind-chapped face. What were these children doing out at this time of night? She pushed at the control to lower the window further.

"Where is your mommy?"

"She's sleeping, but she won't wake up." Tears shone in the child's gray eyes. "Please help her."

Todd rejoined Noelle. The girl abruptly backed up, her expression wary.

"It's all right," Noelle said. "He's a friend of mine. Tell me, sweetie, exactly where is your mommy?"

The child hooked her hand around the boy's mitten. "She's where the ducks live."

"The ducks. You mean at the park?"

The girl nodded, and Noelle quickly filled Todd in on the situation. He set the food down, turned off the ignition, and grabbed the keys from the switch.

"Can you lead me to where she is?" he asked the girl, locking his door and shutting it.

"Will the angel come, too?"

"Angel?"

The little girl pointed to Noelle. "The strawberry angel."

Amusement flickered over Todd's face. "Sure. But we really should go now and see if we can wake your mommy."

Embarrassed, but also feeling a sense of urgency, Noelle got out of the car. They followed the children to the public park located behind the store. The girl glanced over her shoulder twice, as if to make sure they still were there, each time giving Noelle a shy smile.

Near the pond, a minivan sat off the asphalt, hidden behind some bushes. Steam covered the inside of the windows. Todd wrenched open the sliding door. A young woman lay on the seat, twisted up in a blanket, her face shimmering with perspiration.

"Ma'am?" Todd put a hand to her cheek. She didn't stir. "She's burning up. My cell phone's in my jacket. Call 911."

Noelle did so, noticing piles of clothes scattered in the back, two pillows, and a carton containing sparse amounts of boxed food and two oranges. One large suitcase and a small one were stacked near the rear door.

"Where do you kids live?" she asked once she ended the call, already suspecting the answer.

"Nowhere."

The little boy jabbed his elbow into the girl's arm. "Mama said we're not s'pposed t' tell."

The girl looked at him, her brows drawn together. "It's okay, Scottie," she whispered loudly. "She's the strawberry angel, like in my story. She's going to help us."

At a loss to explain the girl's obvious faith in her and her curiosity piqued by the child's strange comment, Noelle did what she could to reassure the children. Soon, sirens wailed in the distance. In a matter of minutes, policemen and paramedics arrived on the scene. One of the officers, Jack, she recognized as a former high school classmate.

"Noelle, is that you?" He let out a disbelieving whistle as he walked her way. "What did they do to you at

Beryl's shop? You look like a costume reject left over from October."

"Wow, thanks, Jack. That's one I haven't heard. But the hair color isn't your sister's doing. It's mine."

In the van's indoor light, she saw him wince. "Sorry. New look from the big city? Never mind. Beryl's always telling me I've got a big mouth. So what's the situation here?" His manner at once became businesslike as he glanced at the paramedics working over the woman. Surprise again lifted his brows. "Todd?"

"Heya, Jack. Yeah, it's me." Todd filled him in on what little they knew while Noelle stood with the children and watched the EMTs strap their mother onto a stretcher. The woman opened her eyes. "Selena?"

"Mommy?" The girl stepped forward, looking uncertain.

Along with her partner, a female paramedic continued to roll the stretcher to the back of a waiting ambulance, all the while assuring the woman that the kids would be well taken care of and she could see them later.

"There's no one for them to stay with." The mother's voice rose to a desperate pitch. "Please don't take me away from them."

"I wanna go with my mommy," Selena cried, rushing forward.

Jack stepped up and put a detaining hand on her shoulder. "You can't ride in the ambulance, little girl. But don't worry. I'll take you and your brother to the hospital so you can be with your mom."

Selena evaded his hand and ran back to Noelle, ducking behind her. She wrapped her arms tightly around

Noelle's waist. "I want the angel to take us." The teary words came muffled, spoken into Noelle's coat.

"Angel?" Jack asked, as if he hadn't heard correctly.

"I think she means me," Noelle said, embarrassed. "Todd?"

"I don't have a problem with it, if Jack doesn't. I'm parked at the mini-mart."

Jack appeared more relieved than put out. "Great. You two—er, four—can meet us there. Phil, you ready?" he called to his partner, who was taking down the minivan's license number.

"Can I ride in the back of the police car instead?" the boy piped up.

"No." Selena shot him a frown as she stepped to Noelle's side. She looped a hand around Noelle's wrist and his. "We stick together, like Mommy said."

Lights flashing, the ambulance sped away. The police returned to their car, and Todd and Noelle took the path with the children to the mini-mart.

Once inside Todd's car, Scottie perched on the edge of the backseat, his arms crossed over Noelle's bucket seat. "What's that smell?" he asked, smacking his lips.

Todd exchanged a look with Noelle. She gave a faint nod, and he glanced over his shoulder at Scottie. "Bratwurst sandwich. Want some?"

"Yeah!" In one motion, the boy grabbed the offering and crammed a bite into his mouth. "Thanks," he mumbled around the mouthful of food.

"Would you like one, too?" Noelle asked Selena.

The girl nodded. "Please, thank you." Her words were subdued, and she was more ladylike as she took her first bite. But after that, the sandwich disappeared much more quickly.

During the drive, Noelle glanced at the children, who gobbled down their sandwiches, barely swallowing what was in their mouths before wolfing down another bite. She wondered when they'd last eaten. Judging from their mom's condition, it probably had been too long.

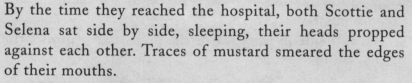

By the time they reached the hospital, both Scottie and Selena sat side by side, sleeping, their heads propped against each other. Traces of mustard smeared the edges of their mouths.

"Oh, aren't they just adorable?" Noelle whispered, a soft look on her face.

"Yeah." Todd studied Noelle.

Selena woke to Noelle's gentle shake, but Scottie snuggled deeper into the vinyl seat. Todd wound up carrying the boy inside, while Selena slipped her hand into Noelle's and walked beside her. The looks Noelle got, with her wild pink hair, light red dress, and white fur coat, ranged from flabbergasted to amused. Some people glanced her way frequently, but pretended not to when they made eye contact. Todd gave Noelle credit for keeping her cool and ignoring the attention.

In the emergency waiting area, the bright lights woke Scottie, and he complained about being thirsty. While Noelle spoke with a nurse, Todd bought two sodas from a machine in the lobby. The kids took them with a polite thank-you but didn't open them.

"Don't you like that kind?" Todd asked.

"Mama doesn't let us have sodas 'cause the sugar makes Scottie jumpy. We drink juice."

"Sorry, I should have asked first." Todd retrieved the un-opened cans and set them on the magazine table beside Selena, then found a machine that contained 100 percent orange juice He bought two. This time both kids eagerly grabbed the bottles, their thank-yous much more enthusiastic.

Noelle joined them, casting a glance at the children who sat out of earshot. "Their mother's being examined. I called Cindy, and she said if the woman's homeless, as I suspect, Haven of Hope will do what they can to help. Only problem, there's no room at the shelter, and I'm not sure what we're going to do about those two if their mom ends up being admitted."

"Has social services been called?"

"I would assume from the police report that they'll be contacted, but I don't know if that's been done yet. Our own social services worker at the shelter is on vacation in Florida."

After a wait that seemed endless, a doctor with iron-gray hair and glasses came from an adjoining corridor. His mouth twitched when he saw Noelle, and Todd detected her slight groan.

"Well, well, if it isn't Noelle Sanders," the doc said. "What have you gone and done to yourself this time?"

"Hi, Dr. Milton. I didn't know you'd be here tonight. I heard you were on vacation." Her expression was sheepish as she explained to Todd, "Dr. Milton's an old friend of my father's."

"I know Todd," the doctor said. "How's the knee?"

"Kept me off the football field," he joked, though that fact still smarted. He'd held such hopes for a career in professional football.

"Hm, yes." The doctor grew serious. "Are you here about the woman brought in from the park?"

"Yes. How is she? Do you know yet what's wrong with her?"

"Now, Noelle, you know the law won't allow me to divulge such information without her written permission."

"Of course. I wasn't thinking." Her brow furrowed as she looked toward where Selena and Scottie sat. "We brought her children. They're sitting right there." She nodded toward the two chairs a short distance away.

"Ah, yes. She hasn't stopped asking for those two." The doctor cast a fleeting glance at the kids. "Under the circumstances, I'll need to give them a quick checkup. Child Protective Services will be contacted, of course."

"I assumed that." Noelle glanced at the children then back at the doc. "Any chance I can speak with her? To ask if there's anyone I can call to take the children? We obviously can't leave them here overnight."

"I suppose it's necessary, but keep it brief."

After Dr. Milton gave both Selena and Scottie a clean bill of health, Noelle herded the two into an elevator, with Todd bringing up the rear. Once the foursome reached their mother's floor, however, the children balked at the idea of staying with Todd in the waiting area.

"Please, I want to see my mommy," Selena begged quietly.

"I'm not sure you can this late, sweetie."

"Please?"

Selena's woebegone expression tugged at Noelle's heartstrings. She darted a look at Todd then moved toward the nurse's station to inquire. The nurse appeared relieved.

"That lady's been fretting over her kids since she was brought up here. I'm sure that seeing them will make all of us rest easier, but I'll ask you to keep it short, and keep it quiet. Most all of the patients are sleeping."

Permission given, they headed to the room. Noelle stood sandwiched between both children, who now seemed frightened by all the hospital equipment and seeing their mom in the midst of it. A plump, middle-aged nurse was fiddling with an IV attached to the patient's hand. A closed curtain shielded the other patient, and Jack stood in front of it in his black, intimidating policeman's uniform.

"Are we interrupting?" Noelle asked him.

"Nah, I just have a coupla questions for the lady. It can wait."

"It most certainly should wait, Officer," the nurse said, her tone clipped. "This woman needs rest. You can come back tomorrow to question her." With that, she whisked from the room, almost running into Todd who stood in the hall by the open door.

The woman's wan, pale face crumpled with worry. Shadows darkened the area beneath her eyes. "Who are you?" she asked Noelle, her anxious gaze dropping to Selena who tightly held on to Noelle's hand.

"Don't let the wild pink hair and outfit fool you," Jack

cut in. "Noelle's good people; she volunteers at the local women's shelter, and her family and mine go to the same church."

"I'll vouch for everything Jack said," Todd added. "All of us are old friends."

"I'm Noelle Sanders. And you are?"

"Miranda Fitzgerald," the woman croaked. "I—I can't pay for this."

"Let's not worry about that right now," Noelle soothed. "I talked to the director of the local shelter, a friend of mine, and she assured me that they'll help in whatever way they can. And for what they can't do, they'll refer you to those who can."

Dr. Milton strode into the room. "Glad I caught you, Noelle. I was about to head home, when I noticed the little one left this behind." He held out Selena's navy coat. The child took it, a sheepish expression on her face.

"Oh, Selena," her mother said, exasperated. "What've I told you about that, honey? First it was your hat and gloves, now your coat. We can't afford for you to lose that, too."

"I'm sorry, Mama." Tears wobbled in the child's words. She sidled closer to Noelle.

"Well, I should be heading home before the little woman starts to worry," Dr. Milton said with a wink. "Say hi to your dad for me, Noelle. I'm hoping we can take another fishing trip in the spring. As for you," he said as his gaze turned to his patient. "You need rest. I'll be back to check on you tomorrow." He looked at Jack. "A word with you?"

"Sure." Jack seemed disgruntled but headed for the

door. The doctor followed him out.

Scottie pulled on Noelle's long skirt, and she bent to hear him. "I hafta go to the bathroom," he whispered loudly enough for all to hear.

"I'll take him," Todd said, reaching for his hand.

"I have to go, too," Selena announced.

"Go with your brother, Selena," their mom said. "I want to talk to Miss Noelle."

"I'll find a nurse to go with Selena," Todd said, looking bamboozled.

Once the two women were alone, Miranda began, "I don't have anyone to take care of the children. Will your shelter take them, at least for tonight or until I can try to make other arrangements?"

"I'm sorry." Noelle wished she had better news. "They're not allowed to take the children without you there, too. Regardless, they're full up right now. I've put your names on a waiting list."

Miranda seemed surprised.

"I've seen enough homeless people to recognize the signs," Noelle gently explained as the woman lowered her head. "It's nothing to be ashamed of, to be without a home. It can happen to anyone."

"After my husband divorced me, I lost my job, then my apartment," Miranda whispered. "Things never got better, so I decided to head to my brother's, hoping he could help us. Then we had car trouble, and so many other things went wrong. . . ." Her words drifted off. "I tried to call him, but the number's been disconnected and I have no idea where he lives, except that it's in the next town—in Fairview. But I've run out of money."

Noelle sympathized with Miranda's plight. "We'll find him." She said the words with assurance, trusting God to give direction as He had so many times in the past. "What about alimony? Don't you receive that?"

"I have no idea where my ex is. He's a trucker, but I don't know who he works for now, since he got fired from his last job. We haven't heard from him in over a year." The woman fidgeted, her fingers plucking at the sheet. "I hate to ask, but will you take Selena and Scottie with you, 'til I can figure out something else?"

Miranda's plea shocked Noelle into silence.

"Please. I've never known Selena to bond so quickly with anyone. She's shy, but she was actually holding your hand. She seems to trust you. And after what that police officer and doctor said, I do, too."

"She thinks I'm an angel," Noelle murmured, still rocked by the woman's request.

Dawning awareness lit Miranda's blue eyes, and the woman smiled for the first time. "Of course. All the more reason I want you to take them. Like I said, I can't pay you, but when I'm outta here, I can clean for you or something. I've only worked retail, but I know how to clean a house."

Her desperation prompted Noelle. "Don't worry about reimbursing me, Miranda. I'll be glad to have Selena and Scottie stay with me."

After blowing kisses to their mama from the doorway of her room, the children left the hospital with Todd and Noelle. Noelle filled Todd in on Miranda's request, and he was amazed at Noelle's agreement to take on a stranger's kids. She was quite a woman. Then again, he'd never known her to deny anyone with a need.

Once they collected the children's suitcase from the minivan, Todd drove Noelle to her car and they transferred kids and luggage to it. He waved away her good night, fully intending to follow her home. She didn't seem surprised when he pulled up behind her at the duplex.

"They're sound asleep," she whispered, "and I hate to wake them. I'll go clear off my bed, and you can carry them inside."

Todd nodded, reaching for the closest child, Scottie, whose thumb slid from his partially open mouth. Inside the duplex, Noelle motioned Todd to an open door and he carried the boy to a double bed, with sheets and a fluffy blanket pulled back. He collected Selena from the car and laid her beside her brother. Noelle pulled off small shoes and coats and Scottie's hat, muffler, and mittens without waking either of the children, while Todd made a third trip for their suitcase and set it just inside the bedroom door. Noelle covered the kids to their necks with the bedding before she and Todd left the room.

Noelle shut the door with a soft click. "It just occurred to me that you've never had dinner. Would you like a sandwich? Or I've got a couple of frozen dinners I could microwave."

Todd studied her glowing face—no longer glowing pink, but glowing just the same. Any food sounded like manna from heaven right now—even breadsticks. But the hour was late, and for him to be in her apartment during this time of the night—or rather, early morning—might be misconstrued by any night owl neighbors.

"I should get home." He saw disappointment flit into her pretty green eyes, and quickly added, "But we still need to set a time to get together and discuss plans for building the set."

"That's right." She brightened. "Can you come by tomorrow?"

"I'll be here after work."

# Chapter 4

N oelle poured steaming coffee into an oversized earthenware mug, savoring the aroma of freshly ground beans. The phone rang. She grabbed it before its persistent chortling could disturb the children, still sleeping, though it was almost noon. "Hello?"

"Miss Sanders?"

"Yes."

"This is Mr. Robison, manager of Cartell's Discount Drugs. I understand you spoke with one of my employees this morning about a misfortune you had regarding a bottle of hair coloring you purchased from our store?"

"Yes, I did." Noelle was still rankled from that call. The woman had made it sound as if Noelle was completely to blame for not noticing the labels on box and bottle were different. Perhaps the woman was partly correct—Noelle should have checked—but the truth was, she'd been too rushed to take notice.

"I overheard the conversation and want to apologize for my employee's discourtesy," the elderly man explained, "as well as to apologize for the incident itself. Two small boys were caught yesterday switching face makeup in boxes. I have no doubt that's what happened with your box, as well. I'm sorry you suffered the brunt of their prank, and to make up for any inconvenience, Cartell's would like to issue you a fifty-dollar gift certificate, redeemable on any item in our store."

She was about to open her mouth and say that wasn't necessary, but a glance toward her closed bedroom door stopped her. "Thank you, Mr. Robison. I'll be in today."

The call she dreaded, the one to her manager, went about as well as Noelle expected.

"What do you mean you can't come in this afternoon?" Rhoda squealed. "Can't you get anyone else to watch those kids? They're not even yours!"

"I know, but I made a promise. I tell you what—you said you needed someone to head those craft classes next month. Give me today off, and possibly tomorrow, and you have your woman."

"That's great. And in the meantime, what am I supposed to do about the wall-to-wall customers and one cashier?"

"How's Darlene working out?"

"Fine. But she's a student and can only work part-time. You know that."

Noelle hesitated. She had no right to offer information before discussing it with the kids' mom first, but she tested the waters anyway. "I might know someone who can help. Only drawback, it would probably be a week or two or more before she could start work." She told her about Miranda Fitzgerald.

"That's one really big drawback, Noelle. The lady has pneumonia, is wired up to a hospital bed—and you think she can be a help to me in what way?" Rhoda's sarcasm came to the fore, a sign that she hadn't gotten her noon coffee break and semisweet chocolate fix.

"I'll see if I can find someone to watch the kids tomorrow," Noelle promised. Though she had no idea who would be available. A door opening behind her and the scuffing of socks on carpet alerted her that the children were awake. "I'll call you later."

"It had better be with good news."

Noelle hung up the phone and turned to face her guests. "Did you two sleep well?"

Selena shrugged. Their clothes from the day before were rumpled, and their golden hair was in snarls. But their eyes were bright, their faces dewy fresh.

"Hungry?" Noelle asked.

Selena tilted her head as if the question posed were a difficult one. "What do angels eat for breakfast?"

"Bet I know," Scottie chirped hopefully. "Cotton candy—'cause it's like clouds. And 'cause it's pink!"

"No." Noelle chuckled. "Just scrambled eggs, bacon, and muffins with strawberry or grape jam. Sound okay?"

"Yeah!" The kids shot like arrows toward the table and pulled out chairs, scraping them over the tiles.

"I'll bet you eat lots of strawberry stuff 'cause you're the strawberry angel, huh?" Selena asked.

Noelle could no longer contain her curiosity. "Why do you call me that?"

"I'll show you." Selena slid off her seat and raced for the bedroom. Noelle heard her unbuckling the suitcase.

Soon she came back with a picture book tucked under one arm. "See," she said, opening to the first page.

Noelle eyed the pink-haired angel in the long, strawberry-colored gown, who hovered amid cottony clouds. The cute, illustrated character was hardly a mirror image, but she understood why the girl might draw comparisons. "I hate to disappoint you, Selena. But I'm as human as you are. I'm certainly no angel."

The child's smile faded and her lips began to tremble as if she might actually cry. Scottie crawled off his chair and tiptoed to stage whisper in his sister's ear. "Maybe she's not s'pposed to say she's an angel. Like in that movie we saw with Kelly."

Selena's face cleared. "Oh—right," she answered just as softly. "She has to be quiet about it, like being a secret agent angel. Her work's top secret."

*A secret agent angel? This was really getting out of hand.* The phone rang—either saving her or interrupting her. Noelle wasn't sure how to view the distraction. She snatched up the receiver. "Hello?"

"Everything okay in nursery land?"

Saving her—definitely. Todd's voice layered a ray of warmth to the somewhat dismal morning. "Everything's just peachy keen." She used one of her grandmother's sayings.

"Sure that's not strawberry topped?" he asked lightly.

She rolled her eyes at his weak joke. Would she ever live this hair-color fiasco down?

"Sorry. Couldn't resist. Your voice sounds tight. What gives?"

She explained the situation at work and her need to

find a temporary babysitter or risk Rhoda's wrath. "I doubt my manager will fire me. She needs me too badly. But I understand where she's coming from. This close to the holidays, working retail is comparable to managing a zoo."

"Let me see what I can do. I might be able to help."

"You?" Surprise raised Noelle's voice an octave. "What about your job?"

"Not me, no. I'm not up for day care duties. But my sister might be willing. I need to run it by her first. By the way, we still on for tonight?"

"Sure." The matter of building the Christmas set could be arranged by phone, but nothing would entice her to forgo a couple of hours conversing with Todd. Former misunderstandings dealt with, they'd gotten along well last night. "Come by around six."

"I'll bring dinner."

"Thanks. That would be great." Noelle hung up the phone and looked toward her two charges, who were seated quietly, heaping spoonfuls of jam onto bran muffins. With them here, surely any lingering awkwardness between her and Todd would melt away.

Todd raised his knuckles to Noelle's door, but stopped short of knocking when he heard a siren wailing inside. Something loud thumped against the bottom of the door.

"Watch it with that thing, Scottie." Noelle's exasperation was evident in her voice. "You almost knocked it into the table with the lamp."

Todd rapped on the door. Within seconds it swung open. Something whizzed past his hiking shoe, followed by a leaping Scottie, who waved a black control box in his hands.

"See what Miss Noelle got me?" he cried, holding up the remote control to the miniature police car that was racing down the short sidewalk, lights flashing, siren wailing.

"Whoa there, sport." Todd grabbed Scottie's coat sleeve at the shoulder before he could run out into the street. "Does that thing have a stop button?"

Scottie took his hand off the knob. The car came to a standstill. Noelle swung the door wider, her strawberry-pop-vanilla hair tied back in a high ponytail. Selena slid into view under her arm. He took note of Noelle's long blue T-shirt and matching pants—with Selena dressed like an Eskimo beside her.

"Hi again, Mister. See my new mittens. Aren't they pretty?" She shoved two pink-and-purple-clothed hands up toward Todd's face. A hat in a similar color and snow-flake pattern snuggled atop her head. "My angel bought them for me when we went to the drugstore, 'cause the man there gave her money 'cause the hair color was wrong."

"Yeah, they're nice." Todd glanced at the mittens, amused to hear the angel reference again. "But isn't it kind of warm inside to wear all that?"

"Oh—I'm *never* taking them off." Selena balled her mittened hands to her chest as if to guard her treasures.

Todd fully focused on Noelle. "Hi."

"Hi back." She returned his grin.

"Sounds like you've had quite a day."

"Oh, you know how it is. An angel's work is never done. And these two don't come with stop buttons. Their motors are gassed up twenty-four seven."

Todd chuckled and held up a sack. "I brought food."

Scottie reached for the other sack. "French fries?"

"No. Chinese."

Both kids stared at him as if he'd spoken the language. Noelle took the unrolled sack from Scottie's hands.

"Egg rolls, egg foo yung, white rice. . . ." Todd counted off.

"And sweet-and-sour chicken," Noelle ended softly, lifting her gaze from the open bag up to Todd. A wondering look filled her eyes.

"Hope you still like Chinese."

"I haven't had any since our tutoring lessons in high school. This'll be like old times. Did you get it from Ming Lee's Restaurant like we used to?"

"Yeah." Todd couldn't help the goofy grin that came to his face. At least she appreciated his efforts, though he'd clearly struck out with the kids. Scottie had retrieved his toy car and both children disappeared inside the duplex.

"Come on in," Noelle said. "I'll pour us something to drink."

As Todd followed Noelle into a small but tastefully decorated room, his mind wandered down another hallway. Although she worked retail now, he was sure that what his father would view as a setback was only temporary for Noelle. Not so for Todd. After his dream of making it to the NFL died, Todd employed short stints of working at a garage, then a gas station before his most recent position of deliveryman.

Could someone as classy and intelligent as Noelle—forget the accidental pink dye job—be interested in the local deliveryman? Todd knew that a lot of women sought the company of men they could look up to—financially sound and smart, like his dad. If that were the case, Todd didn't stand a chance with Noelle.

Too bad, because he was definitely getting interested in her.

# Chapter 5

After giving both kids thick, sloppy peanut butter and jelly sandwiches—the oozing-out-the-bread kind she'd always enjoyed—Noelle rejoined Todd at the table for their Chinese feast. He seemed quiet. Maybe he was just hungry.

"Why'd you quit your job in New York City?" he abruptly asked, his voice sounding a bit strained.

Noelle looked at him, contemplating how to answer. "A year ago I thought I wanted a top position on the team, eventually a partnership, which is where I was heading." She nibbled a forkful of pineapple from her sweet-and-sour chicken and grew thoughtful. "But the company doesn't uphold the values I have. When I finally earned the chance at promotion, I took a step back and looked at where it would lead. I'd had a few spats with my supervisor over too much sex used in selling the products and other moral issues. And I wasn't too happy about some of the clients we had to impress, a beer company to name one. But at the time I thought getting ahead and earning more money were the most important things in life."

"Aren't they?"

She frowned. "You really believe that?"

He was quiet awhile. "No."

"Well, neither do I—now. I eventually realized I was often putting my values on hold to please a client. Being a Christian, I decided I couldn't do that anymore. Bottom line was either I 'stopped being such a prude,' as my former boss put it, or find another place of employment. So I did."

"No regrets?" He fiddled with his milk glass, and she noticed he'd quit eating.

"None. Well, maybe one. I wish I earned as much now as I did two months ago." She made the remark lightly. "But then again money isn't the be-all and end-all of the world. Sure, it helps, but self-respect is more important. And since I quit, I've found I can look myself in the mirror again, even if my freezer isn't stocked with gourmet foods." She blew out a soft laugh. "To sum it all up, I think what's more important than aiming for the highest paying job is to find a job that's a perfect fit, especially when it comes to ethics. I love my volunteer work at the center and being with the kids there. And once the Christmas rush is over I just may find that I love my paying job at the craft store, too." She grinned to show she was kidding again.

Todd slapped his palm to the table. "That reminds me. My sister said she could watch Selena and Scottie tomorrow or whenever you need her, so you can go to work. She has five kids around the same age. They're all staying at my parents' through the holidays."

"Oh, that's great. I should call Miranda and clear it with her, but I can't imagine she'd say no."

"You didn't go to the hospital today, did you?"

Noelle halted her egg roll's progress to her mouth.

"How'd you know that?"

"When Selena didn't include it on the list of things you did, I wondered."

"Ah. Well, they did talk to their mom on the phone. Miranda told me she doesn't want the children to see her with all the added equipment around her and get even more upset than they were last night. She asked that I call her room to let the kids talk to her in the morning and at bedtime."

Selena and Scottie approached the table, their plates and glasses empty. Even the crumbs were missing.

"What can we do now?" Scottie asked.

Noelle thought a moment. "How about each of you draw your mom a picture, and we can mail it to her?"

"Really?" Selena's eyes shone.

"Sure. You'll find colored pencils and markers in that plastic shoe box on the TV stand. Blank paper is in a pile next to it."

The kids scurried away like rabbits excited to find an untouched lettuce patch. Todd and Noelle resumed their conversation and the minutes passed, but she sensed something was still bothering him. Before she could inquire, Scottie and Selena were back.

Noelle eyed them in disbelief. "That was quick."

"We're finished." Selena held up a sheet of paper.

A mother and two children had been drawn next to a decorated house in the snow, with a Christmas tree outside. An angel with pink hair and gown hovered above, holding a star. Noelle felt the blush and glanced at Scottie's picture. A huge turkey—created by the tracing of a small hand—ran from a smiling boy who carried a fork and knife.

Noelle laughed. What different personalities these two had!

"They're both very nice. I'm sure your mom will love them. I'll get stamps tomorrow and mail them first thing," she promised.

"So whatta we do now?" Scottie asked.

"Now?" Noelle was stumped. The clock showed two hours until what Miranda had said was their bedtime. "You could draw another picture, I suppose."

Neither of the children seemed too thrilled with that idea.

"Let me see what I can think up." Noelle took the empty plates and glasses to the kitchen sink. The small funnel she'd used to make orange juice that morning sat nearby. Staring at it, she felt an idea begin to gel.

She spun around with a smile, palms going to the counter on either side of her, and faced the trio who looked at her expectantly.

"How about we make a craft? A Christmas angel."

Selena squealed. "Yeah!"

Noelle was already sliding open the drawer with the various sized plastic funnels, glad she'd bought a set of them. She dug out the largest. "We'll use this for the body, and I have some craft items in a box in my closet. The big brown one labeled 'art supplies.' Todd, do you mind getting it?"

"Not a bit." He set to his task, while Noelle cleared off the table and gathered other things they might need.

"Scottie, will you bring that box of pencils and markers over here, please? Let's see, what else. . ." She stood back, one arm across her waist, her other hand at her chin. Thumb propped beneath, she tapped her forefinger against her lower lip. Surveying the small cache of treasures slowly building on the table as Scottie set the shoe box down, she counted off items. "Scissors, glue, scraps of material—"

"Pink hair," Selena intoned.

Full attention snagged, Noelle stopped her finger tapping. "What?"

"The angel's got to have pink hair—like you." Selena's smile was wide. "It's got to be special."

Feeling the usual dreaded warmth rise to her face, Noelle turned again to study the items on the table. "I'm not sure I have anything pink that would work, Selena." She looked toward the hall closet that held her sewing kit. "But I do have some red tassels I bought on clearance. I thought I might make a belt, but never did."

Todd returned with the box and dropped it on the table. "You really love your sales, don't you?"

"Yeah." Noelle let out a half laugh riddled with embarrassment. "You'd think I would learn by now that clearance isn't always the best way to go."

"That how you got the hair?"

She nodded.

A tender smile tipped his mouth. "Oh, I don't know. Sometimes these things work out for the best."

Noelle eyed him as if he now possessed her pink hair. He walked closer.

"If not for your new dye job"— he lowered his voice for her ears only— "those two might still be living in a van, with their mom in need of a doctor's care. Selena thought you were—what was it she called you? Oh, yeah. The strawberry angel." He grinned. "That's the only reason she approached you for help."

Selena stopped sorting through a box and looked at them,

then scurried to grab her picture book from the couch. She opened to the first page and shoved it at Todd. "See, there she is."

Todd's eyebrows lifted as he drew the book closer. "Wow." His eyes shone with amusement as he glanced at Noelle. "That's uncanny. Pink hair, long dress, and everything."

"Yeah, uncanny." Noelle set to work tearing off the safety plastic from a new bottle of glue. Now that she thought about it, the whole incident was just that. Uncanny. Or maybe God-driven was a better description. Todd was right. Selena probably wouldn't have approached her last night if her hair hadn't been pink and she hadn't been wearing a long gown close to the same color. Not if she was as shy as her mom said. A rapid surge of gratitude showered through Noelle at how awesome God was to bring some good out of her hair-dying catastrophe.

"When are we gonna make this thing?" Scottie asked, sorting through the odds and ends in the box.

Noelle smiled at him. "Right now."

They each pulled out a chair from the table, and soon Noelle was directing them in the necessary steps to make their own, one-of-a-kind, strawberry angel.

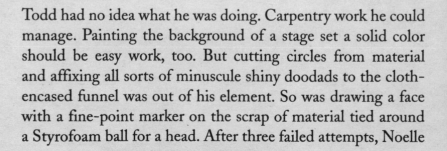

Todd had no idea what he was doing. Carpentry work he could manage. Painting the background of a stage set a solid color should be easy work, too. But cutting circles from material and affixing all sorts of minuscule shiny doodads to the cloth-encased funnel was out of his element. So was drawing a face with a fine-point marker on the scrap of material tied around a Styrofoam ball for a head. After three failed attempts, Noelle took over that chore. Good thing there appeared to be a lot of light-colored material in the scraps bag.

The kids were definitely enjoying themselves. Todd watched Noelle show Scottie how to make the halo from tinsel and Selena the wings from feathers, noticing how relaxed she seemed around the kids. She really liked them, and vice versa. To Selena, Noelle's word was law, and Todd had noticed how the child seemed to shed some of her shyness only when Noelle reassured her that Todd was a friend.

Feeling left out, but not minding so much because the hot, spiced apple cider Noelle had put on the stove was calling to him, Todd rose from his chair.

Noelle looked up. "Where do you think you're going?"

"To dish out some cider?" he asked hopefully.

"Nope. Back to work. You get the final job of hot-gluing the items onto the funnel. I don't think the craft glue will hold the wings on well, and the head could use some help, too."

She handed over the body of the angel, along with its flimsy wings, into Todd's large hand. He held the objects awkwardly, afraid he would crush them. The excess material covering the head had been tucked through the narrow tubing, but the smiling face flopped to one side.

"Slave driver," he teased. Noelle was even bossier than when she'd tutored him in high school, but Todd didn't mind so much. Not if it brought that smile to her face.

"You haven't been doing anything for the past ten minutes," she countered in mock indignation. Her eyes twinkled, while her mouth pouted just a bit—and sparkled, too.

Sitting back down, he reached over to brush gold glitter from her jaw, discovering her skin felt silky smooth to the touch. She jumped a bit, as if shocked.

He showed her the metallic flecks on his finger. "You had some glitter there."

She raised her hand to swipe at the area near her mouth, though the glitter was now gone. "Thanks."

Several seconds elapsed before she looked at him again. "I'll get us some cider while you finish the angel." Noelle headed for the cupboard and began pulling out ceramic mugs. She ladled steaming cider into four of them. The strawberry ponytail swung in time to her actions.

Why hadn't he ever asked her out their senior year? Sure, he'd gone steady with Diane, a girl from the pep squad, for two semesters, but after his accident on the field there'd been a stretch when he hadn't dated much at all. Diane had broken up with him after he'd left the team.

He continued to watch Noelle, appreciating the lines of her slender form and her bubbly efficiency. Truth was, he'd been attracted to her in high school, but he'd been so sure she wouldn't want to go out with someone who was a dunce to her Einstein. Her GPA had been in the top scores, and Todd's. . . Well, he'd graduated from high school anyway.

"Finished?" she asked as she turned, holding two mugs.

"Not yet." Todd picked up the hot glue gun and began attaching items. She set his mug down on a cleared spot of the table.

"You are allowed to take a break," she said, amused, obviously not noticing that he hadn't begun. "I'm really not a slave driver anymore, like I was when I coached you in English Lit."

He finished what was expected of him before taking his first sip. The cinnamon-apple taste warmed his insides but didn't fill the strange emptiness that had crept in unawares.

The children, warned not to touch the angel until it dried, scampered off to watch what was left of a Christmas TV special.

"Why'd you come back to Hartford Falls after you quit your job?" Todd posed the question he'd wanted to ask since day one.

At his abrupt words, Noelle looked up from taking a sip of her cider. He smiled to lessen any unintended sting. "You didn't have to leave New York City. You could have found another job there."

"I suppose." She stared at the mess on the table and took another sip before explaining. "When I went to New York City, I was looking for something. I thought I would find it there. But when I stopped allowing other people's expectations to squelch my own beliefs, my goals changed, and I realized that what I really wanted was here at home all the time."

"And what's that?"

"Miss Noelle!" Selena suddenly screeched. "Tell Scottie to give me the remote."

"I had it first!"

Noelle glanced at the silver and black Art Deco wall clock. "Sorry, kids. Bedtime. Selena, you're first in the bath tonight. Scottie, you can help me clean up. Then we'll call your mom."

"Is the angel dry yet?" The girl ran to the table and reclaimed her chair, kneeling on the seat.

"No, not yet."

Propping her elbows on the table and her chin in her fists, Selena smiled and studied the angel. "It's so pretty. Can we give it to someone for Christmas?" she asked hopefully.

"I think that's a lovely idea. Who do you want it to go to? Your mom?"

Selena shook her head. "I want it for my babysitter when we lived in Sche-ned-aky."

"Schenectady?" Noelle clarified.

"Uh-huh. She once had black hair with a pink stripe in it. And she likes angels. She's got a really pretty shirt that's got an angel on it. It glows in lots of shiny colors."

"But, Selena," Scottie said, coming up to the table. "Kelly went away, 'member?"

Selena sobered. "Oh, yeah. Her dad sent her to charm school. What's charm school?"

"A place where they help young girls behave like ladies," Noelle said as she replaced the items in the box.

"If you remember the name of the school, I might be able to help," Todd cut in. "I have a global tracking device I use at work that can find just about anybody."

"Even our uncle?" Scottie asked, eyes big.

"Your uncle?" Todd cast a curious glance Noelle's way.

"Didn't I tell you?" Noelle slapped a hand to her forehead. "I didn't tell you. So much has been going on." She explained why Miranda and the children had been living in a van.

"It'll be difficult to find him without an address, but I'll see what I can do. You'd be surprised how easy it is to track someone and get information about them, even on the Internet." He grabbed his jacket from the chair back where it was draped. "I'd better get out of here and let you get these two to bed."

"But we never discussed the Christmas set or what time you could come build it."

Todd's movements slowed as he slipped into his jacket. "No,

we didn't, did we? Tell you what, I can probably get Saturday morning and afternoon off if that'll work for you."

"I'll make it work." Noelle walked with him to the door and opened it, revealing how dark the sky had gotten. A light, wet snow was falling. "Thanks for the Chinese."

Her beautiful green eyes seemed to say more. So much more. . . He wanted to kiss her. He couldn't remember ever wanting anything so badly.

"Miss Noelle?" Selena called from a back room. "Can you run the water so my bath won't be hot?"

Todd zipped up his jacket. "I'd better let you go. I'll see you this Saturday. Around ten in the morning okay?"

"Sounds perfect."

With the added coziness of her smile to warm him, Todd headed for his car. But the niggling fact that she was, as his father would say, "out of his league" soon stole even that bit of warmth away.

# Chapter 6

Saturday dawned, freezing but clear, and Noelle quickly herded the kids into her car and drove to the shelter. Once home to the Mackenzie family, built at the turn of the twentieth century, and tucked at the edge of a small wood with a glimpse of the Catskill Mountains beyond, Haven of Hope now belonged to many women and their children in need of a temporary place to stay. The homeless, the battered, the destitute found their way to the sprawling white Georgian to seek comfort, counsel, and aid. Reconstructed to fit the ministry's needs, Haven of Hope had proven a refuge to many, a springboard to help them start new lives. Noelle loved being part of such a ministry and was excited that they'd received enough donations to start building another wing. Presently, they could house thirty, besides the live-in staff, but Cindy hoped to double that amount next year.

The kids crowded close to Noelle as she walked up the circular drive. She felt sorry for the two. Todd hadn't been able to track down the uncle with only a name to go by, and after seeking a telephone operator's help, Noelle discovered that the man had no listing. All they knew about Jimmy Stravinski was that he was a freelance journalist who'd recently moved.

Inside, Cindy greeted them, looking as fresh and elegant, as always, in a soft-yellow and cream-colored sweater and slacks. With a friendly smile she introduced herself to the children then asked Beth, a young staff member, to take them to the playroom.

Selena grabbed Noelle's hand, adhering to her side like Velcro. "No thank you. I want to stay with Miss Noelle."

Beth bent down and laid a gentle hand on her shoulder. "Wouldn't you like to see all the neat toys we have? There's a few kids in the playroom right now."

"No." Selena pressed her face into Noelle's coat. Noelle could actually feel her shaking.

"I'll take her," Noelle said.

Both Cindy and Beth nodded with understanding smiles. They were accustomed to dealing with fearful children who didn't want to be touched or talked to, so Selena's behavior wasn't at all unusual.

"Can I bring my new police car?" Scottie asked, as exuberant as ever, holding up his toy for their inspection.

"Sure," Beth said. "Show me how it works?"

Once inside the cheery playroom, Scottie immediately headed for a round table where two kids were working with plastic building blocks. Both lost interest in the colored squares when they saw Scottie's car, and he gave them a demonstration. Selena walked inside but hung back against the mint-and-ivory wallpaper, as if hoping to become one of the stripes in the pattern. She gripped

Noelle's hand in a death clutch.

Beth bent down to talk to another girl, Skylar, who moved away from playing with a miniature play kitchen and approached Selena. The girl with the beautifully slanted Asian eyes and straight dark hair was two years older than Selena and invited her to play. At first Selena wouldn't budge, but after a few minutes, when Skylar had gone back to pretend-cooking with her plastic dishes, Selena let go of Noelle's hand and crept forward. Only when the child was caught up in baking a cake, per Skylar's instructions, to feed three dolls seated at a play table, did Noelle move silently away, confident that Selena would be all right for the next couple of hours.

Following the bangs of a hammer to what was once a ballroom, she found Todd busy at work. Impressed with the progress he'd made, Noelle voiced an approving, "Wow."

"Oh, hey, I didn't hear you come in." Todd's hammer paused mid bang. A lock of dark hair lay against his forehead, and Noelle fought the urge to reach out and let it curl around her finger. Muscular arms were clearly defined beneath the short sleeves of his blue T-shirt, and she imagined how good it would feel to be wrapped in their protective embrace.

To cover her embarrassment at her runaway thought—and glad Todd couldn't read her mind—she rotated in a half circle, surveying the set in progress in the middle of the high-ceilinged room. "I would have gotten here earlier, but it wasn't easy getting the kids out of the house this morning. It's amazing how many things were missing when it was time to go—shoes, socks, Selena's mittens,

Scottie's coat." Grinning, she tucked her hands in her sweater pockets. "Anything I can do to help?"

"Not sure about now. But when it comes time to decorate the backdrop, definitely ask me again."

"I can hold something for you if you need me to, or play gofer. I'm not scheduled to practice scenes with the kids until after lunch, so I'm free 'til then."

"In that case, I'd welcome your company."

For the smile he gave, she would do anything—pound a thousand nails, saw a thousand boards, paint a thousand backdrops. . .

One half of a stable later, she wasn't so sure. She'd accidentally kicked over the container of nails, then almost gave Todd a black eye when she unknowingly set a heavy can of paint on the end of a wide plank balanced on a metal trash can, just as he bent over, and the board ricocheted upward like a seesaw. Turning now to survey the result of their hard work, she saw that the seven-foot wooden panel they'd just erected was tottering in a slow-motion sway toward them.

"Todd!" she screeched, hurrying to plant her palms against the sheet of wood and try to prevent its downfall. She felt Todd's warmth directly behind as he smacked his hands even higher—causing the panel to catapult in the other direction. Noelle yelped as gravity forced Todd forward—into her—and they both lost their balance. The board slammed to the floor, and they crashed on top of it.

After a couple of stunned, frozen seconds, Todd crawled off Noelle. She felt his hand cover her shoulder. "You okay?"

"I think so." With his help, she sat up—and grew lost

in his rich, chocolate-brown irises, now only inches from hers.

He gazed into her eyes intently for several mind-numbing seconds then lowered his focus to her lips. She did the same, noticing again how well shaped his mouth was. His lips were full but masculine. Entirely kissable.

He moved a breath's pace toward her. She barely tilted her head. The approaching sound of children giggling down the hallway grew louder.

Todd jerked back, his gaze flying to hers. "Guess I didn't use enough nails." His words came out strained.

"Guess not."

Another tense heartbeat passed, as if he were trying to make a decision, before he stood and helped her from the floor. Two of the older children came running inside.

"Miss Noelle, Miss Cindy wants to talk with you about the play."

"Okay, Nancy. Thanks." Noelle still felt shaky—and disappointed—about the kiss that didn't happen. Would Todd really have kissed her? They were rebuilding their friendship, yes, but could he ever be romantically interested in a ditzy female with Pink Fusion hair and a propensity for making mistakes?

Somehow she doubted it—not after remembering the gorgeous and totally together girls Todd dated in high school.

After eating lunch with the staff, Todd walked with Noelle and somehow found himself in the room where she was to teach the children.

"Noelle," Beth said as she popped into the doorway.

"Cindy needs to talk with you again—pronto." With that she was gone.

Noelle turned to Todd. "I should only be a minute. Watch things for me?" Before he could answer, she was gone, too.

*Now what?*

"Hiya, guys." He surveyed the eleven children gathered in the small room, which felt smaller with every passing second.

Scottie and Selena were the only ones to smile back. Some of the kids eyed Todd curiously, others with mistrust, but no one answered his greeting. Judging from what he'd heard of the situations and homes some of these children had come from, he couldn't blame them for not trusting a stranger. But he'd been in worse fixes—when crouched in starting position before a football play and staring at the offensive tackle who easily weighed a hundred pounds more than him. So why was he starting to sweat?

A surly-faced boy bounced a grapefruit-sized ball against a wall, catching it and repeating the process in rapid-fire bangs. "Stop it, Jeremy," a girl ordered and pushed him.

"Make me." He pushed her back.

*This could get ugly.*

Spotting two more rubber balls, Todd scooped them up as an idea struck. "Loan me yours for a minute?" he asked Jeremy.

The boy crossed his arms. "Why should I?"

"Because it's hard to juggle with two."

"Juggle?" a small boy with buckteeth asked. "Like a clown?"

"Yep." Todd began tossing the two balls in the air, in a lozenge-shaped loop, thankful his uncle had taught him years ago, insisting it would help him with his football skills—both to keep his eye on the ball and to catch it.

"Anyone can do that," Jeremy jeered.

"Bet you can't," another boy challenged.

"Bet he can't do it with three," Jeremy shot back.

"Try me," Todd said, keeping his eye on the balls that he kept in constant motion.

The unexpected action of Jeremy lifting his arm in a curve snagged Todd's attention and he lost his timing. Jeremy threw the ball at him—hard. As the other two balls bounced to the floor, Todd took a step back, instinctively putting out a hand to catch the third ball. Stumbling over a chair, balance gone—he fell into it. He missed the third ball, which sailed into the wall behind him, then bounced and rolled past his hiking shoe to land inches away.

The kids laughed, as if watching an old slapstick movie.

Todd grinned. *So, they wanted a clown.*

Amazed to hear peals of children's laughter, Noelle approached the recreational room where she'd left Todd with the kids. Upon entering, she stopped, her mouth dropping open then forming a slow grin.

Todd juggled three balls and missed one—which bounced off his head. The kids laughed again, as he scratched the top of it and pretended to be unable to find the ball that was in plain sight. Two of the smaller children pointed to the blue ball two feet from Todd with giggling shrieks of, "There it is! There!"

Noelle crossed her arms and casually leaned against the doorjamb. She watched his antics until Todd noticed her and lifted his hand in acknowledgment. "Your teacher's back," he told the kids.

"She's not our teacher," one small fry Noelle recognized as Luke said. "She's just supposed to help us learn some stupid play."

"I don't think it's stupid," Todd defended. "The Christmas story is interesting. An adventure. Can you imagine being born in a barn with lambs and goats and cows all around? And kings coming to visit you, bringing treasure?"

"Will you stay and watch?" Scottie asked, and a few other kids joined in with the plea.

"Yes, Todd," Noelle said good-naturedly, uncrossing her arms and walking to the front to join him. "Do stay. I'd love your help. My assistant just called in sick."

"Well, I don't know. . ."

Noelle almost felt sorry for him. She shouldn't have put him in such a spot. Before she could dig him a way out, he shrugged and smiled. "Maybe for just a few minutes."

Just a few minutes turned into more than an hour. While she prompted and instructed those kids with lines, Noelle was thankful for Todd's presence, which made the older boys less prone to act up. Wanting the children to get acquainted with where they were to stand on the stage in progress, Noelle had arranged for a laundry basket to substitute as a manger and a few chairs to stand in for palm trees.

She watched as three-year-old Ginny abandoned her job as shepherdess, walked to the basket, and crawled atop the bunched blanket inside. Popping her thumb into her mouth, she cuddled the doll that would be baby Jesus close to her heart and closed her eyes.

Todd looked at Noelle in confusion. "Her doll?"

"No. She does that when she gets tired," Noelle explained. "Finds a corner to sleep. Once we found her in the laundry hamper, another time she chose a baby crib." She grinned and glanced at her watch. "All right, that's enough for today."

"What about the craft we're s'pposed to make?" Luke asked. "The presents for our moms? Are we gonna do that next?"

"I don't have all the materials yet. I'll pick them up at work Monday, and we'll do the craft next week."

"Can we make another angel?" Selena whispered. She'd been quiet for most of the afternoon and Noelle was glad to see her begin to participate, even if it was just to ask a question.

"We could."

"A strawberry one? Like the one we made to look like you?"

"Maybe." The expected heat rose to Noelle's cheeks.

"What do you mean?" a boy named Trevor asked, but Selena clammed up and dropped her gaze to her feet. Instead, Scottie explained the whole thing.

Jeremy gawked at Noelle. "I was wonderin' why you did that to your hair. It's never gonna come out, ya know. My cousin colored hers—made it real dark pink—and even though the beauty place bleached it and stuff, it didn't go away. She even tried to dye it brown, and it ended up lookin' like a purple Tootsie Pop that had been licked a whole bunch."

A tidbit of information Noelle didn't need to hear.

Jeremy headed for the door, then turned and walked backward. "I know—you can be the purple Toostie Pop Angel! Suckers is better than strawberries, anyways." He laughed and raced out the door. A few other children followed him.

Todd looked at Noelle, his eyes sympathetic. "Are you planning on keeping it that way through Christmas?"

"I don't see that I have much choice with both hair salons in town booked. And I'm certainly not going to try to dye it back myself. After what Jeremy said, I'm not sure I'll try at all."

Todd captured a pink strand that lay over the shoulder of her ivory sweater and held it between his fingers. "It is pretty. Christmas-like."

Noelle wrinkled her nose at him, and he laughed.

"Seriously speaking. The color grows on you. I'm beginning to like it."

Noelle wasn't sure if he was teasing or not, but by the serious look that suddenly entered his eyes, she wished they were alone. If four of the children hadn't been present—one trying to juggle balls while the others watched—he might have even kissed her.

## Chapter 7

"Sing we now of Christmas, Noel sing we here. . ." Selena's hand in hers, Noelle walked up the sidewalk with a group from the center—four staff and a few mothers with their children—as they sang their short rendition of an old French carol. They gathered in a semicircle in front of a decorated two-story house, only one of many homes on Cindy's caroling list of those who'd contributed to the shelter. The porch light flicked on, bathing the area in a golden glow, and she nodded to the children to ring their wrist bells.

"Noel, noel, noel, no-ellll. . ." The exuberant words died on her lips once the door swung open.

"Sing we here, no-elllll," the chorus of angelic voices lifted around her while she went mute.

Positioned in the doorway, Todd smiled at Noelle from where he stood behind his mother, who beamed at the carolers. "Oh, how lovely," the dark-haired woman enthused. "Please, do continue."

The group sprang into a rousing stanza of "Dashing

through the snow," but Noelle's mind accelerated on a careening course all its own. When had Todd's family moved? She didn't remember them living in this neighborhood, and she certainly hadn't known Todd would be here tonight. Todd's sister had picked up the children from Noelle's apartment every workday, so Noelle never visited their home. Tonight, Cindy was the bearer of the list and drove the van to each residence, so Noelle had been clueless about where they were going.

After a few more songs, ending with "Away in a Manger," the group concluded their performance. Mrs. Brentley invited them inside for hot cocoa, but Cindy politely declined, explaining that the last house on their list—Cindy's mom's—had hot apple cider and hot chocolate waiting. Mrs. Brentley insisted they have something and passed out candy canes.

Scottie ran up to Todd. "Will you come with us?"

"Yeah!" two of the other children chimed in. "Come with us."

"I don't know. Can you use a tenor?" Todd asked Noelle.

Giddiness tickled Noelle that Todd would consider joining them. She could only nod, since her tongue seemed to have thickened. But Cindy piped right up, "Sure! The more the merrier. There's room in the van for another caroler. Your mother, too, if she'd like to come."

"No thanks. I think I'll just stay inside where it's nice and warm. You go on and have a nice time." Briskly rubbing her arms over her knit sweater, Mrs. Brentley smiled at Todd, then Noelle, a twinkle in her eye.

*Hmm. Another matchmaker?* Noelle wouldn't put it

past both their mothers to attempt pairing them off, since Noelle knew the women had become fast friends through their work on the committee. Sure, Noelle would enjoy dating Todd. But she doubted Todd would welcome their moms manipulating things.

As the group continued their amateur concert tour, a talcum-fine snow began to blow, adding to the chill. Yet Noelle felt toasty warm as Todd stayed close. When he casually slipped his arm around her jacket while they caroled in front of the mayor's home, her mind went blank. She sought for the next words to the chorus but couldn't remember them. Afraid to even breathe lest he move his arm away, she stood as still as the snowman on the wide lawn.

Todd felt Noelle stiffen and cast a sideways glance in her direction. "Frozen" best described her expression. She didn't seem upset, exactly, rather stunned. Resigned, he lowered his arm from around her shoulders, thinking maybe she was one of those that preferred her own personal space. He didn't want to crowd her, though he missed the feel of her snug beside him.

After visiting a string of other houses, Cindy drove to a retirement center, where they were welcomed with big smiles from those in the recreation room. Two residents sat in wheelchairs while the others sat in high-backed chairs edging the round tables, all of them waiting for the performance to begin.

The carolers sang their tunes, and a number of residents joined in. Afterward, they smiled and conversed with the children. They appeared genuinely happy and grateful for the gift the carolers brought them—the gift of their time and voices. And the children seemed to sense that. It was amazing to see even a troublemaker like Jeremy enter into excited conversation about ice fishing with one of the residents.

"That's sure a pretty dress you have on," a white-haired gentleman who'd introduced himself as Ben said to Selena. He reminded Todd of Barnaby Jones from the TV show reruns, with his hound-dog face, ready smile, and bushy white eyebrows. He even had the Southern drawl.

"Thank you." Clutching her shiny green skirt, Selena inched closer to Noelle. "My angel got it for me."

Ben's shaggy brows sailed high. "Really? Well, that's down-right interesting. I do believe God gives every one of us an angel to help keep us in line." He cast a glance upward to Noelle, amusement on his features. "And this one's yours, huh?"

Selena nodded, loosening up a bit. "She found us in the park and took care of us. So did he." She pointed to Todd.

"We was tryin' to find our uncle," Scottie jumped in to explain. "He moved away but we don't know where."

"Is that right?"

"Uh-huh. He's a jour—jour—he writes a paper."

"You don't say? And does this paper writer have a name?"

"Uh-huh. His name's Jimmy Stra—vin—si. We couldn't remember his last name 'til Miss Noelle called Mommy at the hospital. She got sick."

Ben's carefree manner disappeared. "You mean Stravinski?"

Scottie nodded. "Yeah. It's hard to say."

Ben directed his attention toward Noelle. "We had a young man come here weeks ago to write a piece on the center. I seem to remember Stravinski was his name. I was one of them he interviewed. You might check at the desk before you leave. They should be able to get in touch with him and find out if he's your man."

"I will." A light shone in Noelle's eyes as she exchanged glances with Todd. He also hoped this would be the key to finding the uncle.

The fun evening ended at Cindy's mom's house with hot beverages and homemade goodies the older woman passed around. The phone rang and Todd watched Cindy grab it.

"It's been a good night," Todd said to Noelle as she sipped her cider.

"Yes, it has. I'm glad you joined us."

Todd raised his brows. "Really?"

"Yes. The children like you, and that doesn't happen with everyone."

"Only the children?"

A blush colored her face. "Yes, well, I've enjoyed working with you, too. It's been great so far. Like old times, but new ones, too." Quickly, she took a bite of her chocolate chip cookie. Before Todd could probe further, Cindy joined them, her expression grim.

"That was the center," she explained. "Doc Milton called. The kids' mom had a bad reaction to some new medicine. He didn't go deeply into it, but it doesn't look good."

Both Todd and Noelle glanced across the room at

the two kids who sat beside each other on the sofa. As though somehow attuned to the situation, Selena set her paper cup down and hesitantly walked their way. "Did I do something wrong?"

"Of course not sweetie." Noelle bent to hug the little girl close. "We just need to pray for your mommy. Because God's bigger than any problem that comes against her or you or anyone. Always remember that. Okay?"

Eyes wide, the child nodded, and they all clasped hands.

# Chapter 8

The week before the Christmas play, Noelle and Todd finished details to the set. He'd already spray painted the backdrop midnight blue, and now they both added white dot stars to the surface with small paintbrushes.

"How's the kids' mom?" Todd asked.

"Better now that they've switched medications, but her system is still fighting something. They're running tests."

"Think there's any way she'll be out by Christmas?"

"The doctor says there's always a chance. Each day has brought a little more progress."

"That's good. It must be hard on those two not being able to see her."

"Yes, but Miranda wanted it that way. At least both Selena and Scottie like staying with me, and I don't mind at all. They're well-behaved kids." Noelle stepped back and surveyed her work. "Think I should put more stars in that corner? We want it to look real."

"It's fine."

"Are you sure?" Noelle tilted her head. The scene seemed off balance.

"You know what your problem is?" Todd approached, his voice teasing. "You're too much the perfectionist."

"Am not."

"Are so."

"Right." Enjoying their banter, she flipped her hair. "That would explain this lovely masterpiece."

Todd chuckled. "Didn't you tell me you colored it because you didn't like the way it was and you wanted it to match your outfit? That reeks of perfectionism to me. And this isn't the first time you've changed your looks either. I seem to recall in our senior year, before Christmas break, you got a perm."

"You remember that?" Uncomfortable prickles reminded her of her attempt at a home perm, which had made her look as if she'd stood outside holding a lightning rod during a thunderstorm. Wanting to forget that little catastrophe, she returned her attention to painting. "I always try a dose of self-improvement around the holidays. Sort of a birthday present to myself, I guess."

"I like you the way you are."

Noelle's brush stopped short of the backdrop. Had she heard him right?

She darted a look his way, but he'd returned to painting stars above Bethlehem's hills.

"So when is your birthday?" he asked.

"Christmas Eve."

"You're kidding. The night of the play? That doesn't seem like much of a birthday for you. You should have someone treating you to a steak dinner at some classy restaurant."

"Oh, I don't mind. I'll be with those I love and that's what's important. The kids, Cindy, Mom, Dad. . ." *And you'll be there*, she silently added.

She wrinkled her nose, critically eyeing her work. "I totally got this off balance. It looks like a major galactic explosion in that corner, but like several lonely stars lost their way over there."

"Perfectionist," he teased.

"Hey!" She grinned. Before she thought about it, she dabbed his wrist with her paintbrush.

"Oh, yeah?" He repaid the favor to her hand.

"No fair!" She laughed. "Your dot is bigger than mine!"

Knowing the paint was nontoxic and could easily be washed off with soap, she dabbed his chin. "You look nice with a white goatee." She giggled.

His eyebrows sailed up and his mouth dropped open as if he couldn't believe what she'd done. Then he dabbed her on the nose.

"Todd," she giggled again, wiping the paint away. "Not on the face. Pink hair is bad enough."

"What's the old saying? All's fair in love and war." His low words teased as he dabbed her cheek, then the other one.

"Todd—stop it!" Laughing, she stepped up close, grabbing his wrist to prevent him from adding another white freckle.

The mood changed between them as swiftly as if someone had flipped a switch, and they stood as still as stage props. His gaze locked with hers.

"Todd?" she whispered after an endless moment, her

heart beating faster in anticipation.

The intrusion of his spoken name seemed to decide him. He released her wrist and stepped back, wiping the smear from his chin with one hand. "I should get cleaned up and call it a night. I'll see you at dress rehearsal next Saturday." His easy words didn't match his stiff smile or abrupt movements.

"Okay." Disappointed, she watched him prop his paintbrush in the water can and walk away. What had happened?

At the door, he stopped. Hesitated. Turned.

Before she could think to ask what was wrong, he rapidly bridged the ten feet that distanced them, pulled her into his arms, and firmly kissed her.

Noelle's paintbrush hit the floor.

Her heart still thudded in her ears when he pulled back. "I'd say I'm sorry," he said, his voice low. "But I'm not."

Still mesmerized by his heart-melting kiss and the warmth now simmering in his eyes, she shook her head. "I've wanted you to do that forever," she whispered. "Since senior year, if you want the truth."

With the tips of his fingers, he brushed her hair behind her ear. "I must have been blind then, Noelle. But I've got my eyes wide open now. And I like what I see."

"Even if it's strawberry-topped?"

"Yeah, even then." He smiled.

Their gazes mingled another few seconds before he once more dipped his head. This time his lips settled tenderly, exquisitely over hers. She pressed close to him, wrapping her arms about his neck.

Her fairy tale had come true. The pink angel/princess had won the heart of the dashing messenger/knight.

If only fairy tales could last forever.

The sound of someone clearing her throat returned Noelle to the real world with a jolt, though she felt dazed, as if she'd been abruptly awakened from a dream. She broke away from the wonder of Todd's lips to see Cindy at the door. Todd turned to look, too, keeping his arm loosely wrapped around Noelle's waist.

"Well, it's about time," Cindy said, always to the point, her smile wide. "Sorry to interrupt, but I just came to tell you the news. That tip Ben gave you paid off. We found the kids' uncle."

"That's great!" Noelle exclaimed.

"He just called the center and will be driving here as soon as he can take off from work. He was shocked to hear about Miranda. Since he's temporarily living with a buddy right now—by the way, that's why we couldn't find him—he can't have her move in with him at the apartment. He doesn't make much at his new job yet, but he promised he'd help in whatever way he could."

"Miranda will be so relieved to hear that," Noelle said. "My manager agreed to interview her for a job at the craft store when she's recovered, but I know she's been worried about hospital bills piling up."

"And I have more good news." Cindy fairly beamed. "I called the hospital right after I got off the phone with Jimmy. Miranda's condition has improved—almost a full turnaround. The doctor and staff are amazed."

"That's wonderful! The kids will be thrilled."

"Do you want to tell them or should I?"

"I'd like to. Todd?" Confused, Noelle looked at Todd, who'd just dropped his arm from around her waist. "Want to come along?"

A serious expression replaced his soft-focused one of earlier. "I'll leave that to you, Noelle. I should run a few errands before calling it a night."

"Okay." She tried for a smile but it fell short.

"Bye, ladies. See you at dress rehearsal." With a short wave, he was out the door.

"Don't look so worried," Cindy soothed. "The man's crazy about you. He probably just realized how late it is and that he had other plans, like he said."

"Yeah. Probably." But Noelle's smile felt fake.

Somehow she didn't think that was Todd's only excuse.

"Oh, don't be so nervous," Noelle's mom said, fluffing Noelle's hair over her shoulders. "You'll do fine."

Noelle gave her mother as warm a smile as she could muster. But inside her stomach, caterpillars rapidly metamorphosed into monster butterflies.

Only five minutes until curtain time. For the sake of the play—and the kids—she'd sacrificed any remnant of pride left over from her hair coloring fiasco, donned the Barbie-style gown Cindy had scrounged up at the last minute, and would now take eight-year-old Gwen's place as the Christmas angel.

Yesterday, Gwen's mom decided to take Gwen and visit their estranged family for the holidays. Grateful that the mom was finally willing to mend relationships with her parents, neither Cindy nor Noelle had the heart to ask her to stay one extra day for the play. The bus trip to her hometown would take a day and a half, and they didn't want Gwen's mom to change her mind and chicken out at the last minute. So, thanks to Selena's enthusiastic nomination, Noelle had agreed to substitute. Directing plays she could handle, but appearing in them was a different animal altogether.

Noelle fidgeted with her shoulders, trying to get comfortable despite the gauze wings tied to her back.

"Hold still, dear. I'll fix them. By the way, did I tell you how lovely you look? That silver gown goes well with your pink hair—and the iced glitter you added is a nice touch. Interesting."

Noelle chuckled. Her mother was always determined to unearth the bright side of life. "Have I told you how much I love you, Mom?"

"Not lately," she shot back with a grin.

"Well I do. Love you, I mean."

Her mom's eyes welled up with tears. As if embarrassed, she stepped behind Noelle and began fussing with the wings. "These are still lopsided." Her hands stilled after a moment. "I love you, too, dear."

Noelle smiled upon hearing the soft words and straightened her tinsel halo. Peering through the crack of space between lentil and door, she surveyed the audience. Several residents from the retirement center, there by the children's invitation, filled the front row.

In the second row sat Miranda Fitzgerald, looking pale but recovered. She and the kids had moved into the center yesterday, until Miranda could get back on her feet again. Noelle didn't realize how much she would miss her young guests until they were gone, but she was glad they were back with their mom. Seated next to Miranda was her brother, Jimmy, a gregarious redhead with freckles, and on the other side sat Officer Jack, with one arm looped around Miranda's shoulders. A romance had obviously developed in Hartford Falls.

Noelle sobered when she thought about her own love life.

Since the earth-shaking kiss of four days ago, Todd hadn't tried to kiss her again, though she'd seen him both at church and on Monday, when he delivered a shipment to the craft store. True, neither were opportune times for a kiss, but on both occasions he'd seemed removed, too polite. And yesterday, at dress rehearsal, he'd barely talked to her. Yes, they'd been busy, but this new distance made her wonder. Earlier this evening, she'd caught sight of him standing alone, hands in his back pockets, staring out a window at the faraway mountains and mumbling to himself. Uncertain, she had slipped away, sensing he didn't want company.

From across the room, Cindy motioned to her that it was time to begin, and Noelle turned to the ten-year-old narrator. "Luke, you're on."

The boy nodded, tugged at the bottom ends of his suit coat, and strode onto the stage, head held high. Noelle kept close watch. She winced when Carmen, who played Mary, stumbled on the walk to the manger set, but Jeremy in the role of Joseph grabbed her elbow, saving her. A sight amazing to see, since it seemed those two were always fighting. Noelle listened to the lines, proud of how well the children did. And those without lines didn't miss their cues to act, either.

Noelle straightened. Her own cue was coming up shortly.

"By the way," her mom said, "I almost forgot. Todd asked me to tell you that he needs to speak with you alone after the play. It sounded important. He'll meet you in the rec room."

"What?" Noelle looked back, stunned.

"You're on," came a child's loud whisper.

Noelle blinked, trying to get her bearings. She managed to walk to her spot onstage, where she was to announce to the shepherds the birth of Christ the King. Instead, her mind played back her mother's words.

*Focus. Focus.*

Somehow, she delivered her lines without a flaw, glided to the back, then hurried to grab the silver glittered star from the backstage table, also hoping for clarification.

Her mother was nowhere in sight.

Noelle sighed and drifted to the backdrop. She took the steps up the short ladder placed there so she could hold the star above the stable. Thankful she'd chosen to be in her stocking feet, to lessen the risk of losing her balance, she propped one hand against the sturdy roof while holding the star high. Todd had done a great job on the set and had pounded in double the amount of nails after their misadventure with the panel that first day.

From her perch, Noelle watched the kids, silently mouthing their lines with them, mentally prodding them when they hesitated. Selena and Scottie made endearing shepherds as they slowly walked and knelt by the manger,

Selena holding a stuffed lamb in her arms. As the wise men moved forward with their treasures, Noelle was about to expel a relieved breath when suddenly, three-year-old shepherdess Ginny yawned, laid down her staff, and walked closer to the manger.

*Oh, no!* Noelle cringed. "No, Ginny, no," she whispered as loudly as she dared.

Her words must have been too soft to reach the child. Ginny, as she'd done before, crawled into the manger with the doll baby Jesus, cuddled it close, and prepared to take a nap.

A few chuckles circulated among the audience. A shocked silence prevailed onstage. Narrator Luke, whose line was to end the play, looked up at Noelle, seeking direction.

Noelle thought fast for a fitting conclusion, in light of what Ginny had done. "And so, every Christmas, people celebrate the love Christ gave to us when He came down to Earth as an innocent babe. And in turn, we share our love with Him."

Someone in the audience began to clap. Others stood, and the clapping grew louder. It was obvious everyone now thought Ginny's act was intentional.

Smiling, Noelle stepped down off the ladder. As far as she was concerned, they would never be the wiser.

Todd stood in the rec room, waiting on Noelle. He hoped she'd gotten the message to join him. He hadn't trusted himself to speak to her earlier. As jumpy as he'd been all day he was sure he would have blown everything if he'd tried. While staring out the window at the faraway pine-clad mountains, he had even rehearsed what he planned to say to her, under his breath.

It began to snow, and he recalled the snow on her hair, her lashes, her shining face. . .

Shifting his attention from the window, he shoved his fingers deep into his pockets. Too bad he couldn't remember the words in the order he'd planned them. Memorization had never been one of his strong points.

The angel-funnel decorations Noelle had helped the children make caught his eye. Later, during the gift exchange, the kids would distribute them to their moms. Brown, beige, and yellow angels dotted the spruce tree's boughs. But none of the angels bore bright pink hair.

Todd grinned when he remembered Selena's comment to Noelle, as they were boxing up the special strawberry-haired angel to send to the kids' former babysitter, whom Todd learned was currently residing in Missouri.

"I know you're not a real angel," Selena had said in all earnestness. "But can I still call you my angel?"

The sweetest, softest expression had lit up Noelle's face, and Todd wished he could have bottled up that look in a jar to remember on the gray days ahead. The next several minutes would determine just how many gray days loomed in his future. Hearing a rustle at the door, he turned and inhaled a slow breath.

Noelle was the most beautiful woman he'd ever seen.

Feeling self-conscious because of his direct stare, Noelle walked toward Todd. She knew she looked ridiculous in the angel getup, but she hadn't wanted to risk taking the time to change and have him get tired of waiting for her then possibly leave.

"The play was a success." His voice sounded strained.

"Yes, thanks to Ginny's finale. I can't believe everyone thought it was planned."

"You saved the play with your ending line. It was great. Happy birthday, by the way."

"Thanks." Why did she suddenly feel so awkward with him?

"Noelle, I've got something I need to say—"

Before he could continue, one of the mothers rushed inside. "Have either of you seen Jeremy? They're cutting the cake, and I don't want him to miss out."

Both Todd and Noelle said no, and Jeremy's mom hurried away. Seconds crawled by.

"You had something you wanted to tell me?" Noelle prompted.

"Yes, I. . ." He pulled his hand from his pocket.

"Hey," Jeremy said as he walked in. "Was my mom just here?"

"Yes," Noelle said. "She's looking for you. They're cutting the cake."

"Great! And, oh yeah. Thanks, Mr. B, for teaching me how to juggle. You're one okay dude." The boy shot out of the room.

"You taught him to juggle?" Noelle gave him a warm smile. Jeremy had no father. Teaching the boy had been a thoughtful gesture on Todd's part, considering the way Jeremy had treated him his first day there.

Todd barely nodded. "Noelle. . ."

"Yes, Todd?"

"There's something I've got to get off my chest. . . ."

Noelle felt confused. He sounded so serious.

"There you two are!" Cindy poked her head in the door. "You're missing all the fun. With the way those kids are wolfing down the goodies, I can't promise there'll be anything left."

"Cindy," Noelle said in a voice that clearly implied she was intruding.

Her friend raised one hand. "Don't mind me. I never said a word. I wasn't even here." Her words trailed away as she drifted out of sight.

The second she was gone, Todd blurted, "Will you be my angel?"

"Your angel?"

"I mean my girl." He let out a nervous chuckle. "Angel is on the brain for some reason. This is coming out all wrong. And I'd even rehearsed what I planned to say."

Noelle felt as if she were in high school again, only this time the scenario she'd always dreamed of was playing out.

"You want me to be your girl?" she softly asked.

"For now. With the prospect of moving on to something more permanent down the road."

"Permanent?" she squeaked.

"As in marriage. I love you, Noelle."

She was stunned speechless.

"I know it's too early to discuss the future," he hurried to say, "and I doubt I make as much as your former boyfriends, just so you know. But I hope to move up in the company. I plan to take those computer classes Dad suggested, to help me earn a better position—"

"Todd." Without thinking, she laid her fingers against his lips as she said his name. They were warm and soft and she didn't want to move her hand away. But she did, feeling as if she existed in another dimension, one where time had slowed in a beautiful bright-lit, sharp-focused atmosphere. "I don't care about the money. Yes, I want my basic needs met—everyone does—and it would be nice to live comfortably, but I have no desire to marry a Daddy Warbucks."

Todd hiked his brow. "Daddy Warbucks?"

"The millionaire from Annie. I watched the movie with the kids last week." She thought a moment. "Remember when I told you I moved back home because I realized the things I'd been searching for were here all along? We were interrupted and I never answered your question about what those things were."

He nodded.

"I was looking for acceptance and love for the person I am, faults included. And I accept you for the person you are, too." She giggled, awareness fully dawning. "I can't believe we're standing here discussing the possibility of marriage."

"Then it is possible?" Todd said the words as if he couldn't believe them.

"Of course. Don't you know yet that I've loved you ever since I met you? Even more so, now. I just never thought you'd be interested in a pink-haired ditz like me."

He grinned. "The sweetest pink-haired 'ditz' I know."

"Todd." She felt the blush rise to her face.

"I have a birthday present for you." He opened the

hand he'd pulled from his pocket. Inside was a gold pendant bearing a reddish-pink carnelian gemstone in the shape of a rose. "I've become fond of the color—and it seemed the perfect keepsake for this Pink Fusion Christmas that brought us together."

"Oh, Todd, it's beautiful." She lifted her hair for him to fasten the necklace around her throat. "I'll always treasure it." Touching the rose, she gazed up into his eyes and saw the love shining there.

He slid his hands around her waist, drawing her close, and kissed her tenderly, leaving Noelle with no doubt that dreams could come true. Especially at Christmastime.

"And I'll always treasure you," he whispered in her ear, "my strawberry angel."

# One-of-a-Kind
# Christmas Angel

Materials listed are a guideline. Other items can be substituted if preferred. This is your unique Christmas angel, so customize to fit your personal taste. All listed items can be found at home, or at your local craft or dollar store. This is a fun craft to make with the kids or grandkids!

Parental supervision is recommended.

You'll need:
- Plastic funnel
- Feathers (or angel wings)
- Styrofoam ball (for head)
- Pipe cleaners
- Twist tie (found on bread wrappers, etc.)
- Tinsel
- Pretty material (for dress)
- Flesh-colored material (for face)
- Glue—both craft glue and hot glue gun
- Fine-point markers
- Ruler
- Tweezers
- Decorations for dress (i.e., glitter, sequins, ribbon, lace, buttons, etc.)

# INSTRUCTIONS

Body: Cut a circle in pretty material 5 inches bigger than funnel's wide bottom. To measure, place funnel on wrong side of cloth and with ruler, draw equal-sized lines on cloth radiating from funnel. Connect lines at tops, drawing with pencil, to form a circle. Cut slit in center, same width as funnel's narrow top. If material is type to fray, glue with sewing glue, or hem, if desired. Carefully tug slit over top of funnel until secure. This can be used as either a full dress or skirt. If desired, wrap lace or other material around top for bodice. (Picture shows 4 angels to show variety of ideas). Use hot glue at top to anchor, if needed.

Praying hands: Cut a 2-inch by 6-inch piece of same material and fold around flesh-colored pipe cleaner so that 1 inch of pipe cleaner shows at each end. (You may need to cut pipe cleaner.) Glue length of material together all across bottom to form angel's sleeves. Bend to form loop, then bend pipe cleaner ends and twist around each other for praying hands. (In picture, I gave one of my angels a carol book to hold, also made with pipe cleaners). Slip loop over narrow part of funnel at angle, so "shoulders" are at top back and hands rest at waist. Hot glue shoulders to back.

Head: Cut a circle of flesh-colored material big enough to wrap around Styrofoam ball, so that at least 3 inches of material hangs down after it's tied together. Smooth wrinkles from face area and tie off with a twist tie. Draw face with fine-tip markers (i.e., crescents and lashes for closed eyes and O-shaped mouth for singing angel). Crop thickness of excess material if needed—thin it out—but keep length so material can be inserted through funnel top and pulled down from inside. You'll do this by putting your hand inside funnel, so leave enough material hanging to easily grab onto. (You may need to use tweezers.) Pull until head is flush with top of funnel. Use tweezers to gently push down any excess material through hole. Hot glue where head meets funnel, if needed, and glue lace or tinsel around this to form angel's collar if desired.

Hair: Hot glue curly yarn or tassel to top of head. Glue gold or silver tinsel or shiny pipe cleaner around top for halo. (With a tassel, you may want to wrap pipe cleaner around top "hump" if tassel has one and form an elevated halo.)

Decorate as desired. Hot glue feathers to back for wings. Give as a gift, set your one-of-a-kind angel on the mantel, or use as a tree-topper to remind you that God's angels are watching over you this Christmas and always. And have a Merry Christmas!

## PAMELA GRIFFIN

Award-winning author Pamela Griffin makes her home in Texas, where snow makes a rare visit at Christmastime, but she doesn't let that fact dampen her holiday cheer. Christmas is her favorite holiday, and she enjoys viewing the lights with her kids, making homemade candy, watching old Christmas movies, and all the rest of the gala that this festive time of year brings—especially the friendly get-togethers and family reunions. She loves to write and has written several stories set during the Christmas season. Multi-published, with close to thirty novels and novellas, she gives God the glory for every amazing thing He's done in her writing career. She invites you to drop by and visit her Web site at: http://users.waymark. net/words_of_honey.

# angel
# charm

by Tamela Hancock Murray

*Charm is deceptive, and beauty is fleeting;*
*but a woman who fears the Lord is to be praised.*
PROVERBS 31:30 NIV

# Chapter 1

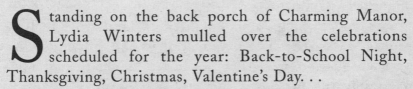

Standing on the back porch of Charming Manor, Lydia Winters mulled over the celebrations scheduled for the year: Back-to-School Night, Thanksgiving, Christmas, Valentine's Day. . .

Valentine's Day. She couldn't remember the last time she'd celebrated the occasion with a date.

"Funny. Charm is my stock-in-trade and yet I wasn't charming enough to keep the love of my life." Lydia ran her fingertip over the rim of her half-empty glass of sweetened iced tea. Perhaps the hint of coolness in the Missouri air, with its promise of a new school year on the horizon, reminded her of the past that had set her mind afire.

She shook memories of Drake Kingston out of her head. Whatever prompted such a thought had to go. Present concerns left no time for such romanticizing about a distant time and place. Drake had long since left the Midwest and hadn't been a part of her life for over fifteen years. He was gone for good. She'd heard talk about his recent plans to return to help his mother recover from recent hip replacement surgery. He had married a woman from his adopted state of New York years ago. Surely he and his wife were happy. She hoped so.

She finished the rest of her tea and mulled over the roster of new students for fall. Running over the final count in her head, she realized all of her classes at Charming Manor were full. Space for a few newcomers would have to be created, a situation that presented itself every year and tested her ability to remain charming under pressure. Finding more slots never proved easy since Lydia's school was located in the house she had inherited from her maternal grandparents. Perhaps the aged four-bedroom frame home, which she had painted pale pink with fuchsia shutters, wasn't really a manor. But to Lydia, living alone in such quarters made her house feel larger than it was. Certainly the two acres surrounding the place, with its vegetable and rose gardens thriving next to the lush green yard she tended, provided more than enough outdoor work to fill her mornings.

"Lydia!"

Hearing an unexpected male voice, Lydia gave a start as she spotted a stocky man wearing a light blue short-sleeved shirt, a dark blue cap, and matching shorts, the uniform of the U.S. Postal Service. She exhaled. "Oh, it's you, Ralph."

He ascended three of the five wooden porch steps painted fuchsia to meet her more than halfway. "Sorry to surprise you, Miss Lydia."

"That's quite all right." Lydia smiled, partly at the way he called her "Miss Lydia" even though he had lived a year or two past the half-century mark. In fact, most of the people she knew called her Miss Lydia, despite the fact everyone knew she hadn't seen her thirty-fifth birthday. She sensed they enjoyed the idea of a resident expert on etiquette, and the amiable honorific seemed to fit.

"You sure must have had your mind on something, to let me sneak up on you like that."

"You're right. I was preoccupied, Ralph."

"No doubt about tonight's party. I'm sure everyone there will have loads of fun. Seems like you'll be having a full house. I saw right many RSVPs come back to you."

"They did." Not wishing to comment on the degree of knowledge he was willing to share about her mail, she kept her voice terse and answer brief.

He smiled and held out a package. "I wanted to make sure you got this."

"A package? Wonder what it is. I haven't ordered anything lately." Lydia set her empty tumbler down on the glass top of a green wrought iron table and remembered her manners. "May I offer you a glass of tea?"

"Thanks for the invitation." Ralph took off his hat and wiped his sweaty brow with it. "Sure is tempting, but I don't have time to stop today." After placing his hat back over a bald spot peeking through strands of hair that appeared to have benefited from liberal application of black dye, Ralph extended the other hand to relinquish the box.

Lydia looked for the return address.

"No return address," Ralph offered, as if reading her mind. "Wonder who it's from."

She turned the package over, searching for a clue. "I have no idea."

"You don't say?" He folded his arms. "Who'd go to all the trouble and expense to mail a package and then not say on the front who it's from? What if your address was wrong? Or what if you'd moved too long ago for the U.S. Postal Service to forward the package? Without a return address, we couldn't send it back. Then whoever it is would think you got the package and then wonder why they never got an answer. They'd have nothing to show for their efforts but a package they didn't know ended up in the Dead Letter Post Office, and no way to reach you on top of that."

"You have a point."

Obviously encouraged by her acquiescence, Ralph puffed out his chest and emboldened the volume of his voice. "If I had my druthers, I wouldn't even deliver a piece of mail without a return address. To my way of thinking, there's no reason not to put a return address. Unless you've got something to hide."

"I certainly don't have anything to hide," Lydia assured him. "And I always use a return address label."

His voice softened. "I know that much, Miss Lydia. Your labels are mighty pretty, too, what with those pink roses you've got on 'em. The perfect flower for a pretty lady like yourself." Lydia surmised that most men who hadn't been given a lick of encouragement would have flushed a bit, or at least averted their eyes for an instant after delivering such a bold pass, but not Ralph.

"Thank you, Ralph." Since he kept looking into her face, she felt obligated to return the favor with a lukewarm sentiment. "What a nice thing to say." Employing discouraging body language to keep him from ascending the remaining two steps, she clutched the box to her chest.

"It's the truth, I tell you." He grinned as he reached into the blue satchel hanging from his shoulder and extracted the rest of her mail. Lydia noticed several catalogs and a few envelopes. Rather than handing them to her, he tapped the rolled up mail on the side of his leg. "So you've got no idea who sent that box, huh?"

"Really, I don't." Her grip on the parcel tightened.

"Well, you're too popular to have any enemies. Although I did notice the postmark is from Independence. You didn't have an argument with somebody there, did you? I sure hope not. A big town like that—especially so close to Kansas City and everything—can harbor an awful lot of nuts."

A half chuckle escaped her lips. "Thank you for your concern, but no, I haven't argued with anyone in Independence."

"I hope not." He tilted his head eastward. "They're close enough for someone to get at you if they set their mind to it."

She chose to ignore the sinister half of his remark and kept her voice cheerful. "Yes, I do recall my state geography."

"I know. I know. Just a reminder, that's all." He sighed. "I guess it's not something that will hurt you. I held your package up to my ear just to be sure, and I didn't hear any ticking sound."

Lydia was amused in spite of herself. She tried not to smile. "Thank you, Ralph."

"Sure is mysterious." He scratched his forehead under the rim of his cap.

"Surely it is." Lydia grinned. He was still tapping the rest of her mail on the side of his leg. If he continued, she speculated he might wear a hole in the top of his blue knee sock. "You're not going to give me the rest of my mail until I open this, are you?"

He shook his head. "Uh-uh."

"All right, then. Come on up."

As expected he leapt onto the porch. Lydia bit her lip to keep from suggesting to Ralph that he might benefit from a semester at Charming Manor as she seated herself on a wrought iron chair that matched the table. She set the package in her lap and studied it. Brown wrapping offered no clues. A plain white label bore her address in bold typeface. The box was compact and lightweight enough to be empty. But who would mail an empty box?

Lydia realized that sliding her fingernail under the packing tape was certain to mar the modest French manicure she had applied earlier that morning. She wanted her nails to appear well groomed but not too daring for the party. She would need her silver letter opener. "I'll be right back, Ralph." She rose from her seat. "Are you sure you won't take a glass of tea? I'll be passing through the kitchen to retrieve my letter opener."

He shook his head. "Nope. Don't have time."

Lydia turned before he could see her grin. If he spent this much time at all of his stops, no wonder Ralph ran late almost every day. Once indoors, she glided through the recently renovated kitchen filled with the aromas of cookies, cherry pies, and puff pastries, and noted that the last plate of chocolate chip oatmeal cookies she had baked appeared to be cooling nicely. A short trip through the hall took her into the study in the back part of the house.

Since her mahogany desk gleamed, free of clutter, Lydia immediately located her letter opener in the top left drawer. Spying one of her long, ash-blond strands of hair hanging from one of the rhinestones set in the handle, Lydia grimaced as she removed the offender and let it float into an empty carved mahogany wastebasket. She slid the silver blade underneath a beige swath of unyielding packing tape. When it wouldn't give way, she stabbed the tape with the tip of the opener. The gap allowed the blade to slice through tough plastic.

"Whoever sent this wanted to make me work to get inside," she mused.

She tore off the brown outer wrapping. Underneath was another layer of paper, this time a green foil.

"That's quite a color contrast," she muttered. "Looks like Christmas in August."

Curiosity aroused, she would have kept going except that she had an audience waiting outside. Nosy or not, Ralph was being a friend to look after her and her mysterious package. For that reason she owed him the consideration of letting him see its contents.

"Careful, Scarlett," she told the white Persian who had snuck into the study. The last time Lydia had accidentally caught Scarlett's tail in the door, the poor cat had avoided her for a week. Once in the hall, Lydia heard her other cat, a Siamese, mewing. "Rhett's waiting for you." The two cats disappeared up the stairs.

When she returned to the porch she discovered Ralph still waiting, leaning against a fuchsia column. His gaze rested on the package. "So what's somebody doing sending you a Christmas gift this early?"

"That's what I'm hoping we're about to find out." Lydia took her place back in the chair. Sliding the letter opener underneath a flap of foil wrap, Lydia removed the green paper and discovered a white box.

"Still seems suspicious to me," Ralph commented. "Where's the name of the store?"

She looked and discovered the moniker CHRISTMAS FOREVER and on the next line, KANSAS CITY, KANSAS on the lower corner, scripted in red. "Must be a store that sells Christmas items all year round." She lifted the lid and took the object, wrapped in tissue, out of the box.

After unwinding what seemed to be an entire batch of tissue, she discovered a round Christmas ornament. On it was stamped a picture of an old-fashioned house, a two-story frame structure much like Charming Manor, amid snow falling in twilight. A horse drawn carriage awaited its occupants. Lydia imagined a party taking place, with everyone sipping hot cocoa topped with sweet whipped cream and munching salted popcorn. The scene sent happy chills through her as she remembered winters past. For a moment, the heat of Indian summer, with its outdoor smells of mowed lawns and gathered hay, dissipated into recollections of the comforting aroma of roasting turkey and the crisp odor of a balsam pine Christmas tree.

She sighed. "It's beautiful!"

Ralph adjusted his silver-rimmed sunglasses and peered at the bulb. "Yep. Sure is."

A note had been placed underneath the ornament. She read it to herself: FROM YOUR SECRET ADMIRER.

"What's it say?" Ralph prodded.

Lydia wasn't sure how to answer. She felt the flush of heat around her collar. "It's rather silly, really. A joke, more than likely."

"A joke?" He set his fist on his thigh. "I don't like the sound of that."

Lydia decided that working Ralph up into a dither over nothing wasn't worth keeping a harmless confidence. "All right. I'll tell you. It says it's from a secret admirer." She let out a practiced giggle to show her embarrassment. "Isn't that the silliest thing you ever heard?"

"I don't see anything silly about it. Nothing silly at all."

As Ralph studied her, Lydia became conscious of her old blue jeans and white oxford blouse fashioned of cotton that had seen one washing too many. Clothes good enough for baking, but not for company. Not even the postman.

"So," Ralph said, "are you gonna put it somewhere on your tree?"

She shrugged. "I suppose so. I don't see why not."

"Depends on whether or not you find out who the secret admirer is, and if you like him well enough, huh?"

"Whoever the admirer is, he has excellent taste. I think I'll put it on the tree regardless."

"Well, that's mighty nice of you. Charming, in fact." He grinned at his own wit. "I guess it wouldn't do me much harm to get a few new ornaments myself. I have a plastic star on the top of my tree every year. It started out red, but you can see silver now where the paint's peeled off in a couple of places. But nobody notices the difference once you get it on the tree. They're all too busy looking for the loot underneath, anyway."

"Now, Ralph. You know there's much more to Christmas than that."

"Maybe to you, but you'll have a hard time convincing most postal carriers—that's the politically correct term. They don't let us call ourselves mailmen anymore. Anyway, my buddies know that gifts are a big part of Christmas whether anyone but the retailers wants to admit it or not. Our bags are so heavy with catalogs before Christmas and we're so loaded down with boxes at Christmas, that we know gift giving is a big part of all the fuss. Too big a part, in my book."

"It can be for some people," Lydia conceded. "I admit, I get caught up in all the consumerism too much sometimes myself. When I do, I try to make a point of spending more time in devotional reading to refocus myself on what's important."

"That's a fine idea, Miss Lydia. No wonder everyone around here thinks you're a fine lady."

"Thank you." Good. Ralph must not have thought she sounded self-righteous when she spoke about her time with the Lord.

He suddenly seemed to remember the rest of her mail. "Well, all this stuff you got today won't help you keep from shopping. You got a whole batch of mail order catalogs. Some even have Santa Claus on the cover." He shook his head as he handed her the mail. "Oh, and you got a postcard from your Aunt Beverly in Florida. Says she had a wonderful time with her Bible group in Jerusalem. Didn't get sick once from the food. Good for her." He gave Lydia a toothy smile.

She took the mail from him. "Thank you." Anywhere else, Ralph would probably have been turned in to his supervisor for reading the mail. She decided not to make a point of that fact. After all, her friendly postman meant well.

# Chapter 2

L ovely party, Miss Lydia."

"Thank you, Ashlynn." The redhead had been one of Lydia's favorite pupils the previous year. She set her gaze for a moment on a similar version of Ashlynn standing just out of earshot. "I look forward to having your sister in my class."

"And she can't wait to begin classes with you as well." Ashlynn sent her the type of self-assured and pleasant smile that Lydia had taught her well.

Mission accomplished.

As Lydia checked the banquet table to make sure plenty of sweetened tea filled the pitchers, she overheard the voice of one of her new students, Jennifer. "I don't know why you wouldn't want to take lessons here, Kelly. Everybody who's anybody around here goes to Miss Lydia's school."

*Kelly?* Lydia wondered silently. So that was the name of the girl with the harsh makeup and vivid hair, the girl who would have stuck out in any crowd, but most certainly within this group of young ladies she planned to teach the niceties of life. No one with that name had appeared on Lydia's invitation roster. She had assumed the new girl was a friend of one of her present students. She'd been waiting for someone to remember her manners and to introduce them. Yet none of the girls claimed to be Kelly's friend.

Then who was she?

Brushing a few stray crumbs from the white damask tablecloth into her open palm, Lydia refrained from shooting Jennifer a chastening look. As much as Lydia appreciated the compliment about her school, Jennifer would have to be taught not to appear as a snob.

Nearing the cut crystal punch bowl, Lydia cut her gaze to the two teens. Jennifer was eating from a plate overloaded with slices of pecan pie, cherry cheesecake, and cookies. Lydia made another mental note about Jennifer. She would have to be taught the niceties of delicate eating, at least in public.

Beside Jennifer was the girl Lydia now knew as Kelly. Lydia cut furtive glances her way to keep her study of the girl from becoming obvious. Kelly held no plate, but kept her arms folded across her chest, barely concealing what appeared to be the logo of a music group. Judging from several skulls and drops of blood, she assumed the group played hard rock. A cloud as dark as Kelly's hair seemed to be upon the girl.

"Then I guess I don't care if I'm anybody or not," Lydia heard Kelly say.

Unable to bear the girl's distress, Lydia interrupted. "Good evening, Jennifer."

The blond's face brightened. "Good evening, Miss Lydia. I was just telling Kelly how wonderful it is to go to your school. I'm looking so forward to your classes."

Jennifer had all the right words down but her tone sounded too icky sweet to convey sincerity. Lydia would have to coach her on not appearing shallow. She decided the lesson could wait.

"I'm glad to hear that, Jennifer." Lydia turned to Kelly. "I don't believe we've met."

Instead of answering, Kelly pushed her hair behind her ear, revealing four ear piercings decorated with alternating studs and small silver hoops.

"Oh, excuse me," Jennifer said. "Kelly Kingston, allow me to introduce you to our headmistress, Miss Lydia Winters."

*Kingston?*

*Kingston?* Lydia swallowed and composed her mouth into a line that wouldn't betray her shock. Her beating heart reminded her of old feelings she thought she had long ago buried. Then again, an image of Drake had popped into her mind just that morning. *No, it can't be the same Kingston family. This is obviously a coincidence.*

"Miss Lydia?" Jennifer asked. "Is everything all right?"

Lydia forced herself to smile. "Certainly, Jennifer."

*Those eyes, black as night. They look so much like Drake's. No, it must be my imagination.*

Jennifer beamed. "Kelly says she'll be a student here this semester."

"That's if my dad can get me in." Kelly refused to

accept Lydia's extended hand or to smile. "But if there aren't any more slots, I'll understand."

Before Lydia could comment, an unmistakable male voice she hadn't heard in years interrupted. "Lydia's an old friend of mine. She'll make room for you, Kelly."

Lydia turned and found herself gazing into ebony eyes she remembered from long ago. Drake's masculine face remained unlined. The straight, pointed nose, mouth that looked as though it was ready to grin at any moment, impish black curls—were all as she remembered. The years seemed to dissolve, along with everyone else in the room. All Lydia could see was Drake. The man who had broken her heart.

Drake tried not to stare. He hadn't approached Lydia until that moment, instead choosing to remain on the porch. As he caught up with other old friends, he had further justified his reticence by rationalizing that she needed to mingle with new students. But in reality, he had been too nervous to go inside. Now close to her, he saw that Lydia appeared even more beautiful than he remembered. His mind took him back fifteen years, to another era.

In high school, she had been a tiny little thing, wispy and shy. But during the summer between their junior and senior years, her parents had sent her to some sort of charm school in Kansas City. He remembered the first day of school during senior year. He hadn't known why at the time, but she had blossomed into a different person. Change was evident on the outside. Her clothes had always been fine as far as he was concerned. He liked how she appeared casual in a T-shirt, usually white, and blue jeans. Her new clothes were still informal but appeared much crisper and made her look more like a young woman on a mission than a teenager worried about homework or getting to her next class. He liked how polished she appeared. Her image hadn't been just a picture on the outside. When he talked to her, he had noticed she didn't shuffle her feet or avoid his gaze. Quickly he fell in love with the new presentation. And just as quickly, she had broken his heart.

He looked back at her now. As poised and polished as ever, she looked even more natural and possessed of fewer airs than she had in high school. Her cheeks, lips, and eyes looked natural, not artificial. A sleeveless dress in a soft blue hugged her curves.

Emotions that evoked an anticipatory shiver and a pleasant roll of his stomach reminded him of the feelings he experienced that September day so long ago. Lydia Winters looked as ravishing as ever.

Winters. Her maiden name. His mom said she never married, even hinted he was the reason why. He prayed that wasn't so.

"It's good to see you again, Lydia." He hoped he had hit the right combination of friendliness yet aloofness.

"You too, Drake."

Her smile seemed so practiced that he couldn't imagine such a cultured woman pining away over anyone all these years. Least of all, him. Mom had to be dead wrong. Too bad.

He poured water on the fiery emotion as soon as it left his subconscious. What was he thinking? He swallowed and tried to compose his expression into one that said he was interested in her only as his daughter's potential charm school teacher. He nodded toward the girls. "So you have a full roster this year?"

"Yes, I am pleased to say."

He allowed his gaze to observe the dining room. "Maybe you should move to larger quarters."

She stiffened. "I'm fine here, thank you. I like to keep my classes small. And I enjoy my place here at Charming Manor."

"We do, too, Miss Lydia," one of the girls, a blond, piped up.

Drake held back a grimace. Great. Not two sentences had left his mouth before he was dispensing advice he had no right to give. No wonder Lydia's chin tilted at him in the defiant way he remembered it used to do whenever she felt miffed. He tried to recover. "I can see why. Come to think of it, your grandmother lived in this house, didn't she?"

"Yes. I inherited this place from her. I suppose it's hardly recognizable since I painted it pink."

"I really like it pink," the blond remarked.

"Thank you, Jennifer," Lydia said.

"I'll have to say, the color does add its own brand of unique appeal." He eyed a mahogany table. "I'm glad to see you still have most of her furniture. Antiques are the only type of pieces that would suit this place."

"I daresay contemporary furniture would seem strange here."

"I agree." A contented sigh escaped him. "I remember that Christmas Eve party she had here. Your grandmother made the best hot cocoa. And do you remember how the whole world seemed covered with snow that night?" The images in his mind took him back so much he looked over to the fireplace, expecting a fire. He almost felt surprised to see no logs burning.

"Yes, I do seem to remember something about that." Her voice didn't convey the tone of a woman reminiscing. Terseness stiffened her face. "A perfect scene. Someone almost could have painted a picture of it."

"Yeah. Someone like Norman Rockwell. Or Thomas Kinkade." He smiled, but instead of returning his smile she cocked her head and studied him.

She turned her attention to her students. "I meant to ask if you girls have tried the jelly roll. Would you like to learn how to make that during one of our cooking classes?"

"I'd love to try it!" the blond replied, not surprising Drake.

Another non-surprise was the way Kelly's dark eyes rolled toward the ceiling and back. His rebellious daughter looked the part, but none of her teachers ever accused her of being stupid. She could spot a fake with no trouble.

"I'll bet the jelly roll is delicious, Kelly. Try some."

She twisted her bright red lips and narrowed her eyes at him to show she knew exactly what he was doing—getting rid of her—but acquiesced. That talk about being on her best behavior was paying dividends. She had agreed in exchange for being allowed to wear those horrible clothes.

Drake let out a deliberate chuckle. "Yes. I seem to remember it was white with black shutters. Not very imaginative." He felt himself blanch. In trying to compliment Lydia, he had insulted her grandmother's taste. At least the girls hadn't heard his gaffe. "Nothing against your granny."

She laughed. "Granny was a practical old bird. She'd be horrified by what I've done here. But I think it's perfect for a charm school."

"So do I." He'd trudged so far into the verbal mud that he figured he might as well see if quicksand awaited. "So your significant other doesn't mind a pink house?"

"Significant other? The only significant other in my life is the Lord, Drake."

*Oh, good!* He cleared his throat. "There's no one on the horizon?"

"No." For the first time that evening, she took a sudden interest in her white, heeled sandals. "But I'm perfectly happy. Perfectly happy." Her crisp voice suggested otherwise.

What could he say? "Um, I'm glad to hear that."

This was not going well. He felt like such an idiot. He should have been more pressing when he asked his mother to catch him up on news in the town before he went to the party. But he hadn't wanted to seem too eager to see Lydia. Not even in front of his mother. She'd always loved Lydia, which had most likely been a prompt for her to mention Lydia's school to him. He'd managed to play it cool so far, but his mother would be sure to pounce on any hint of his interest beyond Kelly's welfare.

His happiness about her freedom evaporated in light of the way her chin tilted again and her emerald eyes looked as hard as those precious stones. He almost wished he hadn't broached the subject. There weren't too many ways out and none of them looked good. He decided to try the road that promised an exit. "I know my daughter Kelly will enjoy her lessons."

"Kelly." She looked over at the girls.

Drake's gaze followed hers. Kelly stood out in any crowd, but she appeared to be more of an outcast in her current environment than usual. Several teenagers milled near her, and like the shallow blond, they all looked as though they had already seen a few semesters of charm school. Their outfits matched, their hair was styled to make them seem as though they belonged in a fashion magazine, and they wore pleasant expressions.

Kelly leaned against a wall. Surely slumping violated etiquette. Still, he felt thankful. He knew Kelly well enough to realize she had summoned all her will to keep her mouth from curving downward and her glance from rolling to the ceiling.

"Yes, Kelly is all mine." He flashed her his best smile and made sure his voice displayed the right amount of fatherly pride. "I'm sure she'll benefit greatly from your school."

Doubt flooded Lydia's green eyes.

Drake wished he could do or say something to remove all of her anxiety, but Kelly's obvious lack of recognizable charm left him with little leeway.

Returning his glance to Lydia, he sensed she didn't need a knight in shining armor despite her barely contained regret that no prince hitched a white horse to a post in the driveway. He wondered why. Standing before him was a slim but fuller figured woman than the teenager he remembered. Years had done nothing to etch around her eyes with wrinkles or harden her face. Nor did she seem dragged down from the cares of life. Who wouldn't want to marry such a beautiful, charming, and successful woman? Such a contrast to his daughter. Could Lydia make Kelly more like her?

"Uh, I know she's a bit edgy looking. But she has a wonderful heart. Really," he assured Lydia.

"I'm sure she does." Her tone didn't indicate much confidence. "I'm afraid I have a full enrollment. I'll have to squeeze her in if I am able to take her at all. And I have a couple of other girls on the waiting list ahead of her."

His stomach seemed to pound the bottom of his gut. After all these years, couldn't she make special accommodations for him? Then again, maybe not. Maybe he didn't have the right even to think such a thing. "Oh, please." He didn't like the whining tone of his own voice, but he couldn't suppress it. "Don't let our past—"

"I'm a professional. I would never let any past relationship I had with a young woman's parent be a consideration, either for or against school admission." She bristled.

"I know that. I didn't mean to offend you." He pressed his thumbs against the outside of his pants pockets. "It's just that, it's so hard without her mother."

He looked at Lydia's unlined face. Perhaps she seemed so carefree because she had never married—or given birth to a beautiful baby who turned into a rebellious teenager. Yet Drake sensed her rebellion hadn't reached the core of her soul. He prayed it never would.

He wished he could take Lydia out for a cup of coffee so they could talk. But he couldn't. He couldn't burden her with his problems. Better to let Lydia get to know Kelly for herself without him expressing his own doubts about her—and himself. He suppressed a sardonic smile. Perhaps he, not Lydia, was the one in need of rescue.

"Oh. I didn't realize you're a single parent." Her mouth slackened and her eyes took on a stricken light but she seemed to recover without delay. "That's okay. I may be teaching an old-fashioned art, but I know a lot of people are divorced nowadays."

"Not divorced. Widowed."

"Oh." The stricken look returned. "I'm sorry."

"That's okay. She's been gone nearly twelve years now."

"No it isn't. It's never okay." Her hand twitched as though she wanted to reach out to him, but she clenched her fingers together instead.

"Thank you for understanding." He deliberately pasted a smile on his face. "I can see why your school is such a success. You obviously know what to say to make a person feel better. So will you find it in your heart to take Kelly on as one of your students?"

"You are aware that this course doesn't last a week or two."

"Yes. It goes all year, after school and some Saturdays."

"Correct. I recommend that my students stay with me throughout the school year. Will you be here that long?"

He nodded. "Yes. Maybe we'll be here forever."

"Forever. That's a very long time."

*Forever.* That sounded good to his ears. Did Lydia feel the same?

"All right, then. I'll let you know as soon as I can," Lydia promised.

"Good. She needs you." Having blurted more than he meant, Drake made a point of taking a sudden interest in a batch of cookies. If he told Lydia the truth, maybe she wouldn't take Kelly. His daughter had been unhappy at the prospect of leaving her friends in upstate New York— friends he didn't like. No matter that Mom didn't really need him so much. He had come to a point in his life where he needed her—to help him with his daughter.

Not that the apple had fallen far from the tree. Maybe Lydia would give him another chance. He had changed. If she would let him show her how much, she wouldn't be disappointed.

# Chapter 3

As the evening drew to a close, Lydia milled around the dining room. Determined to keep her promise to Drake to give him an answer about Kelly, she kept a close eye on the younger girl. Lydia accepted young men but none had shown interest in her school this semester. The girls who had applied possessed evident potential and promised to be eager students.

Kelly was different. If the word "anti-charm" were to appear in the dictionary, Kelly's picture would illustrate the term to perfection. Lydia could see by the way she had applied purple and black makeup and attention-grabbing clothes that she was trying hard to express her rebellion. The girl cried for help. Couldn't anyone else see?

In spite of herself, Kelly's beauty shone through her tough attitude punctuated by ears with multiple piercings. Always willing to look beyond the surface, Lydia hoped Kelly's reticence would prove temporary and she would become bubbly as the evening progressed. Yet even as the hours passed, Lydia could see that Kelly appeared at Charming Manor against her will and failed to make new friends with ease. She halfway paid attention to others who tried to talk to her, and even from across the room Lydia could tell that Kelly answered their queries in monosyllables. Lips painted bright reddish purple made their tightness all too evident. On the opposite side of the room—and on the opposite side of the spectrum—Drake laughed with one of the parents who had gone to school with them both.

*Lord, what should I do? Should I help Drake with Kelly? Or will I do more harm than good?*

The Lord didn't wait to give her a sense of what she should do. She needed to help Kelly. He wasn't going to let Lydia escape her responsibilities.

*Lord, help me fight any romantic emotions I feel. Drake is no good for me. He wasn't then. He isn't now. I just know it. Help!*

Temporary help arrived in the form of a parent with a question. Lydia put off thinking about Kelly and the problems the girl—and her father—promised to present.

The following morning, Lydia drained the last bit of her coffee when she heard a knock. She walked to the door and peeped through the window covered by sheers. "Drake!" She peered at her reflection in the foyer mirror. Her crisp white blouse, black pants, and flat shoes looked satisfactory, but she wished she had splashed a little color on her cheeks and lips before making coffee so company wouldn't catch her with a bare face. Drake knocked once more. She didn't have time for a last-minute makeup fix.

He would have to take her as she was.

When she opened the door, her traitorous heart beat hard as she became drenched in the dark pools of his eyes.

Clad in jeans and a fresh denim shirt, he leaned against the side of the door frame with the easy confidence she remembered. "I hope you don't mind my dropping by like this. I couldn't wait. I have to know what you think. Are we students here or not?"

"There's nothing like getting to the point, is there?" She debated whether to invite him in and decided she'd better not.

"No use beating around the bush."

Lydia stalled. "I'm not sure Kelly needs charm school, if she's anything like you. Last night you barely had a spare minute, so many people wanted to see you."

"They're curious as to why I came back after all these years."

"I doubt they're curious. I have a feeling they already know."

"Because of my mom." He looked at the tip of his boot.

Sensing this conversation might take a few moments, Lydia motioned toward two white wicker chairs. Drake didn't hesitate to seat himself.

"Yes. Everybody has been talking about how she's been hobbling around after that hip replacement surgery. But she's been getting along much better than I ever could have thought possible. I can't believe how quickly she's recovering." Lydia paused. "Care for a cup of coffee?"

He waved once. "No. I had some already, thanks."

Lydia took her own seat.

Drake nodded. "I was happy with how well the surgery went."

"Everyone's been helping. Except I haven't had a chance to do much myself. She's so popular and all. I have been keeping up with her progress through the neighbors, though."

As soon as she spoke the words, she realized how defensive she sounded. If she could have looked charming while smacking herself on the forehead, she would have at that moment. Drake had already referred to their past, and that should have served to clear the slate. So why had she made a veiled reference to things best left forgotten? His mother had been sorry to see them break up, and everyone knew it. Lydia felt too awkward to maintain any contact with Mrs. Kingston. Lydia darted her glance toward a massive oak tree in the yard, hoping against hope to find someone in dire need of emergency etiquette lessons so she could rush over and administer first aid in an ever so charming manner.

*Ha! Look in the mirror. You haven't done such a great job of being an example, have you?*

Drake cut into her self-chastisement. "I did come back to help my mother, and I've appreciated everyone's concern about her health. They're genuine. I can tell."

"I know they are. Everybody around here knows your business, but they care about you. Not like New York, I'd venture."

He thought for a moment. "It was sort of like that in my part of New York. Sure, I didn't know everybody in the Albany-Schenectady-Troy area, but I made friends easily with my immediate neighbors and we all looked out for each other. Upstate is nothing like Manhattan."

"So I've heard."

He cut his glance to her. "You don't have to tell me what you're thinking. You're thinking that Kelly seems like she comes from Manhattan—or, judging from all that makeup, maybe Mars."

"Manhattan. Mars. It's all the same." She chuckled.

"And they'd say, 'Missouri. Mars. It's all the same.' "

Lydia didn't hold back her mirth. "No doubt."

"Sometimes I wonder if they aren't all the same, seriously," Drake confessed. "I tried to shelter Kelly, but it didn't work. She still rebelled and turned from the little girl I knew into an alien."

"That's called being a teenager. At least she agreed to go to the party last night."

"I think it was more to get away from Mother than because she wanted to be here. Oh, I guess I shouldn't have said that." Drake let out a small groan.

"That's okay. I'm not testing you on how charming you are." She winked, and her reward was a smile. "Besides, I need to know the truth about her attitude in regard to taking lessons with me. My course is detailed, and I want my students to enjoy it."

"She will."

"Even if it kills her, huh?"

"I know it's obvious she's a handful. Frankly, that fact embarrasses me. I didn't want her to turn out that way." His gaze bored into her eyes. "And I'm not like that. Not anymore."

"I—I hadn't made the comparison." She tightened her

grip on the armrests.

"How kind of you to pretend to forget." His voice was soft. "I want you to know that since I knew you all those years ago, I found Christ."

A happy little gasp escaped her lips. "You did?"

"Yes." If one of the great masters of art had painted Drake's picture to capture that moment in time, Lydia imagined that a light of the palest shade of yellow would emanate from around his face. She had seen that look of rapture in other Christians. His conversion surely had been sincere.

So the cross hanging on a chain that fell just above the open collar of his shirt was more than a fashion statement.

Her heart shattered.

*Why couldn't you have found Him when I loved you back then?*

"Well," he prodded, "aren't you happy for me?"

She set her mouth into her most attractive smile. "Of course I am. Welcome to the Christian community, my brother in Christ."

"Thanks, but I'm not quite that new at it. I made the altar call years ago. Before Mandy. . ." He looked at the beige rug.

"Your wife." She felt a catch in her throat.

"Yes. That's what's really wrong with Kelly, I think. She never knew her mother. Maybe I should have moved back here then, and at least Mother could have raised her. But I was too busy working, trying to provide her with a good school and home. And what did I get?"

"A goth."

A shadow of a bittersweet smile passed over his lips. "I didn't think you'd know the term."

"Do I seem as out of it as all that?"

"No. You just seem too sweet to deal with the dark side of teens."

"Judging from the looks of her makeup, I take it you mean that literally."

He laughed. The sound lightened her mood as much as she suspected it cheered him. "I suppose that's right." All too soon he turned serious. "I thought by taking her to church every Sunday, I'd be protecting her. But somehow she still managed to connect with a bad crowd. I desperately wanted to do something, but what? I couldn't just quit my job and babysit her twenty-four seven."

"Of course not." She didn't resist the urge to lean over and set a comforting hand on his shoulder. "You did the best you could. And you still are. Look at how you picked up everything and moved here, just for her sake."

"If I can convince her to stay here."

"Don't be silly. You're her parent. She stays here if you say so, right? Unless she has other relatives to go to in New York."

"No. I guess that's some comfort, believe it or not. Once Mandy died, her side of the family didn't want much to do with us, especially once Kelly started rebelling."

Lydia looked for something comforting to say, and found it. "It could be worse. They could be taking you to court to gain custody."

"True. There's no danger in that, at least. Mandy's parents are more than happy living as empty nesters. They enjoy the freedom. And her sisters are bogged down with broods of their own. They're too polite to say so, but I'm sure they welcome the limited contact with Kelly for their kids since they think she'd be a negative influence."

"That's too bad. I see the light in her eyes. I don't think she's hard core."

"That's some consolation," he admitted. "Now if only I can get her away from that crowd in New York. She's pining away for all of her friends. I can't keep her off the phone, and when she's not talking on that, she's chatting with them over the Internet. I've already grounded her for the rest of the week from the phone as it is."

"I wouldn't. That could be a huge mistake."

"Really?"

"Yes. Don't try to stop her. That will only make it worse. For a teen like Kelly, forbidden friendships will just seem more appealing. Maybe she can make friends at church. I—I know your mother doesn't go to church much."

He shook his head.

"Then she won't mind if I invite you to go with me. I attend His Holiness on Main Street. Our pastor offers a contemporary service at ten and a traditional service later. Maybe Kelly would find the contemporary service appealing—or at least less off-putting—since they play modern praise hymns then. You wouldn't believe how many kids go to that service. Some she's already met here last night. The youth group is very active."

"You should go out and pitch your church door to door. You'd fill up the seats so fast they'd have to add an evening service, too."

"Thanks, but we already have one." She took a sudden

interest in the small pearl ring she wore on her right ring finger. "I, uh, I didn't mean to come on so strong."

"You didn't," he assured her. "Or at least, I don't mind. I do have one question, though."

She looked up. "What?"

"Does the youth group have any other goths?"

The query sent Lydia into giggles. "Well, they don't dress like that at church, but I'm sure she'll find something in common with someone."

He nodded. "Maybe she will."

"I'll call the head of the church group tomorrow and find out what they have on their agenda. Maybe they'll be going to an amusement park or somewhere she'd like to go. Even if she doesn't make friends right away, she'll still be doing something fun that will get her mind off New York."

"That's a great idea. Thanks for the suggestion. I really appreciate your help. Even though this is my hometown, it's still not so easy getting acclimated to life here again. I've been gone a long time."

*Too long.* She shook the treacherous thought out of her mind.

"So which service do you go to?" he asked.

She paused. Should she admit that she attended the early service, and that she swayed and clapped her hands to the praise music with as much enthusiasm as the kids half her age? Surely that idea wouldn't hold with her image as a staid etiquette expert. But then again, he hadn't known her as an etiquette expert. He had only known her as a carefree, love-besotted teenager. "I go to the contemporary service."

"Good. Then we'll know someone there." An unsure look entered his expression. "If you don't mind us barging into your Sunday service."

"It's hardly *my* Sunday service. And even if it were, I wouldn't stop you and Kelly from taking part. I don't invite just anyone to join us, you know." She invested that last sentiment with false snobbery and flicked her upturned nose with an affected forefinger.

"In that case, I would be foolish not to take the opportunity to introduce my daughter to the finest society the region has to offer." He rubbed his fingernails against the lapel of a blazer he wasn't wearing and then inspected them with a pretend satisfied air.

"Indeed." She sniffed, enjoying their silliness.

"I'm assuming then, that my fine daughter will find a place in your esteemed school so she can hone the fine manners expected of a lady of her station."

"Of course." Lydia sobered, hoping she wouldn't regret her decision.

Lydia's neighbor Georgia sat at the cloth-covered kitchen table, where she and Lydia had been chatting as Georgia borrowed a cup of flour. Lydia had hoped her neighbor might have a clue about Lydia's secret admirer, but her speculation had revealed little.

Georgia ran a red fingernail over the image on the ornament sent from Lydia's secret admirer. "So you think Drake sent you this?"

"Who else? After all, it arrived just before he did."

"And it was postmarked Independence."

"Yes. He could have stopped off there to mail it so I wouldn't catch on. Trouble for him is, I did."

"You could ask him, you know."

"I've thought about it, but the time never seems right. And what if I'm wrong? I'd really look like an egotistical idiot."

"You're wise to be cautious. I don't think it's Drake." Georgia set the ornament on the table. "I think he's smarter than that. If it had been Drake, he would have mailed the ornament well before he left town so you wouldn't know it was from him."

"But if it's not from Drake, then who?"

"Ralph."

The high volume of Lydia's laughter surprised even her. "I appreciate the belly laugh, but you've got to be joking. Ralph?"

"Yes, Ralph. I've seen how he flirts with you. If he stayed at everyone's house as long as he does with you, it would take him two days instead of one to finish his route."

Lydia made a tossing motion with her hand. "You've got to be nuts, Georgia. Ralph is just being friendly. I'll bet he tells all the women on his route how pretty they are."

"Pretty? He tells you that?"

Lydia wished she hadn't blurted out the fact. "Yes. But I think nothing of it. He's just passing the time of day."

"That's what you think. He never tells me I'm pretty. Case in point."

A quick glance Georgia's way told the tale. The striking redhead never left her house without appearing immaculate and fashionable. Her willowy yet curvy build always attracted the admiring looks of men and envious glances from women.

"There's too much competition for your attention," Lydia speculated. "He must think he has a better chance with someone plain like me."

"Plain? When was the last time you looked at yourself?"

She felt a blush. "You'll say anything to make me think it's Ralph, won't you?"

"He's secure, stable, and has a reliable job. A girl could do worse."

"Yes, he is all those things, and nice, too. But would you settle for that yourself?" Lydia paused. "No, you wouldn't. And if you had, you'd be married by now."

"This is true."

"Besides, it can't be Ralph. You should have heard him go on and on about how the person violated everything decent in the world by not including a return address." She giggled.

"Ah, then he protested too much?"

Lydia squirmed. "I didn't think of it that way."

Georgia pointed at Lydia. "See there? I told you. It has to be Ralph. He's your secret admirer. Well, not so secret, really."

"We'll see. Maybe my admirer, whoever he is, will send something else that will offer me a better clue."

"You really want it to be Drake, don't you?"

"No!"

"Ah, now who is protesting too much?" Georgia sighed. "If I were you, I'd forget Drake. Maybe he's still handsome and all that, but I remember you weren't so happy with him after what he did. And if not for that, he would never have left town and married someone else."

Georgia spoke in a matter-of-fact way, but her words cut Lydia to the quick. "He says he's changed. He was even wearing a cross."

"Oh, is that so? Well, it's been a long time, but I believe people are born with certain personalities and they may alter their habits, but they will always be who they are no matter what. So I would be careful if I were you. I care about you. That's the only reason I say that."

"I know. I wouldn't take the advice of any other woman so close to heart. I know you want what's best for me."

"I do. So what did you decide about his daughter? Please tell me you didn't take her in your class."

Lydia clenched her teeth and formed her mouth into a sheepish curve. "Well. . ."

Georgia groaned.

"She really needs me."

"I hope you're not just telling yourself that."

"No. She really does. You should have seen the way she was dressed for the party. And her makeup! Her lipstick was almost black."

"I've seen that look before." Georgia wrinkled her nose. "I don't like it."

"At least she's willing to wear makeup."

"But you know how it is. She will have just as much trouble getting used to not wearing so much makeup as someone who wears none has trouble getting used to seeing color on her face. Do you really think you'll be able to get her to tone it down?"

Lydia knew what Georgia meant. She had taken on a girl with a similar appearance three years before and, in spite of repeated lessons on tasteful and proper cosmetic application, the girl returned to her former look the next day. "All I can do is try. But there's more to this than makeup."

"I'll say."

"Look, I don't care who her father is, this girl needs help. She has no mother, she's not close to her grandmother, and she hasn't made friends here yet. Through Charming Manor, she can make nice friends and get the support she needs to make a better life for herself."

"So you are being charitable. Good for you."

Lydia wouldn't have tolerated such a snide remark from anyone but her best friend. "I am, as a matter of fact. But I have to say, I see something in Kelly that I'm not sure others do. Not that she seems easy to like. At least, she hasn't been so far. But she can change. I just know it."

"All I can say is, I wish you well."

# Chapter 4

Lydia slid into the pew beside Drake. Kelly was on his other side. A mishap with her cat Scarlett had delayed Lydia, so she barely had time to greet them before the service began. As she swayed to the music and sang familiar lines, guided by the words on the screens, Lydia forgot about her cares and focused on God. Still, she took comfort in Drake's presence beside her as the minister spoke about references to the harvest season found in scripture, focusing on the apostle Paul's letter to the Romans, in which he wrote of his desire to reach his brothers for Christ, adding to his harvest among the Gentiles.

Lydia wondered who had been responsible for Drake's conversion. Or was Georgia right? Had Drake never really changed? Judging from Kelly's appearance, she didn't look as though she had grown up under strong Christian influence. Or maybe her obvious rebellion was a sure sign that she had indeed.

*Lord, give me wisdom.*

After the service they walked together to their cars. Lydia couldn't resist noticing the teenager. To her relief, she had forgone the rock star T-shirt and was wearing one depicting an angel instead.

"So you like angels?"

"No, I'm just wearing this because I don't like them."

"Kelly!" Drake's mouth formed itself into such a straight line that it nearly disappeared. His ebony eyes became hidden under narrowed lids.

"Ask a stupid questio—"

"Kelly, we are still on church grounds," Drake reminded her.

Kelly blanched. "Okay, I'm sorry, Miss Lydia. I was just joking."

"I understand." Lydia bit her lower lip to keep from adding a curt remark that sarcasm doesn't become a lady and is rarely funny. She had to remember that if she wanted a relationship with the girl that could change her life for the better, she would have to become more than just her charm school instructor. This meant she couldn't take advantage of every chance to correct Kelly. "I suppose I could have asked a more intelligent question, or simply complimented your shirt. And I *do* like it."

Kelly's sour look faded into a slight grin before she seemed to remember herself and put her hard mask back on.

Drake stopped behind a sensible Ford that Lydia guessed was several years old. "So where is your car?"

Lydia looked over the horizon. "At the far end of the lot. Serves me right for being late." She shrugged. "I guess I'd better be going."

"Got any plans?"

Lydia wasn't sure how to answer. She didn't have anything more pressing to do than read the Sunday newspaper. Yet even though the last few weeks had been pleasant and she hadn't received any more mysterious gifts, she wasn't sure how far she wanted to take a renewed friendship with Drake. A glance at Kelly gave her the answer. "Nothing too special."

"Good. Want to eat dinner with us?"

How could she answer without sounding self-righteous? "I, uh, I usually try not to eat out on Sundays. Or shop or anything like that." She nodded once toward the church. "Pastor Bart suggested we just rest on Sundays, and I've found his advice to be such a blessing."

"Oh, I wasn't inviting you out. Mom has dinner fixed for us at home. So if you're allowed to eat with friends on Sunday, I know she'd be glad to see you again."

Lydia swallowed. She hadn't seen Mrs. Kingston outside of a crowded public setting since senior year. Since then they had exchanged pleasantries from time to time, but never talked. Not as they once shared their hopes and dreams together. What did Mrs. Kingston think of her? She had liked her, but that was years ago, before the breakup. She wasn't sure she wanted to face her in her own home. "I, uh—"

"Oh, come on. Why, she'd have my head if she thought I'd sat right by you in church and didn't invite you for dinner. And if she found out I invited you and you didn't take me up on it, she'd be liable to come by your house and get you."

Lydia could imagine Mrs. Kingston taking such

action. The thought brought on a chuckle. "In that case, it sounds like I'd better go along."

"So how was the sermon?" was the first statement out of Mrs. Kingston's mouth when they arrived at the Kingston home. The house was just as Lydia remembered—cozy and smelling of pine cleaner.

"It was good, Mom."

"That's what I figured. The Bible's only so big. How many sermons can you get from it?" She eyed Lydia. "Oh, I didn't know you brought a guest."

Lydia couldn't tell from the older woman's expression whether she was glad Lydia was present or not. "Nice to see you again, Mrs. Kingston. I appreciate your willingness to include me today."

"Think nothing of it. It's been a long time."

"Yes, ma'am." She wanted to add "too long" but resisted the urge. "Now what might I do to help you?" She realized she should have brought a hostess gift for Mrs. Kingston—perhaps a loaf of homemade bread or cookies—but Drake's off-the-cuff invitation had left her without time to prepare a suitable gift.

"Not a thing. Now you sit right on down. Kelly helped me set the table before she left this morning. She can get the things to the table now for me. Can't you, Kelly?"

Kelly gave a halfhearted nod but acquiesced.

As they feasted on fried chicken, mashed potatoes, sliced tomatoes, fresh green beans, and cherry pie, the conversation was surprisingly easy and friendly. Every now and again she caught Drake looking at her in a wistful way. She wished he wouldn't. She wasn't ready for a trip down memory lane.

Neither was his mother, apparently. Mrs. Kingston's voice didn't hold quite as much warmth and her smile wasn't quite as deep as it had been in years past. She had every right to be wary. Perhaps she didn't want to get her hopes up for Lydia and Drake—again.

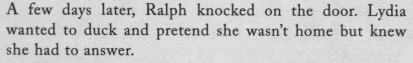

A few days later, Ralph knocked on the door. Lydia wanted to duck and pretend she wasn't home but knew she had to answer.

"Hi, Miss Lydia." His smile was broad as usual.

She didn't have the heart to leave him standing in the rain. "Come on in."

"Don't mind if I do."

Now that Georgia had speculated the unthinkable— that Ralph was her secret admirer—she wished he didn't feel so at home. Thankfully, he didn't wait for her to express any assurances.

"I have another package for you. This time it's too big for your box. So I thought you'd like to have it now, inside, especially since it's raining." He peered through her living room window framed by transparent white lace curtains. Lydia remembered that she needed to change her curtains and rugs to reflect the transition from summer to fall. She watched his gaze travel to the rose-patterned rug. "Glad it's not raining heavy yet. I'd hate to track in on all your pretty rugs. You always keep such a spotless house, Miss Lydia. Always as pretty as you are."

"Thank you, Ralph." Her voice sounded less grateful than

she meant. Still, she didn't add any remarks, not wanting to encourage him more than she apparently already had.

He handed her a box so large she knew she would have to sit down to open it. Yet its dimensions defied its light weight.

"What could it be?"

"I don't know but again, there's no return address. And you know how I feel about that. It must be from that secret admirer of yours."

Did he know because he was sending the packages himself? Or was he just curious? She studied the address label and contemplated whether to come up with an excuse not to open the box right away.

Ralph eyed the brown wrapping. "It's postmarked Kansas City this time. Seems whoever it is stays on the move."

"Kansas City and Independence are not that far from each other," she pointed out. "You should know that yourself."

"Yep. Haven't been to either place lately, though."

"Oh." She wondered if he was saying that just to give her a false reassurance. Whatever his motives, she could tell he wasn't about to budge until she opened it. Rather than argue, she decided to humor him.

Before long she had opened the box and withdrawn a lovely silk flower arrangement of white poinsettias.

Ralph whistled. "Wow, he didn't spare any expense."

"I didn't think you'd know about such things, Ralph," Lydia noted.

"I hope you aren't calling me a cheapskate, Miss Lydia."

"Not at all. I mean, I didn't think you would know about silk flower arrangements."

"Oh. Well, I took one to a sick friend recently. You know her. Opal Kingston."

"Oh. Why, of course I know Mrs. Kingston."

"I met her playing bingo at the hunt club. She won two hundred dollars that night. She's a right nice woman. She's had hip replacement surgery, you know."

"Yes, I know."

"I was taking her to the doctor before her son and granddaughter got back here to help. They're a little late, though. She's walking just as well as you and I do. I think she likes the company, though. I understand her grand-daughter is taking classes with you."

"Yes."

"Well, if anybody can get her straight, you sure can." Ralph eyed the flower arrangement. "This guy has a thing for Christmas, doesn't he?" He looked back out the window. "That sky's looking mighty ominous. I'd better get going."

She set the box aside with one hand and held the arrangement with the other, rising from her seat. "Have a good day, Ralph."

As she watched him depart, she felt more puzzled than ever.

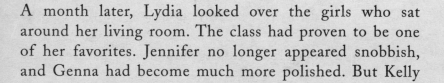

A month later, Lydia looked over the girls who sat around her living room. The class had proven to be one of her favorites. Jennifer no longer appeared snobbish, and Genna had become much more polished. But Kelly still seemed rebellious. She had responded in a lukewarm manner to her makeover lesson, using darker shades with a heavier hand than Lydia recommended. Lydia took a small amount of satisfaction in the fact Kelly had moved to a softer color palette that brought out her gorgeous complexion and shiny dark hair. Her attitude had softened some, but she could still be surly. Lydia knew better than to expect a change overnight, but she couldn't help feeling discouraged at times.

Lydia didn't dare tell Kelly she'd been praying for her.

"Your assignment for this week was to write a bread-and-butter note," she reminded her students. "I am very pleased with what you all wrote." She held up a flower-embossed note. "I have one I'd like to read aloud."

The girls looked at each other, each obviously hoping hers was the chosen note. Lydia read:

*Dear Dominick,*

*Thank you for the wonderful hospitality you presented me with at your house last evening. The escargot, the filet mignon, the chocolate mousse—all were beyond words. I can't believe you flew in a chef all the way from Paris to prepare our meal!*

*And the gorgeous diamond pendant from Tiffany's? What can I say? I will treasure it always.*

*Again, thank you for your hospitality. I look forward to jetting off with you to Jamaica next week.*

*XOXOXO,*
*Kelly*

As she read, groans and giggles filled the living room. But when the others discovered that Kelly had written the letter, some gasped while others nudged her.

"Is that really a bread-and-butter letter?" Jennifer asked. "It sounds more like an engagement letter to me."

Lydia smiled. "Yes, it does sound like this couple is romantic, but as far as thanking him for his hospitality, it meets the requirement. Kelly, I give you an A-plus for creativity."

Kelly beamed for a split second before turning her mouth into an upside-down U. "Yeah, so what? I thought you'd flunk me."

"Flunk you? Of course not. Besides, no one here is a failure," Lydia assured them. "We are all winners."

Kelly sent her stare to the ceiling and crossed her arms.

Lydia suppressed a sigh.

*Stick with me, Lord. I need You.*

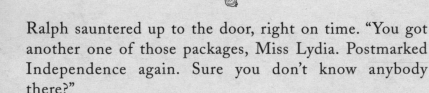

Ralph sauntered up to the door, right on time. "You got another one of those packages, Miss Lydia. Postmarked Independence again. Sure you don't know anybody there?"

"No, I don't."

"Well, somebody there sure seems to like you a lot. Why don't you open it up and see what's inside?"

Lydia arched an eyebrow. "I think you're finding this mystery more tantalizing than I do, Ralph."

"Always thought it might be fun to be an amateur detective. Never had occasion to, though. Not much exciting happens around here."

"I can't say that's a bad thing."

"Nope. I suppose not. So are you gonna open the package?" He tapped his foot.

She opened the brown paper and discovered a box wrapped in silver foil. "It's from the same store as before. The Christmas Store." She set the box on the wrought iron table and lifted its heavy contents. She gasped as she unwrapped red tissue paper and revealed a ceramic Christmas tree decorated with painted ornaments. "Isn't it beautiful!"

"Yep. Whoever it is really likes Christmas."

She couldn't resist. "You like Christmas, don't you, Ralph?"

He shrugged. "It's okay. Mainly more work for me, like I said before. But speaking of Christmas, I was wondering if I could ask you a question."

"Certainly." Her stomach lurched. Was he about to invite her to a Christmas party or dance? Or to his house for dinner? She rehearsed ways to say no before he posed his query.

"Well, it's getting pretty close to the holidays and all, and I was wondering if you might have any suggestions as to what I might get for Mrs. Kingston. I know you know her son."

So the word was out. "Um, yes I do know her son. I didn't know you and Mrs. Kingston were such good friends. I'm glad to hear that."

His face flushed. "Yep, she's a mighty fine woman."

A mighty fine woman. He had said something much like that about her in the past. Could it be that Ralph was interested in Mrs. Kingston romantically? Lydia recalled her mentioning Ralph. The idea of such a romance left Lydia with a warm feeling of relief.

"Yes, she is a fine woman," Lydia agreed. "And I do believe I smelled a whiff of gardenia perfume on her the other day. Maybe she'd like a bottle of that."

"I don't know." He wrinkled his nose. "That doesn't sound too practical to me."

"Well, she did say her toaster's on the fritz, but I wouldn't recommend that as a Christmas gift. At least, not for a lady friend." She winked.

"Maybe not. You always know what to do, Miss Lydia."

Dusting her office, Lydia observed the Christmas-related gifts she had received from her secret admirer. They were all so beautiful and thoughtful. "I wonder who you are, Secret Admirer."

At least he wasn't Ralph. She felt certain of that, after their last conversation where he revealed his interest in Mrs. Kingston. "Maybe it *is* you, Drake."

She wished it were so.

And she wished it weren't so.

She picked up the white silk poinsettia. "It will take more than pretty flowers to convince me you've changed, Drake Kingston."

At that moment, the doorbell rang. Lydia glanced at the wall clock and saw that the hour was early for the postman to be arriving. "Who could that be?"

She answered the door and saw Drake.

"Good. You're up bright and early," he greeted her.

"So are you."

"I was wondering if you'd let me help you pick out your tree."

"Pick out my tree?"

"Uh, yeah. You know. That tradition where you go out and buy a tree and put these colorful things called ornaments on it."

She chuckled. "I didn't know you were even thinking of such a thing." An image of the little tree from her secret admirer popped into her head.

"Huh?"

With his mouth hanging open as it was, Lydia decided not to confront Drake at the moment. "Never mind. Just thinking out loud."

"Well," he said, "I was planning on picking out mine today. I'd be glad to help with yours, too, if you like."

"Kelly doesn't want to help you?"

"She's baking with Mom. Bonding time, you know. They really need it."

She looked at the truck parked in the driveway. "Well, I was planning on going tomorrow, but I think I'd have lots more fun with you today." She headed toward the closet and retrieved her coat. "Okay. Let's go."

Lydia suddenly felt nervous as they drove toward the Christmas tree farm, when she realized they were alone together for the first time since his arrival. He talked easily about his new job at the construction company, about Kelly's new friends at school, about how much she liked the classes at Charming Manor, even about the weather. A casual observer would have assumed they had been friends forever.

"I think we might stay in Missouri," Drake noted as they turned into the entrance of the Christmas tree farm. "She's making good grades at her new school, and she hasn't complained about you putting her through the paces at Charming Manor."

"Really? You might stay here after all?" Her stomach rolled over with a feeling of nervous excitement. To have Drake stay near her forever! Was it too much to ask? What if it were? What if nothing came of their relationship? Suddenly, she realized she didn't want to consider that possibility. Yet the thought that she had developed feelings anew for Drake scared and elated her at once.

"I'm glad Kelly is doing so well here, but doesn't she miss her friends at all? I mean, you said she was having a hard time without them."

"She was at first, and she still struggles a little. But people have been so welcoming here that she seems to be doing much better. I credit you with a great part of her success."

Drake jumped out of the truck and grabbed a small saw from the back. She felt grateful that the necessary motion kept her from having to respond. She had come to appreciate Kelly over the past months. But would saying so make her seem cloying? Better not to make her feelings known too soon.

She exited the truck. Surrounded by evergreens of all shapes and sizes, she felt eager to find just the right one for her living room. The temperature had dropped but the significance of the cold didn't hit her until they'd been out awhile, walking amid the trees.

"I—I'll take that one." Shivering, she pointed to a balsam

that looked to be about nine feet in height.

"Are you sure? Or are you just wanting to get out of the cold?"

"A little of both," she admitted.

"I think this one looks just fine." With several swift strokes, he felled the tree. "I'll take the one beside it. What do you think?"

"It's lovely."

Drake was just as efficient in felling the second tree. Together they dragged their picks to the checkout line.

The farmer scratched his beard. "Two trees? And this big? You two must have a mighty big house."

"Oh, we don't—" Drake protested.

"We're not—" Lydia added.

The two stopped in mid sentence and laughed.

The farmer tabulated their bill. "That's a shame. You two look like you'd make a mighty fine couple."

Lydia was so chilled she was almost grateful to feel heat rise to her face. She noticed Drake didn't seem embarrassed.

"Feel like stopping off for a cup of hot chocolate on the way back?" he offered.

"Won't you let me make you some at home?" she countered. "It seems like the least I can do after you were so kind to help me with my tree."

"You might not say that when you find out all I can do is help you get yours propped up in the stand before I head out. I still have to get Mom's tree in the house." He pulled the car into the parking lot of the diner. "I definitely want to take a rain check on your invite for cocoa at your place. But I've been wanting to see if the cocoa at

Mildred's Diner is as good as it used to be."

"I think it is, but I'm willing to find out." She glanced at the trees in the back of the truck. "Are you sure your mom won't mind waiting?"

"Nah. She's tied up with all that baking. I doubt she misses me at all."

When they entered the diner moments later, Lydia was almost sorry she took Drake up on his offer. All heads turned when the bell on the door rang to signal their entrance. Most of the other diners turned back to their meals and snacks but others—especially those who had known Drake and her for years—raised their eyebrows.

*I guess this is what you call "going public" with a new relationship—or a renewed relationship. I wonder how Drake feels.*

He didn't seem to mind, acting as though he were doing nothing more than he did on any other day.

*That's just what he thinks. I'm just a friend. This is nothing more than a normal stop at the diner for him.*

As they waited for their order to arrive, Lydia chastised herself so much that she could barely register what Drake said. She noticed he flitted from one topic to another without much pause until he tried the cocoa. "Mmmmm. This cocoa is just as good as ever. Even better."

She took a sip of hot liquid, letting the whipped cream topping hit her upper lip. Rich sugary beverage filled her mouth. She swallowed. "You're right."

"How many times did we come here when we were in high school?"

"I can't count them all." She wished her voice hadn't taken on a wistful tone.

"But we can't live in the past. We must live in the present. That's why it's called the present. It's a gift."

*A gift. From my secret admirer?*

Yet something stopped her from expressing her thought.

"Yes, life is a gift. And I want to live life to the fullest," she said.

"Really? You seem scared to me."

"No I'm not." She took a sip of her drink to keep from answering further.

"I hope you aren't. Because life is too short not to spend whatever's left of it with the right person." He placed his hand on hers. The sensation would have felt comforting on any winter day, but she knew the sparks she felt were from more than a desire for warmth. A tingling darted through her, but the excitement of his touch mingled with an awareness of security she had never before felt in Drake's presence.

*Has he really changed, Lord?*

# Chapter 5

Afew days later, Kelly's voice rang out in the Kingston dining room after she bounded in from school. "Dad! Look!"

Drake knew why she was so excited. Kelly had received a package from New York from a street address he didn't recognize. He had been hesitant to pass it on to her. Kelly's old friends weren't above putting a false return address on a package so they could send her—what? Yet if the package proved to be innocent, he would have regretted withholding it from Kelly.

He had fought the temptation not to pass on the package, but to discard it before any harm could be done. Then he wondered if he should have opened it first, and then passed it on to her. Yet either option, while offering him some solace, would have been deceptive. If he chose to be deceptive, how could he expect Kelly not to follow his example? Still, he didn't trust her. Not yet. And he certainly didn't trust her friends. But he had to take a small step before he could take any big ones. He hoped his trust would not prove to be misplaced.

"It's from New York!" Kelly jumped a little, reminding him of Christmas mornings long ago.

"I know. Who do you think it's from?" He tried to keep his voice devoid of suspicion.

"Selena and Scottie, of course! Didn't you read the return address?"

"Yes." He dared not share his reservations, not when she was willing to open the box right in front of him. That showed she wasn't expecting her friends to pull any stunts. He tried not to let his inward sigh of relief reach too deeply into his chest.

Kelly tore open the package and reached into a cloud of white tissue paper. "It's an angel!" She held the angel in her hands and looked at the simple representation, obviously made by the children themselves, as though it were fashioned from 24-karat gold.

He suppressed a breath of relief. "May I see?"

Kelly nodded and handed him the angel. The little figure was composed of an inverted plastic funnel with pretty material over it to make a gown. Her arms were in a praying position, and she held a book in her hands. At her waist was a gold ribbon. White feathers were glued to her back to give her wings. He tapped on her face and assumed it to be a Styrofoam ball wrapped in light colored material. The children had drawn a face on it with a fine-tip marker. They had spared no ink to depict long lashes. Red lips smiled to create a serene expression. A strawberry red tassel for her hair matched her dress. He had a feeling the choice of color was no coincidence. A halo and collar were made from gold tinsel and what looked like one of his mom's doilies was draped over the skirt.

He ran his hand over the silky, yarn-like hair. "She's beautiful, Kelly."

Kelly nodded. "They know how much I like angels." She took the angel as Drake handed it back. He noticed tears in her eyes.

"What's the matter?"

"No—nothing."

"But you're crying."

"Am not."

"Are, too." He kept his voice gentle.

She sniffled as she stared at the gift from a child. "Someone does care about me, after all."

"Of course someone cares about you. We all care about you, Kelly. Don't you know that?"

She shrugged. "I—I guess." Kelly looked into his eyes. Her soft expression reminded him of the little girl he once knew. "You know what? Hardly anybody has been in touch with me since I left New York."

"Don't be silly. You were on the phone all the time."

She shook her head. "You don't understand."

"But—"

"I was fighting with Darrin, all right? Well, mostly fighting. Other than that, everybody else seems to have forgotten I was ever alive."

"Oh, honey." Drake put his arm around her shoulders. As usual, Kelly remained stiff and didn't return his gesture. Still, he sensed she needed a show of his warmth. "You have lots of new friends here. And we'll be staying here long enough for them to be your friends for a very long time."

"Yeah. I guess." She fingered the angel's skirt. "But I was praying to God that someone back home would still care about me. And they do. Selena and Scottie."

"Of course they do, Kelly."

"So God heard me. I guess that means He does care. He really does."

The end of the first semester had arrived and with it, the Christmas party. Lydia always held her celebration before school dismissed for the holiday. All of the girls had performed well on the rudimentary aspects of becoming ladies of charm and poise. The following semester would prove a bit more challenging as they learned finer points, including how to cook mouthwatering appetizers and how to host a party. As a preview she had put the girls in charge of some aspects of the Christmas party.

Looking around the house, she noted professionals couldn't have delivered better results. Pine garland framed each interior entrance, filling the house with a fresh scent that mixed well with the enticing aroma of hot spiced apple cider simmering on the stove. Gold tapered candles lent soft light to the generous living room and adjacent dining room. The Christmas tree she and Drake had selected looked perfect in front of the picture window, lit as it was with white lights.

With the room nearly filled with people talking, Lydia could see the party was well on its way to success. Still, she always felt a twinge of nervousness before each class event lest anything went awry. Since she was their teacher, she felt any failure on the part of her students as her own.

Kelly walked into the living room, with Drake close behind her. Lydia swept her gaze to him. His glance caught hers, a shy smile touching his lips. She could see that he was just as nervous for Kelly as she was. Though Kelly had little to fear, judging by her surprisingly stellar performance in class, she could understand a parent's desire to see his daughter succeed. He had dressed the part, wearing a striking combination of color—a dark suit, white shirt, and red tie.

"Kelly, you look absolutely beautiful. I've never seen you look more lovely." It was true. She was wearing a dress in a deep maroon instead of her usual black shirt and jeans. The streak of burgundy in her hair was gone—an irony since the color would have matched the dress to perfection.

In an unusual move for her, Kelly didn't hesitate to greet Lydia right away.

"You seem to be in a good mood," Lydia noted.

"I am. I got an early Christmas gift today. From friends in New York."

"Oh." Lydia suppressed a worried look. Such a good mood could only be attributed to more contact from the boyfriend back in New York; the one Drake thought was a poor influence.

*Lord, let me be wrong about this. Don't let Kelly go against her father.*

"It's not what you think. I got an angel tree topper from a little girl and boy I used to babysit."

"Oh!" Lydia's hand clutched her chest as though it had a mind of its own before she realized she had shown too much relief.

Kelly giggled. "Had you worried there for a minute, didn't I?"

"I'm afraid so."

"Selena is the one I've been practicing my everyday letters on."

"She's the one who sent you the tree topper." Lydia smiled.

"Yes. Her and her brother Scottie. I knew you'd approve." Kelly's voice held something in it that Lydia hadn't expected—a tone that told her Kelly desired her approval. "Want to see the tree topper?" Kelly didn't wait for an answer, but took the little angel out of its box and showed Lydia.

"She's lovely. Selena must have had some help."

"I think she did. She printed on the card that someone named Noelle showed her how to make it, and Scottie also signed the card. And someone named Todd, too. I guess Todd and Noelle must be friends of the kids' mom." Kelly rolled her glance Lydia's way. "And yes, I will be writing her a thank-you note. Tomorrow."

"Good. Why don't you go her one better? I can give you some of the angel cookies to send to her as a thank-you gift in a pretty Christmas tin. I have some tins left over that I haven't put out and I would be pleased if you took one."

"You do? Are you sure?" She let out a little gasp and widened her dark eyes.

"I'm sure."

At that moment, a couple of the other girls surrounded Kelly, curious and wanting to admire the tree topper. Lydia felt a tug on her arm.

"She sure is excited, isn't she?" Drake asked.

"Yes. She has reason to be. She's received a lovely gift from a friend and she has been a superb student in my classes."

"Believe it or not, her attitude seemed to soften when she got the package."

"I can tell. Her face is glowing." Lydia let out a mock sigh. "And to think I believed the change was due to what she learned at Charming Manor."

Drake lifted his forefinger and pretended to be an old-fashioned etiquette expert. "Poise and charm help one in any endeavor."

Lydia chuckled and watched Kelly talking to the other girls. "Do you know if she hangs out with the same friends at school as she does here?"

"They seem to be calling each other and chatting on the computer a lot."

"Good." Lydia excused herself so she could mingle with the other guests. As much as she wished she could focus her attention solely on Drake all night, she knew she couldn't. Not if she wanted to stay in business.

During the party, she caught Drake studying her on several occasions. Whenever her gaze caught his, he looked away. Could he suddenly be shy after all this time? Or was he sorry he ever took her out to find a tree and then to the diner? She recalled his near confession. Did he still care about her? He seemed as though he did. But she couldn't let him have her heart. Not again.

She noticed Kelly taking a call on her cell phone. Didn't she realize that was a definite violation of manners? Lydia resolved to go over cell phone etiquette again with the girls.

Later, after the party, Lydia summoned Kelly into the kitchen. "Here are the cookies for Selena." She noticed too many were left for her to consume by herself. "Will you allow me to pack you another box for someone else? Darrin, maybe?"

"Darrin," Kelly whispered. To Lydia's shock, tears filled her eyes and trickled onto her cheeks.

Lydia held out a consoling arm. "What's wrong?"

Lydia kept her emotions in check until that moment, when she exploded into sobs. "He—he broke up with me."

"What?"

"He texted me during the party."

"You mean he sent you a text message on your cell phone?" Lydia asked.

Kelly nodded. "How lame is that?"

"Pretty lame. So did he give you a reason?"

"He says he met someone else." Kelly's mouth formed a sneer and her voice betrayed her anger. "He didn't waste any time."

Lydia strode over to her and put a consoling arm around her shoulders. "Oh, honey. I'm so sorry. But you know what?" Lydia stared straight into Kelly's dark eyes. "You've changed so much since you moved here. You've grown into a beautiful young woman that any guy would love to have as a girlfriend. I have to wonder, do you really think you and Darrin still have enough in common to sustain a meaningful relationship?"

"I—I don't know," Kelly admitted.

Lydia had been working with teens long enough to tell what Kelly's tone of voice meant. "Are you really saying that you wish you were the one who broke up with him instead of him breaking up with you?"

"Maybe a little bit." Kelly's chuckle was bittersweet. "But are you really sorry?"

"Sorry you broke up? Probably not. Sorry to see you upset? Yes. Definitely."

"Dad will be jumping for joy."

"He won't be happy to see you hurt, honey."

Kelly shrugged. "He'll never understand."

"Ha!" Lydia blurted. "Of all people, your dad should understand."

"Huh?"

"I've never stopped loving him. And I always will." Lydia gasped. She wished she could take back the words. How did she allow herself to express such buried emotion—emotion she didn't realize she still felt? Ever since Drake had breezed back into town, latent feelings had risen to the forefront of her mind, taking her to another time and place. But to express them to his daughter. . .

What was she thinking?

Kelly's eyes widened. She pointed to Lydia. "So you and Dad—well, I knew something was going on between you."

"No, no. I was talking about an old high school romance."

"This has been going on since high school?"

"Well, not exactly. We dated in high school, but that was years ago. And he did marry your mother, of course." Lydia smiled.

"I hope you don't mind if I don't say I'm sorry."

Lydia felt grateful for the levity that took away from

her mortification. "For your sake I can't say I'm sorry, either."

Kelly grinned at the compliment before turning serious. "You know, I've been wanting Dad to find someone for a long time. And now that I've come to know you, I think he could do a lot worse."

"Thanks." Kelly diasappeared.

A faint smell of men's citrus cologne wafted toward Lydia. She turned and saw Drake standing in the doorway.

*How much did he overhear? Did he hear me tell Kelly I never stopped loving him?*

Her first impulse was to ask Drake but she couldn't. She had to retreat. She was too embarrassed to do anything else. "I—I have to tend to the fire." She headed to the living room and stoked the embers even though the time to let it burn out had passed long ago. She couldn't go back in the kitchen. Not now. She stopped stoking and stared at the dying embers.

*What a fool I am. Lord, I pray he didn't hear me. And I pray he won't come out here and ask me about it. Let him be more of a gentleman now than he ever was in high school. Let him walk out now and forever hold his peace.*

Drake's shadow filled the doorway, illuminated by the kitchen light.

*Let him just tell me good evening. Let him tell me Kelly won't be taking classes next semester. Let him tell me the party was a flop. Anything but that he overheard me!*

"Lydia?"

*Oh, why can't he leave me alone?*

She felt she had no choice but to set her face into an

expression of interest and look up at him. "Yes?"

"Come and sit with me, will you?" His voice sounded inviting. He sat on the sofa and patted the empty cushion beside him.

She felt she had no choice but to comply. "Where's Kelly?"

"She's still putting away the food for you."

"She doesn't have to do that."

"Yes, she does. Isn't it charming for young ladies to offer to help?"

"Yes, but it's not so charming of me to leave her alone to do all the work." She got up. "If you'll excuse me."

He rose. "No, I won't."

She wanted to argue, but the firm tone of his voice stopped her. He reached for her hand, but she didn't accept the gesture.

"I heard what you said to Kelly."

"Everything?"

"Everything. At least, everything that matters to me. I just wish you had confided in me first."

"It wasn't a confidence. I—I didn't know what I was saying. I was just trying to make her feel better, that's all."

"Feel better?"

Lydia wished she wasn't stuck being the bearer of news so upsetting to Kelly but she was grateful that the focus was off her, if only for a moment. "You didn't know her boyfriend back in New York broke up with her?"

"No." His shoulders dropped an inch. "I can see we still have a long way to go as far as getting our relationship to where it should be. I'm glad she has you to confide in. Mom and she have been getting along better, but Kelly still looks at her as someone too old to understand anything."

"Funny. She probably understands more than all of us put together."

"You have to get beyond your teen years to see that, I think."

Lydia nodded. "I wouldn't put too much stock in Kelly confiding in me. I asked her what was wrong and she told me. Besides, I'm sure she would have told you, too, once she got the chance."

"Is that what you think? Don't you remember how she looked just a few months ago? And you have no idea how morose and secretive she was before she left New York. For her to tell any adult anything like that about her personal life shows a huge change in her. A change I'm glad to see." He patted her hand. "A change I credit you for."

"Don't give me all the credit. She's been going to church and making new friends."

He aimed his forefinger at her. "Because of you. And I know she gives you credit, too. I heard how happy she was when she heard your confession."

"There's a big difference between thinking it would be nice for your father to find someone new and the reality if that were to happen. Besides, maybe she was just being nice."

"Another thing no one would have accused her of before." He placed his hand on her shoulder. She tried not to let his touch affect her. She had to protect herself from the ghosts of the past. "But everyone would accuse you of being more than nice."

His words could have been uttered by a casual acquaintance, yet because they came from him, they sent a shiver of happiness through her. She fought her feelings; trying not to remember the day they selected the Christmas tree. She tried not to recall the old flames of the young love they shared so long ago. She tried not to remember how he had broken her heart once. She couldn't let herself be that vulnerable again.

"Lydia, I think you know how I feel about you. It's like I never left."

"Yes. You're right. It's like you never left."

"I'm so happy to hear you say that." His face was lit with love, an expression she remembered all too well. She had seen shadows of such emotion in recent times, but hadn't seen its full flush in a long time. At that moment, she realized how much she missed his love.

She looked over his shoulder, beyond him into the blackness of her backyard. The darkness reminded her of the cold and sent a shiver through her body. She crossed her arms and rubbed her palms against her forearms.

Obviously mistaking her gesture as a plea for his warmth, Drake took her into his embrace. She froze, but he ignored her stiffened body. "I still love you, Lydia. I didn't realize until I came back here how much."

"No." She pulled away. "No. Don't say that."

"Why not?"

"Don't you see? I let you break my heart once. Not again. I'm smarter than I was when I was a teenager. Way smarter." Then why was she talking like a teenager? She clenched her teeth underneath closed lips to keep herself from saying anything more.

"I'm so sorry."

"That I'm smarter?" she couldn't resist quipping.

"No. That I broke your heart as thoroughly as you broke mine."

"Me? How can you even think such a thing? You're the one who was caught stealing, and you're the one who got sent away to military school. I stayed here, by myself. Wishing things could be different. You're the one who left me, by your actions and their consequences. I'll never forgive you!" The strength of her anger surprised even her.

"What do you mean, you'll never forgive me? I'm the one who should be forgiving you."

"What?" She felt her mouth drop so far open it couldn't have stretched another centimeter.

"I wrote to you after I left. I visited you that Christmas. And what did you do? You acted like you never even knew me."

"I—I didn't. Don't you see? You betrayed me! You proved you weren't the guy I thought you were. You never should have stolen from other people. You were nothing more than a common thief!"

He flinched.

"I remember what you told me," she continued, unable to stop herself. "You said it was fine, that those car dealers were covered by insurance and the big companies would be the ones to pay for the stereos and whatever else you took out of the cars on the dealer's lot. But who do you think pays insurance premiums? Why, you may as well have stolen from your own mother!"

"Do you think you're telling me something I haven't heard?"

She realized how self-righteous she sounded. "I guess not. I'm sorry." Embarrassment over just how much resentment she still harbored filled her. She softened her voice. "If only you had stopped to think about what could happen to you—to us—if you were caught. But you didn't. And once you were, it was too late."

"I know that now. But must you lecture me like I'm a five-year-old? Don't you think I was punished enough? Being sent away like that was bad enough, but losing you was more punishment than I ever thought I could bear. And now to have you be so cold after all this time." He paused. "Even the car dealer forgave me and agreed not to press charges, and he's the one I really wronged. You know, his forgiveness is one of the main reasons why I came to a saving knowledge of Christ. He was a Christian, and he walked the talk. You open and close your classes with prayer, encourage your students to enrich their spiritual lives, go to church. Is your charm—and your spiritual-ity—nothing more than an act?"

"An act?" At that moment, she came as close to slapping Drake as she ever could have. But she stopped herself. Striking him, whether or not he deserved it, would accomplish nothing. Instead she clenched her fists by her sides and tilted her chin at him in a way that would have done the most snobbish member of the Social Register proud. "I'll have you to know that because I have relied on my faith, I have done perfectly fine all these years. God has sent me many, many people who care about me. Including Kelly. And their feelings toward me wouldn't be sincere if I were putting on an act. People can see through those things, you know. Especially teenagers."

His features flinched in an almost imperceptible flash. Lydia should have been satisfied that she had slapped him verbally in a way the back of her hand never could, but revenge tasted more like bile than sugar.

She must have heard her name, because Kelly chose that instant to appear. "Hey, you guys, what's going on out here?"

"Nothing," they answered in unison.

"That means something." Kelly leaned against the door frame and snapped her white cotton dish towel. An expectant light shone in her dark eyes. "Come on. Tell me."

"We've got to go, Kelly."

"No we don't. I don't have school tomorrow. You guys can talk all you want."

"No," they answered.

Lydia managed to regain composure. She rose from her seat. "Thank you, Kelly, but we're quite through."

"Yes. We are." Drake's voice sounded colder than the lighted icicles hanging from her roof. "Come on, Kelly, let's go."

Kelly obeyed but glanced at Lydia one last time as they left. At that moment, Lydia realized that Kelly couldn't regret the exchange any more than she did.

# Chapter 6

Traveling home from Lydia's house, Drake wondered about the roller-coaster evening. First he had been a happy party guest, then overheard Lydia confess to his daughter that she still loved him after all these years. The revelation took his heart skyward. Just as quickly, Lydia's biting words of unforgiveness took him to the pit of despair, a pit where he remained with no sure way to climb out. How could Lydia have been so unforgiving? Hadn't she seen the change in him from all those years ago?

From the passenger seat, Kelly ventured a query. "Dad, what happened tonight?"

"I don't want to talk about it."

"I'm sure you don't, considering Miss Lydia said you weren't always such an angel yourself."

"She told you that?" He set his gaze on the road, unwilling even to glimpse at his daughter. How could Lydia have ruined his credibility as a parent? Why did she have to continue to insult him?

"I guess you're not so righteous after all, huh?"

"So you believe her."

From his peripheral vision, he watched Kelly shrug. "I don't have to believe her. I can ask Granny. I have a feeling she'll be honest with me."

"And to think I actually wanted you to have a good relationship with your granny." He let out a small groan.

"So it's true. What did you do that was so bad?"

"Nothing. Nothing really."

"Something bad enough to get you sent to military school. They're threatening Darrin with that, you know," she snapped.

"It would probably do him good."

"Like it did you?"

He swallowed. "If I hadn't been sent away, I would never have met your mother. And I wouldn't have you, the biggest blessing God ever gave me." He pulled the car into the short drive in front of his mother's house.

"But I won't be here forever. In just a few years, I'll be gone."

Drake clenched his teeth under closed lips to keep from showing his emotion. True, he had Kelly for a few more years, but then she would have to fly out of the nest. He put the gearshift into park and turned off the engine. He took a moment to observe his little girl—now on her way to becoming a young woman—and thanked God that by His grace, she had turned from the wayward path she had begun to take in New York. And whether he wanted to admit it or not, he had to acknowledge Lydia's role in Kelly's turnaround.

He didn't exit the car. "Are you really ready for me to

have a new romantic relationship?"

"Yes." She looked at her suede-covered feet. "I think."

"That's a definitive answer. Not."

"I wish I had a mom, but I don't. I hardly remember her."

Her confession left a lump in his throat.

"I don't mean any disrespect," she said.

"I know." He rubbed her shoulder even though he knew she couldn't sense his touch through her coat. "How can you love someone you know only through old videotapes and pictures?"

"I do love her, in a way," she promised. "It's just that, I think you need someone. Maybe it's not Miss Lydia, but you two seem to like each other. And if you want to marry her someday, I would understand. I don't want to hold you back."

He placed his hand on her knee. "I appreciate that. It took a lot of courage for you to say that."

"What? Since I'm a little girl?" Her teasing tone was laced with seriousness. "I can cope. I promise." She looked out the window. "I coped with being stuck out here in the country, didn't I?"

"I think you kind of like it."

Kelly studied the trees. "Maybe." She shuddered. "It's getting cold. Let's go in."

On Christmas Eve day, Lydia heard the crunch of gravel surrendering to the pressure of tires on her driveway.

"Must be Ralph." She set down her dish towel and

walked to the living room. Mail volume had diminished to almost nothing in the past two weeks now that staffs at catalog companies assumed all Christmas orders had been placed. A few cards trickled in each day. She looked forward to taking a break with a cup of herbal tea and reading the news from far-flung friends and former students.

"Looks like you got another one of those packages." Ralph handed her a small box. "Seems to me this secret admirer thing has gone on long enough. He needs to make himself known, don't cha think?"

"Yes, it would be nice. Speaking of admirers, how are things with you and Mrs. Kingston?"

He blushed, and not from the cold air she was sure. "Just dandy. I took your advice and got her some flowerdy perfume the clerk at the store said was popular now. I hope she likes it."

"I'm sure she will." Lydia smiled. And to think she had once considered Ralph might be her admirer. Praise the Lord that Ralph couldn't hear her thoughts. She'd be too embarrassed for words. She fingered the package. "This one doesn't weigh much."

"Maybe your secret admirer is going broke."

"Maybe. I hope not." She opened the outer box and found inside another fashioned of gold cardboard foil, a trademark of her favorite chocolatier. She didn't suppress a triumphant smile. Her secret admirer had to be Drake! The package contained four pieces of exquisite chocolate truffles in a gold box. "Come and meet your secret admirer at 122 England Street at seven tonight."

Ralph let out a low whistle. "Sounds like this is getting serious."

Lydia nodded.

"So you know who it is?"

"I have an idea. But I don't want to say just yet." She bid Ralph farewell as politely but as quickly as she could.

Emotions roiled within her. She was to meet her secret admirer at the Kingston address!

So Drake wasn't mad at her anymore. If he was, he wouldn't keep up this secret admirer subterfuge. Her deceitful heart beat with wild happiness. She didn't want to forgive him, but she knew she had to. The time to forget the past had come and gone. And if she let it slip away, he would be gone forever. She had to keep the date.

Hearing a car pull up in the drive, Drake peered out the window. He watched as Lydia got out. She was so beautiful, as always. Even covered by a full-length black coat with her honey blond hair obstructed by a black hood, he could see her bright face wearing a pleased expression. He felt his heart leap happily into his throat. What was she doing here?

The first thing she did was to offer him a chocolate from a box of four pieces of candy. He accepted a bonbon and let the sweet, creamy, dark goo melt in his mouth. She watched him with the intensity of a person watching the climax of a mystery program. He sensed that she waited for him to say something. What?

"If this is your idea of a peace offering, I'm all for it."

"My idea? I thought it was your idea."

"I don't understand."

"So you mean, you—you aren't the one who sent this candy?"

"No."

"Then you're not my secret admirer?"

"Secret admirer? What are you talking about?"

"The gifts. You didn't send them?"

"What gifts?"

"Well, a little bit before you came back home, I started getting gifts. An ornament, a flower arrangement, candy—all from a secret admirer. They were all Christmas-related. I—I was thinking it might be you."

"Me?"

She looked at the candy she still held. "I remember that you were sent away at Christmas last time. I thought maybe this was your way of saying you were coming home at Christmas. Forever."

"No. You don't mean it. You don't mean you were hoping it was me?"

Her failure to answer emboldened him.

"All right then. It was me."

"Drake. . ." Her tone bespoke an exaggerated warning.

"Oh, all right. It wasn't me. But I wish it was."

"Even after I wasn't very nice to you the other night?"

"I've thought about it. The wounds we suffer with our first loves cut deeper than anything else we bear, I've come to realize."

"First love." She looked at her toes. "You were mine."

"And you know you were mine." He took her hands in his. "And you still are."

She flinched and pulled her hand away. "I—I want you to know I forgive you. I'm ashamed I have to say such a thing after all these years. If I had harbored a more flexible spirit all along, I would have given myself the gift of peace."

"And marriage?" His voice caught in his throat. Even though he had gone on with his own life, the thought of her with someone else was too much to bear.

She looked him in the eye. "No. I had other chances, but no one else felt so right. I chose to remain single all these years, and I don't regret it. If things had been different, I wouldn't be the person I am today."

"And a wonderful person you are, Lydia Winters. More wonderful and beautiful than I deserve. I'll bet your secret admirer is a better man than I am—and the one you really deserve."

A familiar female voice interrupted. "Is that what you think?"

"Mom!" Drake cried. "How long have you been standing there?"

"Not too long, but long enough." She crossed her arms. "Drake Kingston, I'm ashamed of you."

"What?"

"To give up this fine woman that easily."

"What do you want me to do, Mom? Figure out who the secret admirer is and beat him up? That would have been the old Drake. He's dead and gone."

"Who says the secret admirer is a man?"

"What!" Lydia and Drake expressed their simultaneous surprise.

"I mean, what if it's someone who admires Lydia in a different way—a former student, or a well-wisher?"

"Oh." Lydia agreed.

Drake thought for a moment and snapped his fingers when an idea entered his mind. "Kelly! It has to be Kelly!"

"Why do you think it's Kelly?" Lydia asked.

"Because she told me she'd like to see us get married someday."

"Married?" Though Lydia seemed surprised, a little smile of pleasure crossed her lips before she set her mouth back in line.

Drake gave himself a mental kick for mentioning the "M" word in such a cavalier manner. He meant to say something to her when the time was right. Then again, the little smile gave him confidence he'd not had previously.

"Hmm. Someday is probably years down the road in her mind."

Leave it to Lydia to be practical. "Maybe," he conceded. "But I have a feeling she wouldn't mind if it were sooner."

"Kelly!" he called toward her bedroom.

"She's not here," Mom said. "She went to the mall with Jennifer and Genna."

"As happy as I am to learn about her feelings, it doesn't matter in the context of the secret admirer. The gifts started arriving this past summer, before we met."

"So then, who?" Drake's eyes narrowed. "I'll bet it's Genna's father. He can't take his eyes off you whenever you're in the same room together."

"No, it isn't him." Mom seemed certain.

"Then who is it?" Drake challenged her.

"It's me."

"What?"

She nodded. "As soon as I learned you were coming back home to take care of me—ostensibly—I knew I had to do something to get you and Lydia back together. Since the first package arrived at her house just before you did, I thought surely she would put two and two together and figure out it was you. That's what I mean. I wanted her to think it was you."

"Mom!"

"I would have never guessed," Lydia added. "When I came to dinner that first Sunday, I wasn't even sure you wanted me to be there."

"I have to admit, I had a hard time playing it cool."

"You're quite an actress," Drake said.

"Maybe I missed my calling." She winked.

Drake shook his head and smiled. "You know, Mom, you didn't need to do something so silly. But I love you for it."

"I know. I had no idea you'd end up sending Kelly to Lydia's charm school and take things from there. I might have known you'd have the smarts to figure out a way to get her back on your own."

"But, Mom, I really did want Kelly to go to Charming Manor. And she's all the better for it."

"You're right on all counts. But I know you still love Lydia. Mind you, I thought the world and all of Mandy, and I wouldn't take all the money in the world for Kelly. But if things had been different back when you two were in school, you would have been married all along. Life is short, Son. I know that since your father died on me way before I was ready. Now you two take this second chance. They don't come around too often." Mist formed in her eyes. A proud woman, she turned her face away and made a quick exit into the kitchen.

"She's right, you know," Lydia said. "Second chances don't come around too often."

"Are you saying you want another chance with me? I can't promise you the perfect relationship. I can promise you I'll still make mistakes, but hopefully not as bad as the ones I made back in high school."

A wan smile curved her lips. "I can promise you I'll make mistakes, too. I think I've already proven that. All I can do is to say I've learned my lesson. I promise to try not to be so rigid and unforgiving in the future."

"I have a feeling since Kelly is already a teenager, we'll both need to exercise our full capacity for love and forgiveness."

"I want to, Drake." She squeezed his hand in hers. "I really, really want that for us."

"For the three of us."

"For the two of us, first."

"Yes. That is the way it should be." Drake squeezed her hand. "I really do love you, Lydia."

"And I love you, too. I don't think I ever stopped. Not even during those dark days so long ago when you had to leave me."

"I'll never leave you again, I promise. Unless you want me to."

"No, I don't. I know that now."

Drake took her in his arms and kissed her. The touch of her lips proved sweet beyond his wildest imaginings. As he held her, he noticed that Lydia's body was not that of a teenager, but a woman. A woman who loved him. And who always would.

A low whistle interrupted. Drake looked up. "Kelly!"

"It's about time, you guys."

Mom looked in. "I heard a whistle. Does that mean what I think it does?"

"Sure does."

Kelly jumped up and down and ran over to them, a surprisingly childish motion for a teenager who wanted to look sophisticated at all times. She hugged them both. "This will be perfect. Almost like the Brady Bunch."

Lydia's laughter tinkled throughout the room. "I'm not so sure we can be called a bunch."

"Okay," Kelly conceded. "So we don't have six kids."

"At least not yet." Drake smiled.

Lydia's blush told him that their minds—and hearts— had finally become one.

# Angel Sugar Cookies

Be sure to have available cookie cutters in angel shapes or the shape(s) of your choice before beginning.

1½ cups sugar
⅔ cup butter
2 eggs
2 tablespoons milk
2 teaspoons vanilla extract
3¼ cups flour
2½ teaspoons baking powder
½ teaspoon salt

Cream the butter and sugar together in a large bowl.
Add milk, vanilla extract, and eggs to the bowl.
In a separate bowl, mix the dry ingredients together.
Add the dry ingredients to the bowl of wet ingredients.
Mix on medium speed for about two minutes, or until ingredients are combined.
Shape the finished dough into a ball and wrap it in plastic wrap.
Refrigerate overnight.

Ready to Bake:
Preheat oven to 400 degrees F.
Lightly grease the cookie sheets if they are not nonstick.
Roll out the dough, (half at a time) until the dough is ¼ inch thick.
Shape with cookie cutters.
Bake for 9–11 minutes or until the edges turn golden.

Icing:

    1 cup confectioners sugar

    2 teaspoons milk

    2 teaspoons light corn syrup

    ¼ teaspoon almond extract

    3–4 drops food coloring as appropriate to the shape of your cookies

Mix the confectioners sugar and the milk together in a small bowl until smooth.

Add the almond extract and the corn syrup.

Mix well.

Dip cookies or paint them with icing.

## TAMELA HANCOCK MURRAY

Tamela Hancock Murray is an award-winning, best-selling author of twenty Christian romance novels and novellas and seven Bible trivia books. She lives in Northern Virginia with her godly husband and beautiful daughters who keep her busy with church and school activities. When she and her husband married over twenty years ago, the bottom layer of their wedding cake was baked into the shape of a three-leaf clover.

Tamela loves to hear from her readers! Send e-mail to Tamela@TamelaHancockMurray.com.

# angel on the doorstep

by Sandra Petit

# Dedication

I'd like to dedicate this story to
crocheters across the globe.
A special thank-you to those who helped with
Moira's angel pattern, as well as those who
sent me encouragement through
my crochet Web site (www.crochetcabana.com).
You can find more detailed instructions
on Moira's angel (with pictures) at
www.sandrapetit.com. Enjoy!

# Chapter 1

Moira Sullivan patted the shiny red heart sequin onto the angel just as the chimes of the doorbell sounded. Working swiftly, she gathered the rest of the crocheted angels from the end table, hurried to the rolltop desk, and threw all the angels inside, firmly pushing the top down to hide them.

The doorbell rang again, causing her to quicken her pace to the entryway. She ran her fingers through her hair, patted it down, and took a deep breath before opening the door.

"Mr. Corrigan." Moira stood with the door open, finding herself lost in the way the sun highlighted his midnight black hair and deepened his blue eyes.

Tall, dark, and handsome. The old cliché fit Joe Corrigan perfectly.

He nodded at her slowly. "Please call me Joe. After all, we're part of the same church family." He stood quietly, hands in his pockets.

"And I'm Moira." Yes, they were part of the same

church family, but that family was huge and she barely knew him. She suddenly realized she was keeping him waiting in the cold air. She felt the heat of a blush move up her neck. "Oh, I'm sorry. Come on in." She backed away, allowing Joe to move past her into the foyer. "The angel is in the living room. I'll get it."

Instead of remaining in the foyer as she had hoped, Joe followed, chatting as they walked. Moira glanced at Snowflake, her French poodle, hoping the dog might provide some distraction. Instead, he simply lifted his head to give Joe a cursory glance, then lowered his muzzle to rest on his paws and closed his eyes. *Some help you are.*

"It's nice of you to return the angel to Mother. After all, you paid for the desk at the yard sale as is. Mother was so embarrassed when she realized she'd left her angel inside."

"It's not a problem. The angel is hers. It would be wrong to keep it."

Moira stopped at the end table where she had placed Anna Corrigan's angel. It wasn't there. With dismay, she realized she must have put it in the desk with the others. She bit her lip. There was nothing to do but open the desktop and retrieve Anna's angel. That was why Joe was here.

"I was just looking at the angel, and I must have put it in the desk without thinking," she mumbled as she moved toward her newly purchased rolltop desk. *Stay by the sofa,* she mentally commanded Joe. But unfortunately, Joe once again followed her.

"How is that working out? Do you like the desk? Have any trouble with the rolltop? It used to stick sometimes for Mother."

"It's working out fine. The top isn't too much trouble. I just need to jiggle the knobs a bit to open it. Otherwise, I love the desk. It was a terrific find."

Moira took hold of the round wooden knobs and tried to lift the top, but it wouldn't budge. She shifted her weight and wiggled the knob again. *Now? You have to stick now?* She pressed down while lifting, hoping to dislodge it. Without warning, the top flew open. Angels catapulted everywhere. Out of the corner of her eye, she saw Joe's eyes widen. She refused to look at him while they both bent to gather the angels.

"Hey, I know this angel." Joe stood, examining her creative handiwork.

"Oh no," she mumbled, then cleared her throat, stiffened, and walked toward him. "Thank you," she said curtly, reaching to snatch the familiar angel—though not his mother's—from Joe's hand.

Joe moved his hand away, lifting the angel higher so she couldn't reach it. Her five-foot frame was no match for Joe's six-foot frame. Growling, she jumped up. "Joseph Corrigan, please give me that angel!" She felt like a schoolgirl trying to get a favored toy.

"Only my mother calls me Joseph, and of course I'll give it to you. In a second." His gaze moved upward as he inspected the white crocheted angel, obviously noting the distinctive red heart-shaped sequin.

Moira's stomach churned while Joe turned the angel over and over. Joe Corrigan wasn't stupid. She didn't want him to recognize her specially made angel, but she didn't think Joe was the type to let something go until he was good and ready to do so.

Moira crossed her arms, tapped her foot as loudly as she could, and waited.

"My friend Manny Wiseman has one just like this. It appeared on his desk at the real estate office." Joe's brow crinkled, and he frowned. "Manny told me another one of the deacons also received one just like his. And Pastor John. . ." His eyes widened. "You're the undercover angel!"

Moira blinked. "The what?"

"Undercover angel. That's what they're calling her—*you*. The angels appear out of nowhere, in the oddest places, when the person least expects it, and no one knows who's doing it. You know, like an undercover agent." He paused, and his voice became more solemn. "Manny was having a terrible week. He'd gotten some bad news about his health. He went to lunch, and when he returned, there was the angel sitting on his desk. It made his day."

Moira smiled, glad the timing for *that* delivery had been good, if coincidental. "What makes you think I'm this 'undercover angel' person?" she asked, despite the evidence of angels strewn about her feet. "Maybe I'm holding the angels for the real undercover angel. After all, she wouldn't want to be caught with all these angels on hand. Or maybe I got one and decided to make more." She knew she was rambling, but she was running out of explanations for the angels' presence in her home.

Joe rolled his eyes and shook his head. "Nice try, but it looks like they're only going to the Faith Church staff. You're not on the staff. What kind of work do you do anyway?"

Moira's shoulders slumped. She was busted. "I'm a crochet designer. I write crochet books."

Joe's deep voice erupted in a hearty laugh. "Aha! Had I known that, I would have figured it out. Mother never mentioned it."

"She probably doesn't know. I've only just started making enough to do it full time, and I only spoke to your mother briefly at the sale." She sighed. "Joe, you can't tell anyone. It's supposed to be anonymous."

She didn't like the gleam that appeared in his eyes. "Anonymous, huh? Why?"

"Well. . ." *Why indeed?* How was she going to explain this? She took a deep breath. "I just want to show the staff I appreciate them. I don't want credit. It won't mean as much if they know."

"So it's important to you that it *remain* a secret."

"Yes. *Very* important." She stressed *very*, hoping it would make a difference.

Joe quirked one eyebrow, and a corner of his mouth curled up. Moira's heart pounded as she watched him slowly turn the angel over in his hands, inspecting it again.

"Do you think one of these will appear on Gabe's doorstep?"

Moira's heart began to beat faster. "Gabe?"

"Yes. He's the older gentleman who always sits in the back corner. Did you know that once a month, during the week, when no one is there except the pastor, he comes in and washes the dirt and bird droppings off the cross outside?"

"He does?"

"Yeah. Once you get to know him, he's a funny old guy. He doesn't want anyone to know what he's doing. But I know. And I think he should get one of these."

Moira mentally added Gabe to her list of angel recipients.

"I'll give him one, too. What's his address?"

He grinned widely. "If you really want to know, then I guess you'd better cut me in on the action."

"There's nothing to cut you in on," Moira said slowly. "I'm not making any money. In fact, it's costing me materials and time."

"Then there's even more reason to cut me in. I can't make the angels, obviously, but I can help with the expense. And I can help you deliver them. Maybe together we can think of interesting places to stash the angels. You know, sort of keep it mysterious."

"I've been doing fine on my own." She plucked the angel from Joe's hands.

"But you could do so much better with my help."

Moira tilted her head, thinking. This was her idea. She'd made the angels, and she'd already delivered several with no problem. She didn't need Joe's help, despite what he thought. Immediately her conscience chided her. Did she want the credit after all? The mere idea made her squirm. There was nothing wrong with letting someone else help. Joe appreciated the church staff, too. Maybe he just wanted to show his appreciation. *Practice what you preach, Moira.*

On the other hand, Joe wasn't a small person. The phrase "bull in a china shop" came to mind. Slipping in and out without getting caught would be a challenge, but it might also put more fun into her self-appointed job. And what if they *were* caught? While it wouldn't be such a big thing, she did want to do this anonymously.

Yet she doubted Joe would give her much choice. Would he really tell everyone what she was doing? Perhaps out of some misguided sense of fair play. Or maybe just because he could. Though she'd seen Joe at Faith Church for years, they were little more than acquaintances, and she wasn't sure what he would do.

She had no choice. She had to include Joe.

Having made the decision, she was surprised to find the idea wasn't totally repulsive to her. In fact, sharing a secret with Joe might be. . .fun.

"All right, you can help, but you can't tell a soul."

He frowned. "Not even my mother?"

She hesitated. Already the circle of those who knew was expanding. "Can your mother keep a secret?"

This time Joe hesitated. "Well, she does like to talk. Evidenced by our phone bill."

"You live with your mother?"

Joe bristled. "Yes. She's been alone since Dad died, except for me."

Moira quickly backpedaled. "I didn't mean anything by it. Sorry if I hit a nerve. I guess it surprised me because my own parents don't live around here. In fact, they live in separate states."

Joe's shoulders slumped as he sighed. "That's okay. I overreacted. It's just that people always look at me funny when they first find out. They expect a thirty-four-year-old man to be on his own. Really, I *am* on my own. I'm an attorney, and I pay all the bills and cover all the expenses."

*Attorney.* The word leaped out at her. Moira opened

her mouth to speak, but no words came out. She finally forced herself to take a breath and speak calmly. "You're a lawyer?"

"Yes, I'm a defense attorney. I could have moved Mother to my place when she began to have health problems, but she's comfortable in her own home, so I chose to move in with her."

Moira nodded slowly. "It's very nice of you to care for her." It was nice, especially for a man who made his living helping criminals go free so they didn't have to pay for their crimes, regardless of the horrible things they had done. How did a Christian man reconcile that kind of thing with his faith—being a part of the process that allowed the guilty to go free, using whatever technicality and loophole in the law he could find?

Joe's voice was hardly above a whisper as he shrugged his shoulders. "Honor our parents. It's what God tells us to do." Then he straightened and rubbed his hands together, lifting his voice. "So what do we do first?"

*Honor your parents, but otherwise manipulate the truth when it suits your purposes.* Already she regretted her agreement, but she wouldn't go back on her word. She had no choice in the matter. "We make a list."

# Chapter 2

Joe lifted his finger from the doorbell just as the door swung open. Moira reached out to grab his arm, pulling him inside.

"I need you to put these angels together," she said as she dropped her hold of his arm and hurried into the living room, apparently assuming he would follow, which he did.

Joe's gaze moved over the room, where pieces of angels were scattered on every conceivable surface in organized groups. He'd only seen completed angels when he was here last week. Moira's poodle, Snowflake, lay paw over paw, asleep in a corner.

"What?"

Moira turned and pointed to the table in front of the sofa. "I'm almost finished with this group, but there are enough full angels finished for you to start putting them together. The glue gun is hot."

Joe extended his arm to encompass the mass of angels scattered about.

"Moira, what are you talking about?"

She frowned as though it were him who wasn't making any sense when he had no clue as to what she meant. Joe noted the dark circles under her eyes and the harried expression on her face.

"I've made a good start on the additional angels—"

He raised his hand, palm toward her. "Stop. What angels?"

Moira sighed. "Before I started delivering, I made enough angels for the church staff, deacons, and Sunday school teachers. I hadn't thought of all the folks you mentioned, those who work behind the scenes, who don't get any recognition. The ones on the list we made when you picked up your mom's angel. I've stayed up late every night this week so we'd have enough angels to go around. I don't want anyone left out. Since I made all the parts separately, the process went faster. The wings take longest because they're all single crochet, so I'm not quite finished." She paused and glared at him. "Is there a problem here? I thought you wanted to help."

Moira's expression told him she was more than a little annoyed, but Joe had a feeling she was just tired and it was her fatigue that was causing her irritability.

"Sure I want to help, but I thought I would be delivering, not making. I'm not sure I understand what you want me to do. I certainly don't know how to crochet."

She shook her head, and a small frown appeared, causing the sides of her eyes to wrinkle. He thought it was the cutest thing he'd ever seen, even though her ire was directed at him.

"I know that. You don't have to crochet. All you have

to do is glue the pieces together with the hot glue gun. I'll show you. It's really easy, and it will give me time to finish. I'm making a few extra in case we think of more people who should get one."

Joe stared at the pieces. Glue. He could handle glue. His confidence kicked up a notch.

Yet, while it was a good sign that she was asking for his help, he wasn't sure what his status was after he'd blackmailed her into accepting that help. For now, it seemed she had honestly accepted it. He was a part of this project. Now she was handing him the opportunity to show her he was serious.

"Okay, show me what to do."

Moira demonstrated how to attach the head, wings, and red heart sequin to the body. He'd never seen such a small glue gun in his life. It certainly wasn't like his big, old, black, standard model at home. He felt awkward handling Moira's miniature version with his large hands, and squeezing just the right amount of the sticky substance without making a mess was a little more difficult than he'd expected, but not so hard he couldn't do it.

"This is certainly different," he commented. He could attest that it wasn't anything like his day job, standing in a courtroom trying to convince judge and jury of the innocence of his clients.

"Different?"

"I spend most of my time in a courtroom, though I think some of my clients may have had their own personal angels helping out."

When he glanced over at Moira, he noticed her stiffen and wondered what he'd said to cause the reaction.

"Have you ever been in a courtroom?"

"Yes." The word fell from her mouth reluctantly.

*Yes?* Joe couldn't help frowning. When Moira didn't elaborate, he began to wonder if there was a reason the two of them had never seen one another socially. Moira didn't look like a criminal, but over the years he'd come to realize there was no particular look for a person in that position. They came in all shapes and sizes. Should he pursue the subject or wait until she felt comfortable enough to share? There were other reasons, besides being a criminal, that a person could enter a courtroom. Maybe she'd had a speeding ticket, or perhaps she'd sat on a jury.

Moira took up her crocheting, and Joe resumed his job of gluing the angel faces onto the bodies and then joining the pieces to the wings. While he worked, he took every opportunity to sneak a glance at Moira, trying to figure out what she was thinking. Her thick auburn hair fell into her face as she concentrated on her work. She seemed more relaxed as she crocheted. Maybe now that she saw everything would be done, she would be able to slow down and enjoy the process.

Joe glanced down and realized he had glued a wing on upside down.

"Uh, Moira?"

Moira lifted her head to look in his direction. "Yes?"

"I think I may have messed up this one."

He didn't know what he'd expected, but Moira didn't react. She rose from the couch and walked over to examine what he'd done.

"It's upside down. Not a big problem since it's basically the same top and bottom, but it's better if the chenille stem is on top. It's not hard to fix. We just have to reheat the glue, pull the two pieces apart, and reglue them correctly."

Joe was relieved to note Moira's smile. "Right. . .but won't hot glue come out if I use this gun?"

"Yes, but we won't use that one. I have a separate gun, with no glue stick inside, for situations like this."

Joe grinned. "You've done this before?"

"Sure. Everyone makes mistakes sometimes."

Her face was unreadable, but her body stiffened when he leaned over to watch her work. Joe backed up, giving her space. He wondered if there was a hidden meaning in her statement.

Picking up the angel, Moira showed him how to correct the problem. He was determined he wouldn't need to know, however, because he wasn't going to make the mistake again. He knew each individual angel took about an hour to crochet. Moira had worked hard, and he didn't want to be the one who caused her more trouble.

After she'd repaired his angel, Moira showed him how to cut the Styrofoam cones and pack everything for delivery.

"What are the white cones for?" he asked.

"You put the angel on top of the cone so it will stand upright. I could have starched them, but some- times people store their Christmas things in the attic, and some pests are attracted by the starch," Moira explained.

Joe nodded. "These little notes are a nice touch." He held up the small card with a note thanking the recipient, Elizabeth Wright, for her service as church organist.

Moira looked up. "I was afraid they might be too much."

"I don't think so. The sentiment is real, and I know the recipients will appreciate it."

She smiled, but the smile didn't reach her eyes; and Joe wondered if he'd done anything to make her feel uncomfortable in his presence. Thinking back, he thought he'd been the perfect gentleman, but they *were* alone in her home. Maybe that was all it was.

He watched her return to her spot on the sofa where she continued working on the remaining wings. Her nose crinkled as she yawned, and he noticed her fingers, though nimble, moved more slowly. As he watched, they slowed even more, and then her hand stopped moving and he heard a soft sigh. His gaze shifted, and he saw her fatigue had gotten the better of her.

He finished gluing together the last angel, then walked to the sofa.

"All done."

Moira started and lifted her head. "What? Oh, you're finished already?"

"Yes. You can check them later, but I need to get going now. Maybe we could meet Friday evening to deliver some of these?"

"Okay." Moira put down her work and stood to walk him to the door. Even that simple action seemed to take great effort.

"I can find my way out. Why don't you catch up on some of that sleep you lost? I'll see you tomorrow."

He walked to the door, hoping she would return to her seat, but Moira followed him and gave a brief wave as he put his SUV into gear and moved off. Thoughts of Moira's smile occupied his mind as he made his way home.

# Chapter 3

Sitting in the passenger seat of Joe's SUV, Moira glanced at Joe, who sat behind the wheel ready to drive to the home of tonight's undercover angel assignment. They'd spent several previous nights delivering angels. While Joe's ideas were innovative and he had helped her think of many who deserved an angel, it seemed something went wrong with almost every delivery. The recipients were still in the dark about where the gifts came from, but Moira was mentally exhausted at the end of the evening. She was determined not to let the mishaps get to her, however. The angels were delivered, and that was the important thing.

"Who's first on the list tonight?" Joe asked.

"I thought we could go by Jake Simon's house first. He leaves his car unlocked, and he and his wife retire early. We can leave one in his car."

"Jake the groundskeeper?"

"Yes," Moira replied, buckling her seat belt as they prepared to leave.

"Why does he leave his car unlocked?"

"He's hoping someone will steal it," Moira said in all seriousness. "I heard him tell Mrs. Franklin that his wife won't let him sell it."

"Really? If I remember right, that was one of the last Volkswagens off the assembly line, just before the plant stopped production."

"That was a long time ago, wasn't it?" Moira asked the question not so much because she was really interested in old cars, but to stave off an awkward silence as Joe started the car and drove toward Jake's residence.

"Late seventies."

"Wow. And it still runs?"

"It runs fairly well. Jake's an amateur mechanic, so he's able to keep it going. Guess he'd like to put it out to pasture and get something newer."

"Apparently Mrs. Simon disagrees with that philosophy." Moira wrinkled her nose and tucked her hair behind her ears.

As they turned onto Jake's street, Moira pointed to an empty spot at the end of the block, a short distance from a streetlight. "Stop over there. We don't want to park too close."

Joe turned his head and lifted his brows at her command.

Moira squirmed under his gaze. "I just meant that Jake might look out the window, and it would be suspicious if there was another vehicle in his driveway."

"Got it." Joe pulled to a stop at the indicated spot, a short distance from Jake's house, opened his door, and slid from behind the wheel.

Deciding to leave well enough alone, Moira twisted to reach between the bucket seats to the back of the vehicle. The angels sat in a cardboard box, covered with a piece of black felt; so if anyone looked in, they wouldn't be able to determine what the box held. Careful not to flatten it, she retrieved Jake's angel, which had a little card attached with Jake's name and a note of thanks. As she turned back to face the front, the passenger door opened and Joe stood outside, his hand out to help her exit.

Moira's breath caught. She couldn't remember the last time a man had opened any door for her, much less walked around a vehicle to go to the trouble. On their previous deliveries, she hadn't given him time to show this side of his personality. She'd hopped right out as soon as they arrived at their destination. She wished Joe wasn't acting like such a gentleman. He was a lawyer. Just like her dad. Not just any lawyer, but a criminal lawyer. He kept felons out of jail. She resolved not to allow herself to think of Joe as anything other than the person who'd blackmailed her into helping with this project.

Joe extended his hand, and she had no choice but to grasp it or look churlish. He pulled to help her out of the vehicle, since her other hand held the angel.

Once Moira exited the car, Joe released her hand and led the way toward Jake's house.

They had gone only a few steps when a bark sounded somewhere behind them. Moira turned her head to see a large dog coming up behind them.

"Joe?"

"Yeah?"

"There's a dog following us."

Joe glanced behind them. "Pretty big dog, too."

"Maybe he smells cat on me. I was at my friend Elizabeth's earlier, and she has cats."

"Possibly, but he's a bit far for that, I think. I can't tell what kind of dog it is in this light. I can just tell that it's big. Keep walking."

Moira didn't want Joe to think she was afraid, but she picked up the pace anyway. Joe stayed right with her. Keeping close, he moved his hand to her bent elbow. She resisted the urge to shake it off, because she had a feeling it would be smart to stay close to Joe as long as they were being followed by Attila. Unfortunately, the dog also began to walk faster, and the distance between them became less with every step.

"He's still following us," she whispered.

In sync, the two of them walked even faster. The dog's growl was uncomfortably close behind them.

"Joe, he's coming after us!" Moira forgot all she knew about dogs and began to run.

Joe easily ran in place beside her but stayed close. Moira was grateful, because she knew he could have easily outdistanced her and left her to be mauled by the animal.

"I hope you're right about Jake keeping his car unlocked!" Joe yelled.

Moira realized they were in Jake's driveway, coming up to Jake's faded red Volkswagen. Safety was only a few steps away.

Suddenly Moira turned her head to look back, instinct telling her the dog was close. Then everything happened at once. With a loud bark, the large, black dog, which she now saw was a Doberman, rushed toward them. Joe swung open the Volkswagen door, yelled at Moira to get in, and shoved her to be sure she obeyed immediately.

Without worrying about propriety, and wanting to make room for Joe, Moira scrambled past the steering wheel and over the stick shift, landing on her knees on the passenger seat. Caught in an awkward position in limited space, she struggled to turn around to a proper sitting position as Joe slid behind the steering wheel, his knees hitting the dash. The door closed as the dog hit it.

Moira's breath caught at the sight of flashing fangs as the canine tried to get at them. Its sharp bark was ferocious and so loud that it hurt her ears. For a long moment neither of them said anything.

"You have a dog. What should we do?" Joe asked.

Moira shook her head. "I have a poodle. It's not exactly the same thing."

"I wonder whose dog it is." Joe's calm statement triggered her feelings of guilt. After all her talk of being prepared, here they were stuck in a Volkswagen, about to become dog food.

Moira leaned in his direction to try to look out the window at the dog, which had stopped jumping against the door. She hoped Jake's car wasn't scratched. She craned her neck to get a better glimpse of the animal. Maybe it wasn't as big as she'd first thought.

No. It was big all right. She hadn't exaggerated, even in her thoughts. "I don't know, but it certainly would have helped to know about Attila in advance. I'm sorry." She sighed.

Joe chuckled. Moira's eyes widened. She didn't see

anything funny about their situation.

"Why are you sorry? You didn't ask him to chase us into the car. Probably a neighborhood dog that got loose by accident. I've seen it happen a lot. We can call animal control—when we can get to a phone—and they'll pick it up."

"I guess you're right. But now what do we do?"

"I guess all we can do is wait. Maybe Jake will hear the commotion and come out."

Moira had little hope of that, knowing the elderly Jake and his wife were both hard of hearing—not that she wanted Jake to hear anything. That would ruin the surprise. "Listen. He's not making any commotion. He's just sitting there, watching us. And even if Jake does come out, what would we say? If he sees the angel, he'll know why we're here."

Joe's gaze also turned toward the window.

"Wonder how long he intends to stay there," she mumbled.

"Until something else catches his interest and pulls him away."

The dog sat on its haunches, his gaze glued to the door they had disappeared behind. Did the dog realize they were trapped? She knew guard dogs were trained to act just this way, but if this were a guard dog, nothing was going to pull him away.

Forty minutes later, they were still in the car and the dog was lying beside it, seeming to sleep, though they suspected it was just waiting.

"We can't stay here all night," Joe said.

Moira lifted her hand to move her hair behind her ears

but stopped herself just in time. She knew it was a nervous habit, and there was no reason to let Joe know how jittery she was. "I know that."

"Why don't we just blow the horn? Jake will come out and chase the dog away, or at least call someone."

"Jake probably wouldn't hear it, and it would just get the dog barking again. Besides, I don't want him to know we're here. You know how important it is to me for this to be a secret."

"More important than sleeping in your own bed tonight?"

Moira glared at Joe. "Yes. No. Oh, you're impossible."

"Me? Do you want to spend the night in a Volkswagen?"

"Of course not. Don't you have a cell phone?"

"Don't you?" he countered.

"Yes, but it's in my purse. In *your* car."

"Good planning," he mumbled as he sank down into the seat, then crossed his arms over his chest. "It's not a car. It's an SUV."

Moira gritted her teeth. "Whatever." She'd been delivering angels for over a month before Joe was added to the team, and she had never had this kind of problem.

"Look. He's moving."

At Joe's words, Moira turned and stared at the offending animal. He was indeed moving—in the direction of a white cat that had entered his territory.

*Run, cat, run.*

"Come on. We can get out of here while the dog is distracted chasing the cat."

"He'll see us."

"We'll be quiet."

He didn't wait for Moira's okay but opened the door.

"Wait. The angel." Moira quickly set the angel on the dashboard and, as quietly as she could, exited through the passenger door.

The trot back to Joe's SUV was made in relative silence. When they were safely ensconced in the vehicle, Moira gave a sigh of relief. "For a minute there, I thought we were going to be a special dog treat. We should say a prayer of thanks for that cat."

Joe's voice came out of the darkness. "Thank You, Lord, for nudging the cat out at that particular time. It was getting a bit hot in Jake's car."

Moira wondered how much of the prayer was serious and how much of it was simply Joe being funny. She was sure God didn't mind the humor, though.

"I have to say, Joe, things sure have livened up in the angel business since you've joined my efforts. Not that almost getting mauled by a dog is my idea of fun." Moira crossed her arms over her chest tightly and stared straight ahead. "I think I'm ready to go home now."

# Chapter 4

Joe clamped his mouth shut. He should have known better. He'd had Moira on his mind when he returned home and had talked so much about her that now his mother wanted to get to know the new woman in her son's life. He knew the two women had met briefly at the yard sale when Moira purchased the desk, but they were merely acquaintances who attended the same church. He'd long admired Moira from afar and had often wished for an opportunity to get to know her better. God had provided it, and Joe was not going to waste it.

"Joe?"

He shifted his attention back to his mother.

"Yes?"

"I asked you when I could meet this woman."

"You've already met her," Joe pointed out. "At the yard sale. She bought your desk."

"I sold a hundred things to a hundred people that day. And much of what I sold was furniture. You can't expect me to remember every person I met."

"She attends Faith Church just like we do. You see her every week."

His mother tilted her head thoughtfully. "Moira Sullivan. . ."

"She helps with children's church," Joe mumbled.

"I don't have any children in children's church, Joe. Though I wouldn't mind having a grandchild or two there someday soon."

The grandchild ploy. He knew it well. Joe smiled. "I'd like that, too. In God's timing."

She nodded. "So how about dinner on Sunday? I could make that special—"

"I'll have to check with Moira, Mother. I'm not sure when she's available."

It wouldn't do to tell her he didn't think Moira would ever be ready for a visit with his mother. He loved his mother and knew Moira would, as well, once they got to know each other. Until that happened, however, he also knew his mother, who was very outgoing and interested in everything around her, could seem overwhelming.

Knowing what a private person Moira was, he suspected she would need to be introduced a bit gradually into his life and especially to his mother. They didn't yet have the kind of relationship that allowed for family eccentricities.

"Joe?"

He lifted his head again and found his mother staring at him.

"Hmm?"

"You haven't heard a word I've said. Where is your mind tonight? Are you going to invite your Moira for dinner Sunday?"

"She's not my Moira, but if the opportunity presents itself, I'll ask her."

"Where are we going tonight?" Joe glanced at Moira. She hadn't said a dozen words since he'd picked her up. He didn't think she was still annoyed that he'd asked her to join him and his mother for dinner on Sunday. She'd been almost too polite when she said she already had plans.

"I thought we'd stop by my friend Sarah's house tonight and deliver her angel. She's the chairperson of the social committee and is busy planning the Christmas party. She's at a meeting right now, so we could put the angel in her mailbox."

"It's a federal offense to put unstamped mail into someone's home mailbox."

She stared at him. He felt the heat crawl up his neck and knew his face showed his discomfort.

"Only kidding. I mean, it really is a federal offense, but—never mind. That's fine."

*Leave the lawyer shoes at home, Joe,* he told himself.

"I wouldn't want to commit a crime," Moira said. "We can put it in her paper box. Is *that* illegal?"

Joe grimaced. He'd done it now. "That's fine."

They stopped directly in front of Sarah's mailbox since the newspaper box was attached to it. Moira wrapped the angel in tissue and set it toward the middle of the box, with the typed note telling Sarah it was a gift for her work in the Lord's service. This was a much smoother delivery than Jake Simon's had been. Joe smiled at the memory. Again, he wondered if that could be why Moira was so quiet. In hindsight, he thought the whole situation funny, but Moira didn't seem to share his opinion.

"Where to now?" he asked as Moira settled back into the passenger seat of his SUV.

"How about Gabe? Do you have any idea where we could leave his angel?"

"Yes, I do." Joe grinned, turning the vehicle toward the road leading to the edge of town. "Gabe is a creature of habit. He comes to the church every Tuesday to clean the cross unless it's raining. Since the weather is nice today, he should be coming in about an hour. That leaves us plenty of time to put the angel up there."

"You want to put the angel on the roof?" Moira's eyes widened.

"Sure. Gabe keeps a ladder behind the bushes right where the cross is so he doesn't have to drag it out each week. He used a wooden one until recently. Now he has an aluminum one."

"I don't remember the last time I saw a wooden ladder."

"I think he made the wooden one himself. He was quite a carpenter in his youth. Identifies with Jesus the carpenter."

"Is that Gabe's occupation?"

"Not anymore. Gabe's retired. He used to make custom cabinets. Mom hired him years ago to redo the kitchen. He does meticulous work. Same way he cleans the cross. He's involved in other community projects, too."

"Gabe sounds like a nice man. I'm sorry I never took the time to get to know him better."

"He's not dead. There's still time."

Moira smiled, which drew Joe's attention to her mouth.

The shade of her lipstick very nearly matched the color of her perfect lips. He wondered what it would be like to kiss Moira. The way things were going, he feared he would never get that close to her.

"You're right. I'll make it a point to talk to him on Sunday."

Joe nodded, pleased to have been able to make a difference in a life, maybe two. Senior citizens needed friends just as much as anyone else did. Lifelong friends died. Spouses died. Those left behind had to go on, and he knew from watching his mother that it wasn't easy. His ears perked up as Moira spoke again.

"I don't know if I can climb up on the roof. I'm not good with heights."

"That's okay. I can do it. It was my idea."

"How will you get the angel to stay up there until Gabe arrives?"

Joe frowned. "Well, I don't know."

"Joe!"

He cringed at the exasperation in her voice. "I'm new at this subterfuge stuff. Let's just see how it goes. Something will come to me."

"You want to wait and see how it goes? What if it goes badly? Like some of the other times?"

"All of the angels were delivered, even if there might have been a snag or two. We haven't been caught." He suppressed the word *yet* that longed to attach itself to the end of the sentence.

Moira nodded slowly. "That's true. I know sometimes I'm too much of a perfectionist. God's working on me in that area. I'll try to be more flexible, but you'll have to be patient. And maybe you could think things through a bit, too."

"Okay."

He glanced at Moira as he drove along the familiar road. She twirled her fingers through the strands of her hair. It was strangely fascinating to him. He would have loved to sit there and simply watch her fingers twirl, but he had to keep his eyes on the road. He suddenly realized Moira was speaking again.

"I'm glad you brought up folks like Gabe. They don't get recognized for their work, and they should. When I began this project, I made only enough angels to cover the Sunday school teachers, deacons, and church staff. I think I might have already told you that."

"Yes, you did. You must have started working on the angels as soon as you found Mother's—or had you already been making them then?"

"Your mother's angel gave me the idea, but I needed something that could be made faster and still look nice. So I had to design my own. Anyway, back to Gabe. It doesn't seem as though this has been planned out well. Maybe we should think about it some more."

Joe snorted. "Too much planning isn't good. Didn't you just say you were going to try to be more flexible? People have a tendency to do things unexpectedly. You have to adapt. There's always a way. Haven't you ever watched *MacGyver*?"

Her blank look told him she had no idea what he was talking about.

"MacGyver. The guy on TV who could disarm a missile with a paper clip or stop an acid leak with a bar of chocolate." He shook his head when Moira continued to stare blankly at him. "Never mind."

He sighed. The real reason he wanted to help Moira was because he wanted to spend more time with her, and this was a great way to accomplish that while doing something worthwhile. Unfortunately, he'd already flubbed the compatibility test—by questioning her methods, and in a hundred other ways, too.

He admired what Moira was trying to do. It wasn't the first time he'd noticed her jumping in to help others. When the preschool moved to the newly constructed education building, Moira was right there, carrying boxes, setting up classrooms, even running to the local store for supplies that had been forgotten. He liked the way she gave of herself with joy. It was obvious to those around her that she didn't think of helping as an imposition but rather as a privilege.

Though she was quiet and reserved, she was a dedicated Christian. Her faith shone through in the things she did and the things she said. She was always encouraging, always ready with a smile. Always thinking of others over herself. In fact, Joe was impressed that she didn't seem to realize how much she contributed.

Following her example, he appreciated the chance to take his service to a higher level, to do more for both God and the church, but also for Moira. Being with her brightened his days and his life. She made him want to be a better man, to serve God and others just like she did.

As his thoughts tumbled in all directions, he realized why he was still single at thirty-four. He had never met a woman like Moira—a woman who wanted to serve God wherever He led, just as Joe himself served Him. He had always believed God would one day show him the woman who would be his life's mate. With sudden clarity, he knew Moira could be that woman. Now all he had to do was convince her that he was the man for her.

"What made you decide to do this?" he asked.

She was silent for so long that Joe was afraid she wasn't going to answer, but after a few seconds, she spoke.

"I just felt led to contribute in some way." She paused, then continued. "It's a small thing, really. It takes about an hour or so to make an angel, which is why I spent that concentrated time making the extra ones. I still have my regular work to do to keep on target with my current deadlines."

Joe grinned. "You have deadlines?" He regretted the words almost as soon as he said them. To his own ears, his question sounded disrespectful of her job, and he hadn't meant it that way. He cleared his throat. "I mean, I didn't realize there were deadlines attached to designing."

Moira's voice was clipped as she responded. "If I want to eat, I have to produce. I have contracts for two books right now, and I have lessons to plan for the class I teach over at Barbara's Craft Shop. I'm scheduled to speak at a Crochet Guild convention in February. I have to get all the materials together."

As she warmed to her topic, her tone grew livelier. Her face flushed, and her slim hands moved in all directions as she talked. Did she realize how attractive all that energy and joy made her? A lump formed in his throat.

"You seem to enjoy your work."

"Yes, I do. Crochet has always been a part of my life.

My mother taught me years ago, before she and Dad started having problems. It's helped me through a lot of tough times. I find it relaxing, and I love designing. Don't you love your work?"

"It's a paycheck." The words tumbled out without him thinking about them.

"A job should be more than a paycheck."

"Some are, I guess." He didn't really want to talk about work. Much of it he couldn't share because of confidentiality issues, but there was no way to stop her questions without being rude.

"If you don't enjoy it, why do you keep on doing it?"

Why did he? Joe spared a second to glance in her direction. He'd wondered the same thing himself on more than one occasion.

"I guess because it's what I was trained to do. I went to law school. I got a degree. I passed the bar. I practice law. It's what I do."

Moira opened her mouth but closed it before any words came out.

"What?" he asked irritably. He hated when people held back what they really thought. Clients did that often, usually when they were hiding something he wasn't going to like when he heard it.

"I was just going to say if you're not happy, you should find something that does make you happy. You're only what. . .thirty-five? You'll be working a long time. Why not do something that gives you pleasure besides income? Something you can be proud of."

"Thirty-four. Not everyone can have fun while they work. And I *am* proud of what I do." He could hear the irritation in his voice. This wasn't the way he wanted things to go. He wanted to get closer to Moira to enjoy the time with her, not cause dissension.

He had to admit that fun was part of the reason he'd wanted to do this. *And we will have fun.* He'd see to it. Moira would not regret letting him in on her project. A change of subject was in order. "So does your mother still crochet?"

He knew immediately it was the wrong thing to say. Moira's face fell.

"Yes, when she can. She can't afford a lot of extras since the divorce, and she won't accept my help."

"Have they been divorced a long time?"

"Since I was a teenager. They're not Christians, and when they began to have trouble, they didn't have the Lord to lean on. Things went from bad to worse."

"Marriage is certainly hard enough. Without God, I don't know how people do it." He paused, hoping a subject change wouldn't seem too abrupt. He didn't think Moira wanted to talk about her parents' situation. "Do you think we have enough angels now, or will you need to make more?"

She brightened some and nodded. "I think we do, but if I have to make a few more, it won't be a problem. I'm really glad you thought of adding these folks to the list."

It was the closest she'd come to saying she was happy he had joined the project.

"Glad to help." While he didn't need acknowledgment, he was pleased she wasn't regretting her decision to include him.

"Looks as though we've arrived."

Joe looked out the window and realized they had indeed arrived at the location of their next undercover angel adventure. He hoped this one went smoothly. Visions of Attila the Doberman flitted through his memory, and he sent up a whispered prayer that there would be no Attilas in this delivery.

# Chapter 5

Moira felt somewhat better when they found the ladder just where Joe had said it would be—behind the bushes in front of the church, just under where the cross was attached to the wall. The cross was thick enough to hold the angel, so they wouldn't need anything with which to attach it, particularly since it wouldn't be up there very long.

Joe set the ladder close to the outer wall of the church, just even with the horizontal bar of the cross. The ladder was tall and reached almost to the top of the cross on the front of the building.

The cross itself was made of fiberglass and attached to the brick wall just below the point where the two sides of the roof met in the center. Because of an interest in the church history, Moira knew it was a Latin-style cross with three short arms and one long one, the style most associated with Christian churches. An outdoor floodlight brightened the white cross at night so anyone passing would be reminded of the Lord's sacrifice.

Standing in front of the cross, Moira realized it was larger than it had seemed at first. It was also higher.

"Are you sure you want to do this? We could think of another way to get Gabe his angel." Much as she wanted Gabe to have an angel, she didn't want Joe to get hurt. Of course, Gabe did this every week, but Gabe was used to it; and Joe was used to being in a courtroom, not on a ladder.

"Of course. It's not a problem. Look, I've made sure the ladder is secure, though you can stand here and hold it if it makes you feel better." He pointed to the ladder, waving his arm at it. "The rule is, you angle the ladder about a quarter of the total length. This ladder looks to be about sixteen feet, so I've angled it four feet from the wall."

"How do you know that?"

Joe laughed, the sides of his eyes crinkling with humor. "I have a roof, and I have a ladder. Just because I'm not a carpenter by trade doesn't mean I don't do any outdoor work. In fact, I enjoy working with my hands."

Moira felt the heat rush to her face. "I guess that didn't come out quite right."

"It's okay. We should get to it, though. Gabe could come by anytime now." Joe glanced toward the road and then up to the roof.

Moira nervously followed his gaze. "Maybe we should come back another time."

"Moira, we're here. We're doing it." He pulled a handkerchief out of his pocket. "I'll even clean off a spot so the angel won't get dirty."

"Good idea."

Resigned, Moira handed him the angel and positioned

herself below the ladder, ready to steady it if needed.

Joe climbed up to what Moira thought was a ridiculous height.

"You don't have to go all the way up," she called.

Their eyes met as Joe looked down at her. "I know. But I thought it might not be so noticeable from below if it's at the top. It's white and would look like an extension of the cross."

It made sense, but Moira was still nervous, watching him balance on the ladder as he cleaned the spot where he was going to place the angel. She held tightly to the ladder, willing it to stay in place, her eyes on the rung in front of her.

"Moira!"

Joe's shout made Moira look up quickly. Was he falling? To her surprise, when she lifted her head, she saw Joe was no longer on the ladder. He had climbed to the roof.

"Gabe's early. Put the ladder down and come to the back of the church. Hurry."

Against her better judgment, Moira quickly returned the ladder to its hiding place where Gabe would hopefully not notice it had been moved. Though awkward to maneuver, at least the ladder wasn't heavy, which was probably why Gabe had opted to use this one.

She glanced toward the highway where Gabe was just pulling into the long driveway leading to the church parking lot. She quickly said a prayer that Gabe had not seen her removing the ladder or Joe on the roof. She hurried around the building, wondering how Joe was planning to get down from his perch.

When she arrived at the back of the church where Joe

had parked his SUV, she found him sitting quietly on the lower edge of the roof.

He pointed toward his SUV and made driving motions with his hands. Moira tilted her head as she attempted to figure out what he was trying to tell her.

Joe grimaced and pointed emphatically toward the SUV. Then he pretended to be driving and pointed straight down, where Moira was standing.

She could almost feel her eyes widen as she realized what he was asking. He wanted her to drive the vehicle underneath where he sat so he could use it to get down. How high was an SUV? Not as high as a ladder, she was sure. Joe was about six feet tall. Glancing at the SUV, she estimated it to be somewhere shy of six feet high. The single-story church building had eight-foot walls. There was a good chance if Joe could make it to the edge of the roof without falling, he would be able to make it to the roof of the car without injury. She hoped Gabe was so engrossed in his work cleaning the cross that he wouldn't pay attention to any noise they made. She wondered how long it would be before Gabe saw the angel.

There really wasn't a choice, however. Joe couldn't stay up on the roof forever. Moira determinedly made her way to the vehicle, slipped inside, and realized she didn't have Joe's keys. She walked back and looked up at Joe. He was dangling the keys from the end of his fingers, a smile on his lips. He motioned for her to back up, then threw the keys down in front of her. Moira cringed at the clanging noise that erupted in front of her as the multiple keys hit against one another. She could only be grateful they landed on the ground and not on the nearby cement.

Moira maneuvered the vehicle as close as she could get without hitting the bushes that surrounded the entire building. It was a good thing Joe had long legs, because he would need every inch of them for this.

Once she was in place, she turned off the engine and stepped outside, listening for sounds of someone coming to investigate the noise. Hearing nothing, she turned back to the wall of the building.

Moira held her breath as she watched Joe carefully descend to the edge of the roof, turn himself around, and very slowly ease himself over the edge to dangle close to the SUV. He stretched his legs to reach and dropped onto the luggage rack. A gasp escaped as she heard the soft plop of rubber shoes on metal.

Quickly moving toward him, she whispered, "Are you okay?"

Joe turned and slid off the car, then faced Moira. "I'm fine. And I didn't even dent the roof."

Moira rolled her eyes. "I was afraid Gabe would hear."

"Even if he did, he probably thought nothing of it. People are in and out of the church all day long." Joe slid into the driver's seat and started the vehicle. "Let's drive around to the front and go inside."

"What? Are you crazy?" After this close call, she couldn't believe he wanted to advertise their presence.

"As a loon," Joe said, chuckling softly.

"Joe!" She spoke as loudly as she could, with all the emphasis she could put into a loud whisper, but Joe paid her no heed. She slid into the passenger seat as Joe brought the SUV down the side street behind the church, out onto the highway, and back into the parking lot. He waved at Gabe, who was on the ladder, cleaning the lower portion of the cross. It didn't look as though he had found the angel yet, but it was hard to tell from this distance.

Joe slid out of the driver's seat and walked around to open the door for Moira. Again, she was impressed with his courtesy, much as she wanted to continue to be annoyed with him.

He leaned down and spoke softly in her ear. "If we're just arriving now, we couldn't possibly have put the angel on the cross, could we?"

Understanding dawned, and Moira nodded. The man was insufferably correct.

They walked inside, and Moira consulted Anne, the church secretary, about the preschool portion of the Christmas pageant, while Joe talked with the pastor about some legal matters. Moira had committed to helping the choir director, and since she was also part of the adult choir, she was doing double duty that night.

Joe had just returned to the office, when the outer door opened and Gabe came rushing in.

"Look. I got one. It has my name on it." Gabe's eyes were shining, and his face was flushed.

"One what, Gabe?" Anne asked.

"An angel. I got an angel."

He held it out, and Anne took it from him. Moira leaned in to have a look. It looked like the time outside had not harmed the angel any.

"It's just like the one I received a few weeks back— with your name on it and the little note and everything. Guess our undercover angel has been busy," Anne said.

Anne then turned to Moira. "You should get one, too, Moira. You're always doing things for the church." Her eyes twinkled. "Better keep an eye out."

Moira laughed uneasily. Would she have to give herself an angel to keep suspicion away? The idea didn't sit well with her. "I don't do any more than anyone else." She turned to Joe and gave him a warning look. "Ready to go?"

Joe nodded, and they left together.

"That was exciting," Joe said as soon as they were out of earshot.

Moira sighed and turned slightly in her seat to face Joe. "Your idea of exciting is not the same as mine. I was scared to death you would fall off the roof. Why didn't you just climb down when you saw Gabe?"

"Not enough time. You needed time to move the ladder before he arrived."

"I admit that I would like to keep this anonymous, but not at the expense of your life."

"I wouldn't take that kind of chance. Trust me. Besides, even if I'd jumped off the roof, the most I'd have done was break a leg. It would hardly be life threatening. It's only one story high."

Moira sighed and looked out the window. Trust him. How could she do that? She didn't know Joe, not really. She knew he was a gentleman and a Christian. She knew he was successful at his job and he loved his mother enough to move in with her. Those were all good things. But she didn't really know him. She didn't understand how he could spend his days defending criminals and his weekends in church.

Joe's voice interrupted her thoughts. "Who's our next recipient?"

Moira stared out the window silently, contemplating the question. At the moment, she thought the best answer might be "no one."

# Chapter 6

Each second of silence passed like an hour. Joe began to fear Moira was not going to answer his question. He hoped she wasn't having second or even third thoughts about his participation in this project.

"I can't do another one now. I have to go home and get ready for the Sunday school Christmas party."

Joe's heart did a flip as he realized God was giving him the perfect opportunity to take his relationship with Moira to a higher level. "I was planning to go, too. Why don't we go together?" He held his breath as he waited for her answer.

"I don't know. If people see us together. . ." Her voice trailed off, and Joe wondered what she was thinking.

"If you're worried about the angels, I don't see that as a problem. There's no reason for anyone to suspect the undercover angel is anything but a single person working alone. In fact, maybe going together would be a good cover. I think people should see us together. Isn't the party at Elizabeth Wright's house? The organist?"

"Yes. Elizabeth is a friend of mine. I was going to go early and help her set up."

"I'd be glad to add my hands if I can be of help."

"Well. . ." Her voice trailed off. Unable to resist, Joe glanced over at Moira to see the emotions flying across her face. His mind raced. He knew he'd better do some fast-talking if he were to convince her they should appear at the party together.

"Come on. You've seen how handy I can be." Perhaps he was pushing things, but he was desperate.

"I guess it would be okay."

Joe reined in the whoop he wanted to let out. He held his breath for a second before allowing himself to respond. "That's great. What time shall I pick you up?"

"Five would be good. Everyone is supposed to bring their favorite finger food. All I have to do is make punch and set up the plates and such."

"Isn't Elizabeth on the angel recipient list?"

Moira turned her head to look at him. "Yes," she said slowly. "What are you thinking?"

"We'll be right there in her house. With a lot of other people. Easy enough to drop an angel in her lap, so to speak."

Moira groaned, and Joe chuckled. At least she hadn't changed her mind. But for now, the mission of distributing the angels was of lesser importance. He had a date with Moira Sullivan!

From what Joe could see, the party was a tremendous success. The Wrights had a large, two-story home with an open area downstairs ideal for entertaining. They had obviously spent a lot of time decorating and getting the house ready for the party. It looked to Joe as though most of the church family was in attendance. He and Moira had decided that when Moira was ready to drop the angel in an inconspicuous spot, she would let him know and he would provide a distraction. In the meantime, he intended to spend as much time at her side as he could. He didn't know if it was good or bad that Moira didn't consider their being together a date, because he certainly considered it one.

He stood off to the side and watched her interact with the other guests. She could have been the hostess the way she made sure no one was left out. He could appreciate the effort she was making. Moira certainly had a mission heart.

Eventually she broke away from the group and headed his way. Joe straightened and waited, not wanting to seem anxious to have her at his side.

"What are you doing, standing here by yourself ? Have you eaten?" she asked.

Her smile brought a smile to his own face. "Not yet. It looks like they have a nice spread, though."

Moira nodded. "Yes, they do. I'm starved, and I'm afraid I've done too much talking. My mouth is dry. Let's go get something."

His heart speeded up as Moira took his arm. Her touch, though light and friendly, caused his heart to speed up. Was it possible Moira could come to care for him? He was beginning to fear that when all the angels were delivered, he wouldn't see her again. It scared him how much he looked forward to being with her. He'd never felt this way about any other woman, but he wasn't sure if he was ready to make a long-term commitment. He had his mother to think about, too. The woman he chose for his wife must agree to having his mother in her home. Two women living under the same roof. He vaguely remembered a saying about that being trouble.

"Joe?"

He turned his head and smiled at Moira. "Yes?"

"I asked if you would like some of these chicken nuggets."

He glanced down at the food. "Sure. Why don't we each get a plate and just go around the table. Looks like there's enough to feed an army here. I was expecting chips and dip. I didn't realize they'd have actual food."

"Elizabeth loves to entertain. This is her one big bash of the year. Later she'll play the organ and we'll sing praise songs. She doesn't let anyone forget *why* we're celebrating."

"Sounds nice." Joe picked up a plate and began to add a few items to it.

A short time later, plates filled, they meandered back to the living room.

"Well, if it isn't Joe Corrigan."

Joe turned to see Clark Anvil, a prosecuting attorney with whom he often battled wits, coming toward him. He bit back a groan. He didn't want to talk shop tonight. He didn't want Moira to be bored. Yet he couldn't refuse to talk to the man.

"Clark. Nice to see you." What was he doing here anyway? Joe knew Clark didn't attend Faith Church. Perhaps he was a friend of the Wrights. Assuming it wouldn't be polite to ask Clark what he was doing there, Joe simply extended his hand to the other man.

Joe glanced at Moira and found the smile she'd worn all night still in place.

"And who's this lovely lady making you look good?"

Joe maneuvered himself closer to Moira but turned so he could look at both her and Clark. "Moira Sullivan, this is Clark Anvil. He's also an attorney."

Moira nodded at Clark. "Merry Christmas, Mr. Anvil. How nice that you could be here with us this evening."

"Please call me Clark. Elizabeth was gracious enough to invite me. I didn't realize Joe would be here, though. You may not know this, but he's a formidable foe in the courtroom. We're usually on opposite sides. I can't say I'm ordinarily happy to see him. Have you ever seen him in action?"

Joe watched as Moira blinked and bit her lip. "Um, no, I haven't. I would imagine he's good at his job, though."

"Good? I'd say he is. If you ever have need of an attorney, I would recommend him."

"I hope I won't ever need one, not for the courtroom anyway." The smile remained on her face, but Joe sensed that Moira was uncomfortable with the topic.

Clark laughed loudly, and Joe cringed. "You've got a wise woman there, Joe," Clark replied.

A blush stained Moira's cheeks, and Joe wondered what part of Clark's statement embarrassed her. "She certainly is that," he said.

"Do you only work in the courtroom, Clark?" Moira asked.

"The courtroom is the final step. There's a lot of preparation that goes on beforehand, but of course we all have staff to help with that part. Right, Joe?"

"Actually, I prefer to do as much of the research myself as I can, though I obviously can't do it all. It helps me to understand my client better if I've done the background work. Then I know the case inside out." Joe squirmed. *Did that sound too pretentious?*

Clark snorted. "Listen to him. That's why you work so hard." He turned to Moira. "This guy could write his own ticket if he'd only take some of these high-profile cases." He shook his head. "I've never understood why you don't go after those, Joe."

"I can't properly defend a guilty client."

Clark splayed his hands out in front of him. "Everybody gets a defense, innocent or guilty. It's the law."

Joe nodded slowly. "Yes, it is. And I agree with it. I just don't believe they would get the best defense from me if I knew my client was guilty." He kept his eyes focused on Moira, wondering what she thought of the turn of the conversation. "I realize there can be extenuating circumstances. . . ."

"You only defend the innocent?" Moira's voice was soft and hesitant. "How do you know they're innocent?"

Joe shrugged. "That's a tough call sometimes, but I do the best I can with a clear conscience."

Her smile disappeared, and a small frown creased her forehead. "But do you always have a choice?"

"I run a private practice. For the most part, I choose my clients."

"That's true," Clark said. "But if you want to build a career, there are political advantages to having your name well known, your reputation secure."

"I have no political aspirations," Joe said testily. It was true. He had never desired to go into politics. He was content with his lot as a defense attorney. In point of fact, he wanted to expand his services to help those who normally couldn't afford an attorney.

Clark shrugged. "To each his own. I'm just as glad to hear it. No competition when I jump in the ring." He turned to survey the room. "Time to shake some more hands." He faced Moira once again. "You two have a nice evening."

Moira's head bobbed up and down slowly. "You also."

When Clark was gone, conversation lagged. Joe wasn't sure what Moira's silence meant. Did she want to marry a man who was in the political arena? Did she think he was not ambitious enough? He didn't think she was the kind of woman who wanted the things a high-profile life would bring.

"It's pretty crowded," Moira said. "I think it's time to drop the angel. I saw a spot on the end table, just behind the picture of Elizabeth's twins, that will do."

"Okay. I'll provide your distraction. Give me a minute or two."

He walked off toward the grand piano in the corner of the room. He had an idea that might distract not only the guests but Moira, as well. He needed to salvage what was left of the evening.

Sitting down, he began to play one of the few songs he knew how to play, albeit badly. A few of the guests noticed and sauntered his way. He grinned. "Where's Elizabeth? It's been a long time since I've played. I don't think 'Chopsticks' is suitable for Christmas."

"There she is," someone in the crowd called out. With little coaxing, Elizabeth joined the crowd that now surrounded Joe.

"You do a much better job than I do," he told her with a smile, as he slid off the bench so she could sit down.

"But I've heard you sing, Joe. How about accompanying me? Do you have a favorite tune?"

Joe smiled. "Why don't we all sing?"

Moments later, Elizabeth began to play an introduction; and Joe positioned himself within eye contact of most of the guests and where he could also see Moira, who stood with her oversized purse open and ready.

At Elizabeth's nod, Joe opened his mouth and began to sing.

All heads turned his way. Some joined him, and others hummed along. Out of the corner of his eye, he saw Moira drop the angel onto the table and then step away to concentrate on the singing, along with the other guests.

*Thank You, Lord, for this opportunity to worship You in such a setting.* He closed his eyes as he poured out his heart to his Lord and Savior.

When the song ended, there was a hush as everyone absorbed the meaning of the words they had sung. Then a burst of applause sounded.

Joe smiled and pointed to Elizabeth. "It's not me. It's the Lord who provided such fine accompaniment. Let's all gather round and praise Him for His mercy and love."

Elizabeth took the suggestion and began to play a song they had sung often in church services. Soon everyone was gathered around the piano, calling out songs. Elizabeth was an accomplished pianist and had no trouble keeping up.

Joe felt more than saw Moira appear at his side. Seconds later, her hand was wrapped around his arm; and when he looked down at her, it was to find her looking up at him, a smile on her face as she sang out with the others.

Yes, this was the woman of his heart. The woman God surely wanted him to spend the rest of his life with.

# Chapter 7

The Christmas spirit was in the air all around Moira as the church family gathered together for their annual celebration. A large Christmas tree stood in one corner of the room. This was the Angel Tree, which for weeks had been filled with cards, each one holding the name of a child in the local area. Moira was glad to see the tree was now bare, which meant that each of those children had been taken care of by someone in the church community.

Moira glanced first toward the front of the church, where the pastor was preparing to lead the service, then to the side where Joe's mother sat visiting with a neighbor. She spotted Joe kneeling down next to a little girl who was showing him a doll that Moira assumed she had received as a Christmas gift. He glanced up, and their eyes met. Moira motioned casually to let him know she wanted to speak to him. Joe said a few words to the little girl and stood, turning to walk in Moira's direction.

"Hi. I'm glad you're here. I wanted you to meet my mother—officially."

Moira blinked. *Meet your mother? I don't think so.* Meeting his mother spoke of a closeness she wasn't quite ready for. She didn't say the words but rather pulled Joe to the side so they could talk privately.

"I brought an angel for the Nativity set."

It was Joe's turn to blink. "What Nativity set?"

"The one Manny and his family are going to put out as Pastor John reads the Christmas story." It was a tradition at Faith Church that the Nativity set was put up on Christmas Eve, each piece brought out as Pastor John read the story. Of course this year there would be no angel, since the original had been lost. Moira planned to fix that problem tonight.

"Oh. That's right. I heard the angel was missing in action. Ruined by a roof leak, wasn't it? Didn't they replace it?"

"It happened during the summer. Stores weren't selling angels then, and I think they meant to replace it later, but you know how that is. It was just forgotten. Anyway, I heard Pastor John talking about it when I was at the church earlier. Someone had promised to get one but for some reason was unable to. The staff wasn't informed until the last minute. I had one angel left over, so—"

His eyes widened. "You're going to leave one of the angels tonight? With all these people here?" Then he laughed. "You surprise me, Moira."

Moira crinkled her nose at him. "We left an angel at Elizabeth's in the middle of a Christmas party. I think we can handle this."

A mischievous smile appeared on Joe's face. "You're right. What's the plan?"

"Follow me," Moira whispered.

She glanced around to make sure no one was paying attention, then moved casually to the front of the sanctuary, heading to the small room off to the left. Thankfully, it was empty. This room led to the choir room, which was open, but since the choir was not performing tonight, Moira assumed people would not be going in and out of the room.

"Here it is." She pointed to the Nativity set, which waited close to the doorway.

Joe studied the set thoughtfully. "Where do you want to put it?"

Moira stood in front of the Nativity set, examining it carefully. Her thoughts turned to the little babe asleep in the manger. What a life He had ahead of Him. The joy of childhood and then the pain of His undeserved death on the cross. She was grateful God loved her so much. The little she could do on this earth was nothing compared to what God had already done. She sighed.

"Here. Watching over the baby." It was the perfect place, of course.

She opened her purse and pulled out the angel with the shiny red heart sequin, the trademark of the undercover angel. *Angels*, she reminded herself. Joe was an undercover angel, too. She handed it to Joe, and he knelt to place the angel next to the manger where Manny would be sure to find it.

A soft gasp caused both of their heads to jerk up.

Two pairs of eyes widened as they saw Joe's mother standing in the doorway. Moira's heartbeat doubled. She looked at Joe, who stood quickly, his hand squeezing

Moira's arm gently as he passed her to move to his mother, his hands motioning to quiet her.

"Mother, it isn't what you think—"

"It's you! You're the undercover angel. Or should I say 'angels'? My own son. And I never knew." Anna Corrigan shook her head. "I'm a crocheter myself, son. The angels are unique. I've been watching them pop up unexpectedly and admiring each one and how they're made." She frowned and then slapped his arm. "I can't believe you didn't tell me—"

"Moira wanted it to remain anonymous." His eyes narrowed as he looked at his mother. "And we *still* want it to remain anonymous."

Anna wouldn't meet his gaze.

"Mother." Moira could hear the warning in Joe's voice, but she knew there was nothing they could do to stop Anna from spreading the word if she decided to do so.

Anna walked past Joe and stopped at Moira's side. "I know you bought the desk at my yard sale, but I don't believe we've ever been formally introduced. I'm usually with the senior ladies, though I've seen you at church before, of course." She extended her hand. Moira gently laid her own hand inside it, and Anna gave it a hearty shake. "I'm Anna Corrigan. Nice to finally meet you, even if it was by accident." She turned slightly to include Joe in the conversation, her eyes boring into him. "Joe, have you invited Moira to the house after the service?"

"I was just going to do that," Joe began.

"No time like the present, son. You'll come, won't you? The family is meeting there for supper. Well, everyone but Liza. She can't make it. My sister promised a big pot of hot chocolate to warm us up, though. Everyone is looking forward to meeting Joe's girl."

"Mrs. Corrigan—"

"Anna."

"Anna—" Moira hoped her feelings didn't show on her face. She didn't do well in crowds of people she didn't know, and she was still processing the shock of their being discovered in the act—by Joe's mother, no less.

"Moira may already have plans, Mother," Joe interrupted.

Moira turned to Joe. "It's not that. It's just. . ." Her voice drifted off as she tried to think of how to get out of the invitation without being rude.

"Will you be visiting with your parents, dear?" Anna asked.

Moira started, then frowned. "No. My mother lives in Denver, and my father lives in New Jersey. We haven't been together for Christmas in years." Even before the nasty divorce, they hadn't really been together. Her parents had married too young, before they knew what they wanted in life. Moira was determined not to make the same mistakes her parents had made. She would wait until she was ready to marry. She would wait for the right man, the man God chose for her. And she would know him a lot longer and a lot better than her parents had known one another.

"Then come and be a part of our family tonight. You can have a peaceful evening. No cooking, just eating and visiting." Looking at Anna's warm smile, Moira couldn't seem to make the word *no* come out of her mouth. The woman was sweet, even if pushy.

"All right. For a little while." It was a compromise, she

told herself, a chance to convince Anna not to give away their secret. But if she was honest, she had to admit she wasn't quite ready to give up her last night in Joe's company. After all, she didn't have to marry the man to enjoy being with him for just one evening, did she?

Anna leaned to the side and spoke near Moira's ear. "That's a lovely dress, dear."

"Thank you." For some reason, the compliment unnerved Moira. Anna moved off, and Moira wondered yet again how she had ended up here, in Joe's living room on Christmas Eve.

She, Joe, and Anna had huddled together during the crowded Christmas Eve service. There had been some murmuring when the angel was put in place, but no one seemed to suspect her or Joe of being involved.

Surely Anna would keep their secret. Joe would see to it. He knew how important it was to Moira.

*Joe.* Though they had been partners in the undercover angel venture, now that all the angels had been delivered, there was no further reason for them to get together. *Just in time,* she thought. Before things got out of hand and she became too dependent on seeing him. She had enjoyed spending time with Joe more than she thought she would. Though she was attracted to him in some ways, it was much too soon to think of a romantic relationship.

Moira wondered what her mother would think of Joe. Though her mother had married a lawyer, and their family had enjoyed the fruites of his labor, it had not turned out well for her parents. While having money was nice, Moira realized it was more important to have a man after God's own heart. A Christian who would put God at the center of his life and love his wife as Christ loved the church, just as the Bible says a man should. A man she could be sure of and could depend on in good times and bad. Not a man who would leave her after a few years as her father had left her mother.

She was sure God had a woman in mind for Joe, but she was just as sure she was not that woman. Though he was a good Christian and a good man, she didn't want to be involved with a lawyer, even if he did defend the innocent. And even if he claimed he had no political aspirations, he could change his mind and she could end up in the public eye.

Joe would find another woman to spend his life with. She frowned. Irritatingly, the thought of Joe with someone else made her want to squirm.

If Clark could be believed, Joe didn't go after his cases based on what they could do to further his career. She and Joe hadn't discussed it, but as she'd gotten to know Joe better, she realized he had a high work ethic. He believed in justice. And he trusted God. Moira felt her lips lift in a small smile. One would have to trust in the Lord, given how many times they'd almost gotten caught delivering angels.

A touch at her elbow brought Moira back to the present. Joe was standing beside her, a grin on his face. "Sorry. Pastor John had some questions about the church property sale. He's anxious to get started on the new building for the preschool, and this was the first step. We kept missing each other during working hours. This was my first opportunity to talk with him."

"I thought you were a criminal lawyer."

Joe's eyebrows rose. "I defend the accused. I wouldn't call them criminals." He shook his head. "Even so, I know a bit about other aspects of the law. This is a pretty straightforward sales contract, but I told him I'd have a buddy of mine look it over, just to be sure."

Moira nodded. She couldn't help admiring the way Joe looked. The blue background of his sweater brought out the blue in his eyes, while the snowflakes reminded her of past Christmases, before her parents divorced. Snow was a rarity in the South, but when she'd lived in Colorado, she could look out her window at mountains topped with white. The navy blue dress pants allowed Joe to keep his lawyer image despite the snowman on his chest. Of course she knew he was the same person no matter what kind of clothes he wore, but his more casual outfit made her forget for a little while what he did for a living. The more she knew of Joe, the more she saw the kind of person he was—one with a great deal of honor and love for others.

"It's nice of you to help him out even though it's Christmas Eve."

"I didn't mind."

They were quiet, both watching the group of people moving around the room. Anna roamed from group to group, making sure everyone had something to eat or drink, much like Moira did when she was with her own friends.

"Remember when. . ." Joe's soft voice rolled over her as he began to reminisce about the delivery of Jake's angel and their run-in with the Doberman.

"Did you ever find out what happened to the dog?"

Moira asked.

Joe nodded, leaning in closer so they wouldn't be overheard. "Animal control picked him up soon after we called it in. Turns out the dog was let out accidentally. The owners picked him up at the pound that same night."

"Good. I'm glad he didn't have us for supper, though."

"I have to agree with you there."

A soft chuckle escaped from Joe's throat, and Moira smiled. She liked being able to make him laugh. She'd never been good at telling jokes, nor did she have anyone to share them with, even if she were a comedienne. Joe had changed her—for the better.

Joe sighed, and a shadow crossed his face. Moira tilted her head as she watched him.

"Is something wrong?" she asked.

"Wrong?"

She shrugged. "Never mind. You just had this look on your face."

He suddenly seemed uncomfortable and shuffled from one foot to the other. He must have realized what he was doing, as he suddenly stopped and resumed their conversation. "I was just thinking about our adventures delivering the angels. Did we accomplish all you'd hoped?"

She lowered her voice, remembering that some of these people were members of their church. "All the angels were delivered. I think we did well, partner."

"It certainly gave the church something to talk about for a few months. It's almost a shame to see it come to an end."

*Yes, a shame,* she thought, but she didn't say it. Out loud, she said, "I think we covered everyone we could in the time we had."

"I think so, too. There's always next year, or maybe we could do something for Easter."

Moira felt the blood drain from her face. This was just what she'd been afraid of. Joe wanted to extend their partnership. "Next year?"

"Sure. There's no reason to give it up, since you obviously enjoy it so much. It could become a Christmas tradition at Faith Church."

"I don't think that's a good idea."

"Why not? Didn't you have fun?"

"Sometimes it was fun. Sure."

"I know we sort of started off on the wrong—"

"Moira. Come and say hello to everyone." Anna suddenly appeared beside them. She put her arm around Moira and pulled her into the center of the room where a group of women stood waiting. "This is Moira Sullivan. She's here with Joe. She crochets for a magazine." Anna turned and motioned toward another woman who appeared to be about Moira's age. "This is Joyce, Joe's cousin. She crochets, too."

With Anna leading the conversation, Moira soon found herself involved in a discussion of designing and the process of publishing. Moira noticed Joe easing his way to a gathering of young men, where he became involved in a conversation of his own. She didn't see much of him the rest of the night, though their eyes often met. He would give her a smile, and she wondered if he knew her discomfort at being the source of attention in a group of people she didn't really know. Yet she was surprised at how easily she adapted to Joe's family. While she expected her own friends to ask about her work, these people didn't know her, yet they seemed genuinely interested in what she had to say. Still, she knew Joe's relatives considered them a couple, and that wasn't true. She felt a twinge of guilt at not setting them straight.

After a while, Joe appeared at her side. "Ready to escape?" he whispered.

She nodded, continuing to smile at the young girl with whom she was talking.

"Sorry, Judy, time for us to head out," Joe said.

Everyone expressed regret as they made their way to the door, but Moira was aware of winks and smiles among the company.

Regardless of what his family wanted, Moira knew she had to make sure Joe understood that theirs had been a partnership of convenience and she was not ready for or interested in anything more. She cared for him as a brother in Christ, and she thought they'd become friends; but nothing more serious could come of it—at least not now.

They drove in silence to her home, but the silence was not an uncomfortable one. Rather, Joe put the car heater on to ward off the stiff December chill, and Moira was content just to sit and enjoy the quiet. She knew she should bring up their earlier conversation, but she couldn't seem to make herself shatter the peace.

Joe pulled up at the curb and walked around the car, as she'd come to expect. She sat waiting until he opened the door for her.

"Thank you," she murmured.

She took his hand and slid out of the passenger seat.

He didn't relinquish her hand but held on to it as he walked her to her door.

"I hope my relatives didn't annoy you too much."

Moira looked up at him. The streetlight cast a glow so she could see Joe's face, though part of it was in shadow. She knew she had to say something. Yet still she hesitated. The sound of Snowflake barking at the door gave her a few seconds to think.

"He's happy you're home," Joe said, tilting his head in the direction of the door with a smile.

"Yes. But when I go inside, he'll curl up and go right to sleep." She knew she still hadn't answered his question. He was giving her an out by changing the subject; but she'd really had a good time, and she wanted him to know it. "I enjoyed meeting everyone at the party. They're an interesting group, and they were all nice. I didn't feel too out of place."

"I'm glad, because I was serious earlier about continuing our partnership. But I don't really want to wait until next Christmas to deliver angels, though we certainly can do that."

"Joe," Moira began, "I've enjoyed delivering angels with you, but I thought I'd made it clear from the beginning that that was all it was. You gave me little choice, as you recall. We were partners. But the angels are delivered now, and while I'd certainly like to remain friends, I don't think I'm ready for anything more than that."

"I see." She thought he did see, because his face fell. Her heart beat faster. He still held her hand, and now he lifted it to his lips and kissed it. "I'll respect your wishes, but, Moira, I'll ask you to pray about it. While I don't presume to speak for God, you've been on my heart, and I think God isn't through with us."

Moira forced a smile to her lips. "I know He's not finished with me. I have a long way to go."

"We all do. You know that's not what I meant."

He pursed his lips and looked at her, his eyes sad and his shoulders drooping.

Moira suddenly felt an inch tall. "I'm sorry. I don't mean to make light of it."

"Is it me particularly you don't want to have a relationship with? Is there something about me that puts you off?"

Moira hesitated as she remembered the first time Joe had visited her home. She gently pulled her hand away from his. "I admit I was concerned about your occupation."

"You don't date lawyers?"

She turned to her right so she didn't have to look him in the face. "I haven't dated any lawyers except you." Moira took a deep breath and lifted her eyes to his. "You remember I told you I'd been in a courtroom before? What I didn't tell you is that my father is a lawyer. Whatever else he's done, he shines in the courtroom." She sighed. I don't understand how a Christian could defend a person who has committed a crime. I know you tried to explain, but I'm not sure I really understand even now."

Joe shuffled his feet and sighed. "As I told you before, as far as I can tell, the people I defend *are* innocent. It's not always easy to tell, and sometimes I make a mistake in judgment. When that happens, I'm honor bound to give the best defense I can regardless. That's the way our system is set up. Innocent or guilty, everyone gets their day in court. I don't defend my occupation. It's what I do. I'm sorry if that's a problem."

His speech left her feeling guilty somehow. "I'm glad you've chosen to help the innocent, but I can't help the way I feel. My father's occupation and his political aspirations were a part of their later problems. I know you've said you're not interested in politics, but you may change your mind one day."

"I doubt that, but God controls the future. Not me. If He led me that way, I guess I'd go." Joe sighed deeply. "This is it then. It's been nice working with you," he said stiffly.

He stepped back and waited while she opened her door.

She picked up Snowflake and watched from her doorway as Joe walked slowly back to his car and drove off.

Her heart sank as she realized what she'd done. She'd sent him away. Joe Corrigan was finished with Moira Sullivan, by her own choice. It was what she wanted, wasn't it?

*Merry Christmas.* Her eyes welled with tears. What was wrong with her? It was the right decision. She remembered quite well what had happened to her parents. She knew it happened over and over again to many others, as well. People threw relationships away as they did old clothes. She didn't want that. She wanted a relationship that was God-centered and life-long. It took time to build that kind of relationship. If her parents had taken that time, perhaps they could have weathered their problems.

There was time for that to happen. She was still a

young woman, and there was no hurry to marry. Maybe Joe felt the same. Maybe when she was ready, Joe would be ready, too. *Maybe.*

She closed the door, set Snowflake back on the floor, and walked to the bedroom. Slowly she lay down on the feather bed she had impulsively treated herself to just last month. Closing her eyes, she allowed herself to enjoy the softness beneath her, remembering all the good things the television salesperson had said about the bed. Then she turned over and reached to her nightstand for her Bible. There was only One who would be able to help clear her thoughts. The One who cared for her more than anyone else could. He would never lead her astray. She could trust Him with her life and her love.

She fell asleep, the Bible still in her hands.

# Chapter 8

Moira walked into the church, accepted a bulletin from the greeter at the front door, and proceeded to the fellowship hall. The first Sunday in February was her class's turn to provide breakfast. The informal meal was also a time to welcome new church members and for present members to catch up with one another. As was her custom, Moira filled a cup with coffee, sugar, and a bit of milk, grabbed a doughnut, and turned to see which of her classmates had arrived. Sarah was in a group at the other side of the room, so Moira headed in her direction. As she got closer, Sarah looked up, her eyes widened, and a pink tinge ran up her neck. Moira paused, confused, but then Sarah motioned for her to join them.

"Moira." Sarah greeted her a little too enthusiastically. The other class members turned, mumbled a greeting, and moved off to get seats.

"Was it something I said?" Moira tilted her head and looked at her friend.

"Of course not." Sarah's voice was unconvincing. "It's

just that it's almost time to start. Let's get a seat." Sarah led the way, and Moira sat down beside her.

Throughout the class, however, Moira had the feeling people were looking at her. When she glanced around the room, faces quickly turned away. It was an unsettling feeling. She was obviously an object of interest today. She was glad when the bell rang and class dispersed. She realized she hadn't gotten much out of today's lesson.

She was moving quickly toward the door when, suddenly, Sarah grabbed Moira's arm and pointed. "Oh, look, there's Joe Corrigan."

Moira gazed in the direction Sarah motioned. There was Joe, standing in the aisle, holding a young child and talking to a woman, whom Moira assumed was the child's mother. Joe was laughing, and though he was too far away for her to see them, she could picture how his blue eyes crinkled when he chuckled. Joe enjoyed life and laughed often. He'd made her laugh, too, and she missed that.

Joe leaned over and kissed the cheek of the woman he was talking to, and then the two of them slid into a pew, continuing their conversation. The child laid his head on Joe's shoulder and appeared to be going to sleep.

"Let's go over and say hello," Sarah continued.

But Moira hung back. "No. It's almost time for the service to begin. Besides, I need to wash my hands. They're sticky from the doughnuts." Any excuse was better than having to meet Joe's new love interest.

Moira quickly moved off in the direction of the ladies' room, and Sarah followed. Moira frowned as she hit the soap dispenser.

"I didn't know you knew Joe Corrigan," she said casually

as she turned on the faucet and stuck her hands beneath the spray of water.

Moira watched Sarah's face in the mirror and saw a light blush form over her face.

"I don't know him. I thought you did," Sarah said. She glanced at her watch. "It's time for the service to start. We'd better get going."

They hurried to the sanctuary, but Sarah paused at the entry, looking around the room. "There's Joe. Do you want to go sit with him?" she asked.

Moira stared at her. "Why would I want to do that?" *Particularly since he's with another woman.* She turned to face her friend. "Sarah?"

Sarah sighed. "You could have told me. I'm your best friend." She shrugged. "Oh, forget it. Let's just find a seat."

Sarah moved into a pew before Moira could gather her wits to respond to her friend's strange statement. Moira joined her on the seat and stared at the words in the bulletin, but her eyes wouldn't focus. Sarah seemed to think she and Joe were a couple. Why? She didn't recall seeing Sarah at the Christmas party at Elizabeth's house. That was the only time Joe had been with her in public. Maybe someone else had seen them together there and commented on it. Moira knew rumors sometimes developed a life of their own. Were the church members talking about them as a couple?

A couple. Of course they weren't a couple. Joe was here with another woman. Moira's mind whirled. *Doesn't Sarah think that's strange?*

Moira sighed deeply. Thoughts of her time with Joe

wouldn't leave her. She had about given up fighting it. No matter how hard she pushed the images from her mind, they immediately returned. She couldn't believe thoughts of him were still stuck in her head like this.

Moira rubbed her temples. A headache threatened to overwhelm her. She felt a lump in her throat. Joe had moved on. She'd told him in so many words that she wasn't ready for a relationship. Apparently Joe was ready for one, and in the short weeks since they'd last spoken, he'd taken steps to find a woman who shared his desires.

A whine sounded from the microphone as the pastor began to make the announcements, and Moira forced her attention to the front of the church. She stood with the rest of the congregation as they began to sing praise and worship songs. Though she tried, she found she couldn't join in the singing. The words caught in her throat, and her voice cracked. She moved her eyes over the words and took them into her heart. The song was about God working things out when there didn't seem to be any way things could work. Would God make a way for her? And if He did, where would that way lead? Was it too late for her and Joe?

Moira knew that God was always at her side. She constantly relied on His strength and love. But she also felt that God expected each one to do his or her part. She had turned Joe away. What if God had put Joe in her path for a different reason than delivering angels? What if God meant Joe to be her future husband and she had turned her back on His will? How could she be sure? And did it even matter? Joe was with another woman. She had no right to change her mind now.

Trying to focus on the sermon, Moira found that her thoughts kept drifting as her eyes caught sight of Joe. His attention was on the pastor, and he appeared to be drinking up the words of the sermon. Moira sighed.

She realized how much she missed Joe. It wasn't just the fun they'd had delivering angels she missed. It was the encouragement, the support, the caring. She pictured Joe walking around the car to open the door for her. Such a small thing, and yet it was just another extension of his personality.

Even if she wanted to begin a relationship with Joe, it was too late. She'd pushed him away, causing a distance between them. Joe was respecting her wishes. He had not contacted her since Christmas, though he'd been polite and friendly whenever they ran into each other at church. He had other things in his life besides her. His actions did not depend on her, nor did she affect his decisions.

Right now, however, she needed to put her mind where it should be. She was in the house of the Lord and needed to concentrate on Him. *Help me to focus, Lord. You deserve my entire concentration.* Determined, she opened her Bible and focused on the pastor.

"Hey, Joe."

Joe glanced up and moved to the side to make room for Manny Wiseman and his wife.

"Who you got there?" Manny whispered.

"This is my nephew, Aaron." Joe patted Aaron's back. His sister, Liza, had come for an unexpected visit, and Joe was happy beyond measure that she'd agreed to attend church services with him. Since her husband died, she'd pulled away from the Lord. This was the first time she'd been open to renewing that relationship, and Joe determined he would do everything he could to make her comfortable here and encourage her to open herself to God's healing powers.

"Getting a little practice in before having one of your own, huh?"

Joe looked at Manny, for once at a loss for words. *What a question.* He wasn't even dating anyone, and Manny was asking if he was preparing for a family of his own. Manny looked away from Joe, and Joe followed his gaze to see Moira sitting across the aisle.

As he held little Aaron, Joe admitted to himself that he did yearn for a family of his own. He'd hoped Moira would be the mother of his children. He thought he was doing God's will when he approached her about a relationship. How could he have been so wrong? Could it be true that Moira really didn't have any feelings for him?

He again looked across the aisle at the woman of his dreams. Her eyes were focused on the front of the church. Did she ever think about the time they'd spent together?

He sighed deeply, knowing he should be paying more attention to the pastor and less to his own thoughts. God would take care of everything. Whatever happened, if God was in it, it would be right. He had to trust the Lord.

One thing he did know was that he wouldn't push Moira. If she wasn't ready, if she didn't want a relationship, whether with him or anyone, he wouldn't force the issue. He knew, however, that it would be a long time before he felt the same way about another woman.

The service was about to conclude, and for the first time in his life, Joe was anxious to leave the church building. Being so close to Moira and unable to talk to her, except for a simple greeting, was driving him crazy. He wasn't sure if he would be able to maintain his distance if he stayed at Faith Church. Perhaps it was time for a change.

Pastor John walked to the front of the church, replacing the song leader at the podium.

"Today there is something special I'd like to say."

Joe's ears perked up at the unusual opening. Though he was quite active in the church and a personal friend of the pastor, he had no clue what was coming.

"You all know that myself and members of the church staff received special gifts during the past Christmas season." He paused. "These gifts were delivered anonymously, with a note of encouragement addressed to each recipient." He looked around the room, and Joe felt the heat of a blush crawl up his neck as the pastor seemed to look directly at him. "Philippians 2:3 says, 'Do nothing out of selfish ambition or vain conceit, but in humility consider others better than yourselves.' I think those who provided this message of hope and encouragement took this verse to heart."

Pastor John moved to front center stage as he talked. "Though the angels were delivered anonymously, someone has already let the cat out of the bag. I think most of you know who these good-hearted people are, so I don't think I'm stepping on any toes by talking about it. I think it is important their generosity is publicly recognized in this time when it seems honesty and integrity are in short demand, when instant gratification is the mode of the day, and most focus on their own needs. They have shown us there are still those who think of others above themselves." He smiled, and his eyes moved from one side of the church to the other. "An angel gave the good news about Jesus' birth to the shepherds, guiding them to Joseph and Mary in Bethlehem. Our undercover angels brought the good news of hope and encouragement to everyone here in this church by their selfless acts." He smiled. "Moira Sullivan and Joe Corrigan, I just want to say thank you, on behalf of all the recipients of the beautiful angels you provided us."

As the church family broke into applause, each one turning to locate Joe and Moira among the congregation, Pastor John moved back and the song leader nodded to the organist to begin the final hymn.

Joe was grateful Pastor John hadn't called them to stand with him, though he wasn't sure if it was any better to have their names announced to the congregation. He tried to see how Moira was taking the news, but she remained facing the front. She would be furious, he knew, and she would know how the pastor discovered their secret. There was only one person, other than the two of them, who knew the truth about the undercover angels. His mother.

# Chapter 9

Moira forced a smile to her face as she tried to leave the church. She'd never known it could be so hard to smile. People kept stopping her to ask about the angels. She repeated the story a dozen times, each time condensing it just a little bit more. She now had it down to about a half dozen sentences. Inside, she fumed. How could this happen? No one knew. No one. Well, Joe knew. She frowned. And Joe's mother.

That was it. It was Anna. It had to be. She'd told someone, or many someones, and the news had gotten to the pastor. She'd almost died when Pastor John thanked her and Joe for delivering the angels, essentially telling everyone that they were the undercover angels. She couldn't be angry with him, though, because she now understood why Sarah and the other women in her Sunday school class were talking about her. It wasn't about her romantic relationship with Joe but about her and Joe delivering the angels together.

Her head ached. Maybe they were talking about both.

It would be logical for people to assume they were working together because they were a couple, even if that wasn't the way it was.

She couldn't let people continue to think that. Joe would be upset, and so would his girlfriend, yet she didn't know how to set things straight. She would have to talk to Joe about it.

"Moira."

She whirled around at the familiar voice. Joe stood not two feet in front of her. Another step and she would have walked right into him.

"Joe."

"I'm sorry. I know you didn't want this to get out. I'll talk to Mother. It had to be her. No one else knew." He spoke softly. She assumed he didn't want to say anything negative about his mother in the crowd of church members, many of whom knew the family.

"Never mind. It's out now. It can't be undone. Just let it go." It wasn't exactly what she felt, but she knew it was the right thing to say; and she knew she *would* feel that way eventually.

Joe took her arm and gently led her out to the parking lot. The crowd moved off as soon as Joe took her away, as though they understood the two of them needed time alone. Time alone for what, she didn't know, as there wasn't much else that could be said.

"I know you're angry," Joe began.

"Shocked. Surprised. Yes, angry. But I will get over it."

"I can only apologize. I had no idea Mother told anyone. She's home with a cold today, but I will talk to her. As you've already said, however, it can't be undone."

She realized Joe didn't fully understand why she was really upset. She had to set him straight. "Joe, people think we're a couple."

His eyes narrowed. "I don't see why, but if they do, we'll set them straight on that. But. . .would it be such a bad thing?" His smile almost undid her.

"Of course it would! Won't your girlfriend be angry?" Moira frowned, nonplussed at his attitude.

"What? My girlfriend?" His eyebrows rose. "What girlfriend?"

Moira took a deep breath and motioned toward the woman in question, who was walking across the parking lot toward Joe's car, carrying the little boy Joe had been holding.

Joe turned his head to look where she was pointing. Then he burst out laughing.

Moira's shoulders slumped. This wasn't funny. Joe had a terrible habit of laughing at things that weren't funny to her. Didn't he realize how this would look to another woman? Maybe he didn't. Men were a bit dense sometimes about things like this.

"She isn't my girlfriend," Joe finally managed.

"She's not?"

"No, Liza's my sister. Come on. I'll introduce you." He started off toward the woman and child, but Moira stayed where she was. When he realized she wasn't following him, he turned back. "What's wrong?"

"I—thank you, but no. Please give her my apologies, but I need to go." Moira suddenly felt as though all the air in the parking lot had been sucked into the clouds above.

Her heart and head were both pounding. She had to get out of there.

Joe was not seeing another woman. Joe was still free. And she was back in the fire—with a decision to make.

She swung her car door open and slipped behind the steering wheel, started the car, and headed out of the parking lot without a backward glance.

Joe stomped from one end of the living room to the other. Liza gave him a threatening look, and he set his feet down more gently as he paced the room. Aaron was sleeping, and it wouldn't do to have a grouchy two-year-old in the house.

He couldn't get Moira out of his mind. He'd talked to his mother, and she admitted telling one of her friends about the angel deliveries; but she seemed honestly surprised the news had traveled so far. She apologized profusely and offered to apologize to Moira, as well. Joe wasn't sure if that was a good idea or not. Moira hadn't taken the announcement well. He was sure she would never speak to him again, and the thought pained him more than he could say.

Even after she had told him she wasn't ready for a relationship, he still harbored the hope that one day she would be ready and that she would consider him in that light. He was sure they could work out her problems with his job. To be honest, he wasn't all that happy with it either. He'd been toying with other ideas lately, and maybe this was as good a time as any for a change. He would have liked to consult with Moira before he made any decisions, however, but now it didn't look like that was going to happen anytime soon.

The doorbell rang, and he growled. He didn't want to see anyone, but he couldn't let the person continue to ring the bell and wake up Aaron. Mother was resting, and a quick glance told him his sister was on the phone.

He hurried to the door, forcing down his annoyance so he could greet their guest properly. However, when he swung open the door, no one was there.

Frowning, he glanced up and down the sidewalk, thinking perhaps the person had thought no one was home and walked away. But no one was in sight. Then the sun reflected off something shiny on the top step leading to the doorway.

An angel.

Not just any angel, but an angel with a shiny red heart sequin.

He remembered the first time he'd visited Moira and his comment about an angel appearing on Gabe's doorstep. He squatted down and lifted the angel from its perch. He knew they had given out all of the angels Moira had made. She must have made this one especially for him.

What was she trying to tell him? The other angels had been delivered to give hope and encouragement. He smiled as he stood, bringing the angel with him. Was that the message meant for him?

He lifted his eyes and noticed Moira's white car, parked nearby. Moira stood next to the car, waiting.

She wouldn't have to wait long. Long strides took him to her side in seconds.

"Hey." He placed his finger under her chin and lifted her face so he could see her eyes. He didn't know what else to say. He hoped she would talk. . .explain. His heart hammered against his ribs.

Her eyes were sparkling. "I wanted to deliver angels to show how much I appreciated the church workers. Well, there's one church worker who didn't get one. Someone I appreciate more than any of the others. Someone who was always there for me, who taught me how to laugh, who loves the Lord above all else. Someone who captured my heart, despite my best intentions." She smiled as she said the last, and Joe returned her smile.

"But he's a lawyer," he pointed out, his tone tentative.

She laughed and winked. "Well, not just any lawyer."

"I love you," he said softly. Lowering his face, he touched her lips with his, gently savoring the kiss.

"I love you, too, Joe Corrigan."

He pulled her to his side. "Let's go. I think we have a lot to talk about."

Walking beside the woman who had stolen his heart, Joe thought he was the luckiest man alive. *Thank You, Lord.*

# Moira's Angel

For more detailed instructions, please visit my Web site at www.sandrapetit.com.

Materials: Small amount worsted-weight white cotton yarn; F crochet hook; #16 needle; white chenille pipe cleaner; small red heart sequin

Size: 5½ inches tall with 5-inch wingspan

Skill level: Intermediate

Time: 1½ hours

Special stitches: Shell = 3 dc; corner = (shell, ch 3, shell)

# ABBREVIATIONS

beg = beginning

ch = chain

dc(s) = double crochet(s)

dec = decrease

hdc = half-double crochet

hk = hook

rnd = round

sc(s) = single crochet(s)

shell = 3dc

sl st = slip stitch

sp = space

st(s) = stitch(es)

wk = work

yo = yarn over

Body: Make a 3-round granny square as follows:

Ch 5, join with sl st to form a ring.

Rnd 1: Ch 3, work 2 dc in ring, (ch 3, shell in ring) three times, dc in top st of beg ch 3.

Rnd 2: (Ch 3, 2 dc, ch 3, shell) in same sp, (ch 1, in next ch 3 sp wk corner) three times, hdc in top of beg ch 3 (8 shells).

Rnd 3: (Ch 3, 2 dc) in same space, (corner in next ch-3 sp, ch 1, shell in next ch-1 sp) three times, then ch 1, corner in next ch-3 sp, ch 1, join with sl st to top of ch 3, finish off, leaving a long end loose for sewing sides together (12 shells).

With right side facing you, corner at the top, fold sides so they meet in the center to form a cone shape. There will be a "skirt" hanging lower than the rest. Starting at top, leaving the top ch 3 open, insert needle in first dc of first shell and whipstitch sides together. Finish off. Sew in ends. Turn piece inside out, pulling right side to the front.

Border: Holding body upside down, attach yarn with a sl st in sp to left of center joining at bottom of skirt. Ch 3, 2 dcs in same sp. Skip first dc of next shell. In center dc of that shell, wk 1 sc, (shell in next sp between shells, skip one dc, 1 sc in next dc) twice. At point of skirt wk 5 dc, skip next dc, in next dc wk 1 sc, (shell in next sp, skip one dc, 1 sc in next dc) twice, shell in final sp, join to top of beginning ch. Finish off. Sew in ends on *wrong* side.

Wings: Special Stitch: Sc dec: Insert hk in st, yo, pull through (2 loops on hk), insert hk in next st, yo, pull through, (3 loops on hk), yo, pull through all 3 loops.

Row 1: Ch 11, sc in 2nd ch from hk and in each ch across (10 scs).

Row 2: Ch 1, turn, sc in each st across (10 scs).

Row 3: Ch 1, turn, sc in first st, sc dec over next 2 sts, sc in next 4 sts, sc dec over next 2 sts, sc in next st (8 scs).

Row 4: Repeat row 2 (8 scs).

Row 5: Ch 1, turn, sc in first st, sc dec over next 2 sts, sc in next 2 sts, sc dec over next 2 sts, sc in next st (6 scs).

Row 6: Repeat row 2 (6 scs).

Row 7: Ch 1, turn, sc in first st, (sc dec over next 2 sts) twice, sc in next st (4 scs).

Row 8: Repeat row 2 (4 scs).

Row 9: Ch 1, turn, (sc dec over next 2 sts) (2 scs).

Row 10: Repeat row 2 (2 scs).

Row 11: Ch 1, turn, (2 sc in next st) twice (4 scs).

Row 12: Repeat row 2 (4 scs).

Row 13: Ch 1, turn, sc in first st, 2 scs in next
2 sts, sc in last st (6 scs).

Row 14: Repeat row 2 (6 scs).

Row 15: Ch 1, turn, sc in first st, 2 scs in next st, sc in
next 2 sts, 2 scs in next st, sc in last st (8 scs).

Row 16: Repeat row 2 (8 scs).

Row 17: Ch 1, turn, sc in first st, 2 scs in next st, sc in
next 4 sts, 2 scs in next st, sc in last st (10 scs).

Row 18–19: Repeat row 2 (10 scs), do not finish off.

Border: Ch 1, turn, 3 sc in first st for corner, sc in
next 8 sc. Insert hk in last stitch (corner st),
yo, pull through (2 loops on hk). Place chenille
stem along side (this will be top of wing); with
hk above stem, yo and pull through, completing
a sc. Wk 2 more sc in same st. Sc in each row
along side, covering stem as you go. Bend stem
as needed to follow shape of wing. At end of row,
wk 1 sc in corner st, clip leftover stem (at both
ends) being careful not to clip threads, then complete 2 more sc for corner. Sc in next 8 sts, working over loose strand so you don't have to sew it
in later, wk 3 scs in corner, 1 sc in each row along
side. Join with a sl st. Finish off. Sew in ends.

Head: Rnd 1: Ch 4, join with sl st to make a ring, ch 3, wk
9 dcs in ring, join with sl st to top of beg ch (10 dc).

Rnd 2: Ch 1, wk 1 sc in same st, (2 scs in next st)
around, join with sl st to top of beg ch. Finish
off. Sew in ends.

Halo: Starting about half an inch in, wk scs around stem of 6-inch piece of chenille wire (note: work over beg strand so you don't have to sew in); leave about a half inch unworked (20–25 sts). Do not finish off. Carefully insert stem from left to right through holes at the uppermost part of body (near point) behind the front stitches. This would be the space where there is no shell. Take care that the stitches don't get caught as you're pulling it through. Holding stem up, above the body, bend the two pieces together and wrap ends around one another so they won't move as you crochet over them. Be sure stitches sit up around the outside, not the inside. Finish covering the un-worked portion with sc stitches. When complete, sew ends in, then turn so that the join is at the bottom, where it will be hidden by the head.

Assembly: Glue head (right side in front) to top of body. Glue body to wings (right side in front), making sure the halo is above the head and the chenille stem on the wings is at the top. Glue the red heart sequin over the angel's "heart."

## SANDRA PETIT

Sandra Petit grew up in southern Louisiana and lives in the New Orleans area with her husband of more than twenty years and her two teenage, homeschooled children. She believes God's timing is always perfect and welcomes the opportunity He has given her to share her faith through tales of romance. She prays that each of her readers will experience the love and joy of having Jesus in their lives and invites you to visit her Web site at www.sandrapetit. com.

# an angel for everyone

by Gail Sattler

# Chapter 1

Trent Johnson tipped back his head and smiled.

"Hey, Trent. It looks great."

He nodded to acknowledge Pastor Mark without looking at him. His smile dropped as he pressed his fists into the small of his back and stretched. "Yeah. It's even better than he said it would be. And bigger, too."

Beside him, Pastor Mark sighed. The shuffle of winter outerwear told Trent that his pastor also felt the effects of what they'd done. "I can't believe we got it in here. This is the biggest Christmas tree I've ever seen. Indoors, anyway."

Again, Trent stretched his sore back, this time twisting from side to side to get the kinks out. The tree was so heavy that it had taken three men to drag it inside, and that was only after they bound the branches tighter because it was too full to get inside the double doors of the church building. "I know. But it will be easier to get it out, because we'll be able to cut off some branches."

Pastor Mark groaned. "It's not even decorated yet, and

you're already talking about destroying it."

Trent looked up to the twelve-foot ceiling, only three inches above the top of their newly acquired Christmas tree. "Actually, I was a little worried we were going to have to trim it to get it to stand upright. I have my chain saw in my car." He craned his neck back again. "How long do you think it will take to decorate?"

"I have no idea. All I know is that Stephanie promised that the committee would have the tree and the room done in time for the banquet Saturday night."

Trent checked his watch. It had taken longer than expected to get the tree upright, and then he and Pastor Mark had to get it properly secured and positioned so it would be ready for the decorating committee's arrival, which was supposed to be fifteen minutes ago.

Pastor Mark smiled as he again looked upward. "The tree really looks great, Trent. You really outdid yourself this year. For a while, though, I didn't think we—"

The door creaked open, and the clacking of running footsteps echoed in the large, empty room. "I'm sorry I'm late! I'm so glad someone is still here!"

Trent spun around to face the newcomer. As soon as he saw the face of his neighbor, he froze.

Kim Warner had lived next door to him since before he could remember. Years ago, when they were both in high school, she'd had a cute crush on him, which wouldn't have been bad except that she'd been born and raised in a Christian home and he hadn't. She'd always been a good girl and a good person. He hadn't been so good, and while her attention had been tremendously flattering at the time, now that he was older and had accepted Christ, he was glad he hadn't taken advantage of her. Now at least he could look her in the face without guilt.

He'd always thought she was nice, and lately he'd been starting to think about finding the woman who would be right for him—but that woman wasn't Kim. A few of the other men from the college and career group had their eyes on her. When she decided to settle down and get married, she deserved to spend her life with someone of the same caliber, and that person wasn't him.

He forced himself to smile. "Hey, Kim. It's good to see you. But it looks like you're not the only one on the decorating committee who's late."

Kim Warner gave him a nervous smile, and with the smile, her cheeks flushed. "I have some bad news. When I arrived at Gary's house to pick him up, I found out that the reason he wasn't in church yesterday was because he's in the hospital with appendicitis. He's okay now, but he's not going to be in any shape to be decorating any tree, the church's or his own. Yesterday Sylvia had to go out of town on an unexpected business trip, so I knew she couldn't do it."

Trent frowned. "But what about Ellen? I was talking to her last week, and she told me she was going to help with the decorating, as much as she could anyway."

Pastor Mark smiled. "She had her baby yesterday, a month early, remember?" His smile dropped. "But no one told me about Gary, and I was at the hospital without seeing him."

"He was in emergency surgery Sunday afternoon," Kim said, "so you wouldn't have been able to see him even if you had known."

Pastor Mark pulled out his organizer and tapped in a note to himself. "I'll call in the morning and see when I can pay him a visit." His hand froze in midair before he completed his entry. "If the committee is down by three people, then that means. . ." He let his voice trail off.

Kim nodded. "That means I'm the only one who is healthy and available."

Trent felt his pastor's gaze upon him, heating up the skin on his face. "Surely there's someone else who can help?"

But even as Trent asked, he already knew Kim's answer before she said it.

"No. This year we want the banquet to be an outreach to the community and not just for our own church members. Everything is being provided by volunteers, including some of the food, in order to keep costs down. I think everyone in the church is doing something, even if it's just folding napkins. I already tried to find someone else to fill in for Sylvia, then Ellen. There's no one left. Everyone else who can do something is already busy on another committee."

Trent was on another committee, but it was a committee of one. He had volunteered to acquire a tree, and he had. It had taken weeks of hunting, but he'd found a good, healthy tree that a farmer was going to cut down in order to expand one of his outbuildings. After much negotiation, it was only when Trent offered to buy the man and his family tickets to the banquet that the farmer finally agreed to cut it down carefully, in one piece. Then, to Trent's surprise and delight, the farmer not only gave the tree to the church free of charge but even helped deliver it and haul it inside.

Trent personally didn't care if the decorating would be sparse. He didn't even put up a tree at home, because he lived alone. His mother gave him a wreath every year to hang on his front door, and that was good enough. But the congregation expected traditional decorations, and the farmer would expect his donation to look good.

Trent looked back up at the huge, plain pine tree, then down at Kim. If he didn't volunteer, Kim would have to do everything herself, and that wouldn't be a good thing. He didn't want her to risk injury by working alone. Not only would no one be there to hold the ladder, but even if she made it to the top rung, she was still too short to reach the top of the tree—not to mention she would have to decorate the room all by herself.

But he'd already sacrificed too much time finding the tree. His Christmas shopping wasn't done, and he hadn't sent out a single Christmas card or e-mail. He also hadn't taken his mother out for dinner, something he did every year during the holiday season.

But if he didn't help Kim, no one would. For all she'd done for him—and everyone else—she didn't deserve to be left high and dry.

He gritted his teeth, then forced himself to smile. "I think I can find the time to help decorate the tree with you."

Kim's eyes widened. "You would?" she gasped.

Her surprise almost hurt his pride. "Of course."

"Are you sure you have time?"

"Yes." *No.* But sometimes there were choices to be made, and this was one he had to make. Kim was one of the main reasons he'd started attending church and then came to know Jesus as his Lord and Savior. She always sacrificed her time to help others learn about Jesus, and since the banquet was supposed to be an outreach to the community, this was a good time to follow her example.

If he had to justify the time, he told himself that if he had to be on any more committees, this one was best because he lived next door to the only other committee member. For the work they needed to do at the church, they would drive together, so there would be no impatient waiting; and for anything they had to figure out together, once he had his coat and boots on, he could be at Kim's door in twenty seconds.

Also, years ago, she'd hurt herself because of him, and he'd always felt like he owed her something. Now he could finally pay her back.

"Wow." Her eyes lit up as her voice trailed off.

All Trent could do was stare. He hadn't seen Christmas lights as beautiful as Kim's sparkling green eyes. He wondered why he hadn't noticed before.

"That's wonderful!" she chirped as she held out a brightly colored gift bag. "I brought the first thing to put under the tree, and that's the party favors I made to give to everyone."

Pastor Mark cleared his throat. "It looks like you two have everything under control. If I don't talk to either of you before then, I'll see you Saturday at the banquet. Have fun."

They both waved as Pastor Mark made his way out and the door clicked closed behind him.

# Chapter 2

Kim Warner tried to control the frantic beating of her heart.

Pastor Mark's words echoed through her head. "Have fun," he'd said.

She didn't know if she could have fun with Trent. She'd lived next door to him nearly all her life. During her teenage years, she'd developed the most insane crush on him. For a while she thought she'd grown out of it, but when he started attending her church, those old feelings came back; and the reasons she'd fallen in love with him in the first place hit her tenfold. Now, as an adult, those same qualities, plus the fact that he'd become a believer, made her love him even more.

But to him, all she would ever be was the ditzy sixteen-year-old who'd built a ramshackle tree house just so she could talk to him over the fence one summer, then had broken her arm when the structure collapsed with her in it. He hadn't ever taken her seriously before that, and he certainly hadn't afterward, not even as an adult.

Trent looked at her. She couldn't read his expression, but he didn't look exactly eager to help.

"You don't have to do this, you know. It will just take longer, but I'm sure I can do it alone." If she worked every evening until Saturday, up to the time everyone who was bringing food started to arrive.

He turned his head and fixed all his attention on the top of the tall tree. "No. I happen to know from a good source that your sense of balance gets exponentially worse the higher you go. I could never forgive myself if something happened to you. Especially if you were here all alone just because you were being stubborn."

"I've overcome my fear of heights."

His face tightened. "I think the jury's out on that one. I remember vividly the day you developed that fear of heights, and for good reason. Let's get started. Saturday will be here before we both know what hit us."

She knew what he was referring to. Memories of that day came back in a rush, none of them good. Her parents hadn't been home, nor had his. She didn't know what had made the day worse—the mind-numbing pain of breaking her arm in three places and trying to tell him she wasn't hurt too badly, or the terror of being in the car with him as he drove like a madman to the hospital, less than a week after he had gotten his driver's license.

Now she worked in a nice safe office on the first floor, and the most innovative projects she made were knitted or crocheted crafts, done while she was sitting safely on the couch in her living room. In reasonable light.

She stared up into his face. "Trent? Are you okay? You seem a little pale."

"I think I've been standing inside too long with my coat on." He shrugged it off and tossed it against the wall, and when he did so, some of his color started to come back.

"But. . ." Her voice trailed off as she looked closely into his face. She'd always thought that being too warm would make a person flushed, not pale, making her wonder if perhaps he was coming down with the flu.

Before she could think about it anymore, he extended one open palm. "As I recall, the decorations are in the attic. If you'll give me the key, I'll get them for you. I know you can't reach that high."

Without giving her a chance to respond, he plucked the key from her fingers, turned, and left the sanctuary, which also served as the banquet hall and activity room, depending on the arrangement of chairs and tables that day.

She followed him down the hall and up the flight of stairs leading to the storage area. He reached up and unlocked the trapdoor in the low ceiling, then pulled it open and tugged the rope to bring down a folded-up, hanging metal ladder.

He turned around. "Stay here, with both feet on the floor. I'll hand you down the boxes of Christmas decorations," he said, then climbed up into the storage area.

His footsteps echoed down from the ceiling. She heard the grumble of words she couldn't make out, and then the footsteps above her stopped.

Kim shuffled closer to the opening, rested her hand on the ladder, climbed up one step, and froze, not daring to raise her foot off the thin rung. The slight sway made her nauseous. She struggled to push the sensation away, tipped back her head, and called up through the opening above her. "Trent? Are you okay up there? What's wrong?"

The tips of his boots appeared in the opening, and way above his boots, his head appeared as he leaned slightly forward and looked down. "Do you remember in the spring, when those squirrels got into the attic?"

Kim remembered it well. One Sunday morning the entire congregation had quieted for prayer, and suddenly the mad scampering of many tiny feet had echoed through the sanctuary. Pastor Mark had prayed for the animals to find another home, and then someone had gone into the attic to scare them all away while a few of the men from the congregation patched up the hole where they'd come in.

"Don't tell me they're still up there," she called upward.

"Not at the moment, but I can certainly see where they've been. It looks like they came back for a while—or something else got in here after they were gone. There are holes in all of the boxes. Stuff is falling out, and some of the boxes fell over, and everything inside is broken. And some stuff, well, it looks like they were either nesting or had babies in there for a while, because the contents are, well, uh. . .not very clean."

"Is anything still good?"

"I don't know. I want you to be prepared for what you see, and please, stand back so you don't get hit with any debris."

When they had everything down, Kim almost cried. Most of the garland was either crushed or soiled in some place, and when one part of the length was ruined, the whole piece was ruined. One of the boxes that had fallen over contained the glass ornaments, which now were all broken. Some of the ornaments were made of either wood or a flour-and-water mixture, and most of those were chewed. Many had been made by Sunday school classes over the years and were made of paper and macaroni. Most of those were either eaten or shredded, and those that weren't shredded smelled funny.

Trent ran his fingers through his hair. "What are we going to do? We were supposed to start today."

Kim straightened and rested her fists on her hips as she scanned all the boxes around them. "I don't know why, but I have lots of money left over in my budget for making the gifts for the guests. I suppose I could use it to buy new decorations. Although usually we buy that kind of stuff after Christmas, when it's half price."

Trent checked his watch. "It's actually getting pretty late. Is there anything in that bag we can decorate with? I hate to waste the night."

"Not really." Kim sighed. The only thing she'd brought were the gifts meant for the banquet guests.

They pushed the ruined boxes to the side and returned to the multipurpose room, where the gift bag she'd brought sat next to the tree. She pushed the tissue paper aside, reached inside, and pulled out one of her creations. "This is all I brought."

"What is it?"

Her cheeks burned. "It's a beaded angel, silly. I made a bunch of them for the guests. We're going to give one away to everyone who comes, as a memento of the evening."

"But it's so small."

"It's not supposed to be big. I think they're cute, and they turned out just like they were supposed to."

"I guess. I suppose they are cute. You did a nice job." He smiled, then reached into the bag, but he froze as his fingers touched the pile of angels inside. "If those are supposed to be mementos for the guests, there aren't many in here."

"I made the exact number Stephanie told me to."

"What are you talking about?"

Kim dug through her purse and pulled out the crinkled piece of paper that Stephanie, the church secretary, had given her. "Here's what she said." Kim began to read. " 'This year we're going to give one small gift to everyone who attends the banquet, instead of larger gifts to only a few lucky winners. We decided on these beaded angels. Here are the instructions and the money for your supplies. Just bring back receipts and the change. We'll need you to make thirty.' "

Kim lowered the note. "It's really strange that she made such a mistake with the money. I had way too much, but she didn't say to buy anything else." Just in case she missed something, Kim flipped the paper over, but as it had been every other time she checked, it was blank.

Trent crossed his arms over his chest. "Something isn't right. Stephanie is usually meticulously accurate, especially with money. Didn't you think that was a little odd? Also, don't you think thirty is a strange number to ask for?"

Kim shrugged her shoulders. "Not really. I'm sure she has other people making them, too. I just don't understand how she could make such a mistake with the money."

Trent sucked in a deep breath. "I know how many tickets we had printed, and they're all gone. Can I see that note?" His brows knotted as he reread it. "This note is really badly written."

"Yes. When she was writing it, her pen was running out of ink and she couldn't find another one. I had to go. I was already late. That's the best she could do. But it's okay. I know what it says."

"I have a bad feeling." Trent ran his fingers over the number. "Last I heard, we're expecting over 270 people, and that was a couple of weeks ago. Can you see how the pen made an indent on the paper? I don't think she was scribbling to make the pen write. I think she only wrote the actual number down. The pen actually did spit out a bit of ink. The way I see it, this doesn't say thirty; it says three hundred."

"But that's not possible. How could she think I had time to make three hundred beaded angels?"

"Maybe she assumed you'd ask other people for help if you needed it. Just how much money do you have left over?"

If Kim didn't feel sick enough after her attempt to go up the ladder, she felt doubly so now.

Without a word, she pulled her calculator out of her purse and refigured the amount of money needed for the new number of angels.

The final total bought her near the edge of having to run to the washroom. Her voice came out in a rough croak. "If I was supposed to make three hundred, that leaves me with under five dollars in change. I think you're right."

She looked up at Trent. "Once I got good at making

these angels, each one took me twenty minutes to do." She frantically began punching more numbers into the calculator. "Not including the shopping time, it will take me fifty-four hundred minutes to make the rest. That's. . .ninety hours. . . ." Her voice totally failed. She punched in a few more numbers. "That's nearly four whole days, if I don't eat, sleep, or go to work. But I can't even start until after I go shopping to buy the rest of the supplies, and we need the angels finished for supper time on Saturday. Today is already Monday. That's only five days away."

Trent laughed weakly. "I said earlier that Saturday was going to hit us before we knew it. Now it feels really creepy, having said that."

She turned and looked blankly at the plain, oversized tree. "And $4.57 isn't going to buy many decorations. Our budget for the banquet was already stretched to the max. There isn't any money left, and I certainly don't have enough time to make all those angels."

"We have to decorate. What am I going to do?"

# Chapter 3

Every second felt like an hour while Kim waited for Trent to reply. Not that she really expected an answer. She knew he wouldn't have one. If she had to, she knew she could buy some new decorations for the church and put them on her credit card, then work it out with Stephanie later.

But she couldn't put the time it would take to make 270 angels on her credit card.

She looked again at the note. It now seemed obvious that she should have known she would need more than thirty angels, but as usual, hindsight was twenty-twenty. This time she felt even more foolish than when she fell out of the tree house. At least then she could use youth, a complete lack of mechanical aptitude, unbridled enthusiasm, and an extreme case of puppy love as an excuse.

Now none of those applied, except, in a way, the puppy love—although as an adult, she really didn't believe in puppy love anymore. But she did believe in love. Yet no matter what she did, either in the neighborhood or at church, Trent never seemed to notice her.

She looked up at Trent.

She couldn't remember a time when she didn't like him. For years, ever since she was fifteen, which was ten years ago, she'd gone through various stages of trying to get him to notice her, but he never did. Many times she'd given up and gone on with her life. Then, sooner or later, her feelings for him came back and she found herself in the same position. And every time was the same as the time before. He simply never noticed her. Now, after all these years, she finally had his undivided attention.

She was sure that God truly did have a sense of humor. The only other time she'd had his full attention was when she was writhing in pain on the ground. Now, ten years later, instead of physical pain, this time it was mental. This wasn't the way it was supposed to happen.

"It's more than obvious that I'm going to have to call for reinforcements. Do you have any idea who has a few hours they can spare before the banquet?"

He gave a short, humorless laugh. "A few hours?"

"At this point I have to tell myself that every little bit counts. Otherwise I should just give up."

Trent shook his head. "No, I didn't mean it that way. You're right, of course. Are these things hard to do?"

"No. They're actually pretty easy. Stephanie gave me really simple instructions to follow."

"Do you think I could do it? If so, you have your first volunteer."

"Really?"

"Unless you think I'm completely incapable."

Her cheeks flamed. She'd always admired his intelligence,

but more than that, he had an innovative way of thinking that she found just as fascinating now as she had ten years ago.

"Of course I don't think that. I just know how busy you are, with night school and everything."

"I have an assignment that has to be in after the Christmas break, but I think I can spare a few days. And it will only be a few days. So don't worry about it. I'm nearly done anyway, so it will be easy to make up the lost time. I can just take my books to work and read on my lunch breaks."

Kim shook her head. "I don't know how you do it."

"I have to support myself, so I have to work. That leaves night school. It will just take a little longer to get my certificate. After that I can go for my apprenticeship, and onward I'll go."

Kim was happy with her office job, even though she knew she didn't have much opportunity for advancement. She was happy, most days at least, and the office was on ground level.

She turned away from Trent and focused on the huge tree in the corner. "Actually, if you help, that should really make a difference. I think I can probably get a day off work, and if so, I'll see if I can get the ladies' coffee group that meets Wednesday mornings to do some. If everyone can do even four or five each over the two-hour meeting, that will make a big difference."

"That's a good start."

"I feel better already. I think this is doable. And now, about the decorations." She glanced around the room. "A little garland would go a long way if we only looped it around the walls. But the tree is another matter. It's huge, so it's going to take a lot to fill it. Wait a minute. . . ." Her voice trailed off as images started to form in her mind, like snow gently falling down, landing on the tree, and taking shape, transforming from a blur into a surreal picture—almost real enough to see.

"I have an idea!" she exclaimed as she spun around to face Trent.

At the sudden volume of her voice, Trent flinched and stiffened.

Again Kim spun around and stepped closer to the tree. She reached out and fingered one of the branches, then tipped her head back to see all the way to the top.

"We can decorate the tree with the three hundred beaded angels! Can you imagine how pretty that will be? Picture it. The deep green of the tree, the shimmering white beads of the angels, the rich gold of the halos, and the delicate fluff of the white lace wings. . . . It's going to be gorgeous! All I have to do is add a gold loop on the back to hang them, and they'll be perfect! Then we can pick them off one at a time and give them away to everyone as they leave. The tree might be left bare, but it won't matter, because the banquet will be over."

"I'm not so sure that's what Stephanie had in mind, but the idea has potential."

Before he had a chance to turn down the idea, Kim quickly balanced one of the small beaded angels on one of the branches. "See?" she asked as she stepped back. "Doesn't that look nice?"

Trent didn't move from where he stood. "Actually, you're

right. The white on the dark green does look good."

"I've got a gold star at home that's too big for my small artificial tree. I can bring it here, and the church can use it." She clasped her hands in front of her chest and spun around on her toes. "I think it will be perfect! I feel so much better now. I bet I can even get one big spool of gold thread with the money I have left. I could even stay within my budget."

"Maybe, but that doesn't change the fact that we have an awful lot to do before it's going to happen."

Kim checked her watch. She tried not to get too excited at his automatic *we*, which meant that they were in this together. "The stores are open late every night until Christmas, including weekends—the craft store, too. If I can make it before they close, I might be able to start tonight. At this point, every twenty minutes is one more angel. Bye!"

She began running to the door but stopped after a few steps and turned around. "I almost forgot. We left the wrecked decorations in the hallway. We can't leave them like that."

Trent waved one hand in the air. "I can pick through the boxes and take out anything salvageable. You go. I'll be fine."

With a quick nod, Kim turned and ran out the door.

She did manage to make it to the craft store without a speeding ticket just as the clerk locked the door.

Kim held up the directions and pressed the paper to the glass. "Please, you've got to let me in!" she called out loudly enough to be heard through the glass. "I know what I need, and I have to get all this stuff tonight!"

The clerk looked up to the clock, then at the directions. She sighed and pulled open the door so Kim could enter.

"I shouldn't be doing this. I'm supposed to stand here and let people out and tell anyone new to come back tomorrow. But if you promise you'll be fast, you can get what you need."

"Thank you!" Kim said without stopping.

Since she had already purchased the same materials a few weeks ago, she knew exactly where to find what she needed. She threw everything into a basket and hurried to the checkout, very proud of herself that she wasn't the last person in line.

She said a special thank-you to the woman who was still posted at the door and hurried to her car. But before she went home for the night, Kim had one more stop to make.

The coffee shop. She needed a large mocha grande. Maybe two. It was going to be a long night.

# Chapter 4

Trent slowed his car, hit the switch for the remote garage-door opener, and pulled into the driveway to wait for the door to open.

While he waited, he studied Kim's closed living room curtains.

He couldn't see her, but he knew what she was doing.

Trent drove into the garage, but instead of going inside the house, he stared through the opening of the still-raised garage door.

Despite the time, he knew Kim would be at it for many, many more hours.

He sighed, tensed, pushed the button to close the door, then ran the length of the garage, ducking under the door as it descended. Once outside, he straightened. He waited only until the bottom of the door touched the ground, then, patting his keys in his pocket, he walked next door and knocked.

"Trent? What are you doing here? Don't you have to get up early for work in the morning?"

He forced himself to smile. "Yes. Don't you?"

"Well, yes. But I, uh. . ." Her voice trailed off.

"You weren't thinking of pulling off an all-nighter already, were you? There's no need to panic, at least not yet. Is there?"

She ran her fingers through her hair, something Trent knew Kim only did when she was stressed.

"I figured it all out in the car," she muttered. "Between my coffee breaks and my lunch break, I can make three angels every day at work. If I work at these until midnight, then I can do nineteen or twenty each evening, and if I get up early, I can probably get one done while I'm eating breakfast. That way I can probably do twenty-four per day." She sucked in a deep breath and went on. "If I start tomorrow"—she started counting on her fingers—"and if I get Wednesday off, I can do another twenty. If you help me for three hours a night, plus what I figure the ladies' group could do Wednesday morning, and then what we could do Saturday before the banquet, that makes 282." Her eyes brightened, and she actually started to smile. "So if I can do eighteen tonight, even though I'm starting a few hours late, then it really is possible. I'll just stay up until I'm done."

Trent sighed. Maybe panic had started to set in. The way she was tossing around numbers did nothing to help calm her. The fact that she had memorized all the figures told him that despite her words, she wasn't as sure as she tried to appear that she could actually do it.

Now it was Trent's turn to run his fingers through his hair. "May I come in?"

Her cheeks darkened. "Of course. Would you like some coffee?"

As they walked into the kitchen, he saw two large, empty paper cups from the local coffee shop, in addition to a pot of coffee on the counter that was down by half.

He shook his head. He thought he'd detected a tremor in her hands. A strange feeling rolled through his stomach, making him wonder if it had been too long since he'd last eaten.

Trent extended one hand toward the counter. "This isn't the solution, you know. It's not worth killing yourself. The banquet isn't going to be a failure just because you don't get all the angels done."

"That's not the point. I said I would do this, and I'm only as good as my word. As it is, the decorations have been ruined. I can't let this be ruined, too."

"That wasn't your fault."

"No, but that's not the point. Everything has to look festive and cheerful. It's Christmas."

Trent shoved his hands into his pockets. He didn't want a pack of wayward rodents to spoil anything in Kim's Christmas. "I was thinking that I'd buy some new decorations on the way home from work tomorrow. That will at least solve the decorating crisis. But since you've got it all figured out, if I can help you tonight, that's only a dozen each. I think we can do that and still get to bed at a decent hour. We both have to get up for work tomorrow."

Kim smiled, which suddenly made the concept of staying up until the wee hours and going to work with not enough sleep seem like not so much of a sacrifice.

"Are you sure you want to stay?"

"If I wasn't sure, I wouldn't have asked. Show me what to do."

Her smile widened.

Trent forced himself to keep smiling, He'd never done such a thing before, and he really didn't know what he was doing. However, he didn't want anything to ruin the Christmas season for Kim. She was already stressed, and he couldn't see her getting any calmer until the angel situation was at least under control. If this was what it would take to make this Christmas a good one for her, then he would do it.

He walked to the kitchen table, which was strewn with bags of beads, ribbon, a spool of gold wire, and a pile of clipped lace pieces. Another pile to the side showed she'd already completed three angels that evening.

Trent glanced at the clock. If he got to bed at 1:00 a.m., then they had another three hours, which meant they could make nine angels each. It was a bit short of what she needed, but it was a start, and much better than if she had to work alone.

"I'm going to warn you; it took me longer to do the first one, so don't feel discouraged. It only took a couple, and I was up to the top speed of twenty minutes each."

He rubbed his hands together. "Then let's get started."

He copied her movement for movement as she strung the first row of beads on the wire, then double strung each subsequent row to give it the right shape.

"This isn't so hard," he said as he tightened everything up when he finished the single bead at the top of the triangle, then checked the clock.

"That was the easy part. Now we do the arms. The smaller beads are harder to do."

Trent picked up a bead and was about to string it when the phone rang.

Kim's eyebrows quirked. "I wonder who would be phoning at this hour. I hope nothing is wrong."

While she hurried to the phone, Trent closed one eye and poked the wire at the hole.

And missed.

After a few more attempts, he took a deep breath, held it, and finally poked the wire through. No longer fully concentrating on the tiny hole, Kim's laughter registered in his mind. He wasn't going to listen to her conversation, but the small laugh indicated that whoever was calling didn't have bad news. He hadn't realized that he'd become tense until he felt himself sag at the confirmation that nothing was wrong.

Trent picked up a second bead, held his breath, and poked the wire at it until he finally got it through, too.

This time, as he let his concentration on the bead lapse, he couldn't help hearing Kim tell the caller that she really had to get off the phone. Yet instead of hanging up, she continued to protest, indicating that the caller wasn't giving up easily, despite the late hour.

Trent picked up the third bead and held his breath, but this time he froze with the wire in midair, still pointed at the microscopic opening.

Each arm contained seven beads, and the halo contained ten beads of the same size. If it was taking him this long to string the smaller beads, his angels were going to take a lot longer than twenty minutes each.

Briefly he considered taking some beads to work and doing them there on his breaks. In order to do what he'd promised, Kim's frantic figuring had counted on him producing a certain number a day, and at this rate, he was going to be lucky to make one.

Suddenly he understood why it was so important to Kim to get the required amount done for the banquet. He was feeling the same way about getting the number done for her that she'd counted on from him.

"Sorry I took so long. That was Katie from work. I can't believe she'd be calling at this hour; but she needs a ride to work in the morning, and she asked if I could pick her up. . . ." Kim's voice trailed off. "What are you doing?"

"Yes!" Trent muttered between his lips as he got the third bead on the wire.

He lowered it to the table, being very careful to place it so there was no chance of his hard work coming off.

"I'm almost done with one arm."

She narrowed her eyes and leaned down to inspect his handiwork. "You're not almost done. You've got. . . three beads. . . ." Her voice trailed off again.

He sighed. "You were right. It's harder than it looks. I don't know if I can do this. Or if I can, I can't do it as fast as you're going to need." He glanced at the clock. "I don't know how you can get one finished in only twenty minutes."

"You weren't trying to thread the beads, were you? For the smaller beads, you leave them on the table, brace them with your finger, and then poke the wire through, like this."

In seconds flat, she had all six beads for her angel's one arm on the wire. He could see how doing it her way made sense. He hadn't considered there could be more than one way to string a bead.

She looked up at the clock. "We still have lots of time, but we should get back at it."

Her graciousness in the face of his foolishness impressed him.

He watched, then copied Kim's method, agreeing without saying so that she was right. It took him as long to do the arms as it did the rest of the body, but he did get them done.

It was a relief to add the head, which was the easiest bead to do, being the largest.

"Now we do the halo."

Trent sighed. "I know. With the same size beads as the arms. Maybe I will take you up on that coffee. But I do have to set a limit. I should be out of here at one o'clock, or I'm going to be useless at work tomorrow."

"That's actually longer than I expected you to stay. I'll set the timer. We can meet back here after supper tomorrow to do more."

Her smile widened. Something in Trent's stomach went haywire, making him wonder if he'd somehow passed his limit on the amount of coffee he'd consumed.

"We can do this," she said, and as she smiled, cute little crinkles appeared at the corners of her eyes. "Now I know that everything is going to be okay."

# Chapter 5

I t's not going to work." Kim's voice cracked over the phone.

Trent froze.

They'd recalculated the time they needed because Kim had forgotten to include how long it would take to decorate the tree before the guests arrived on Saturday. But because he'd agreed to go to her house straight from work, and he could make eighteen per day instead of twelve, it was still reasonably possible that they could indeed meet their goal.

However, it was Wednesday afternoon, and for some reason, she was calling him at work.

"I don't understand," Trent mumbled in response.

"First of all, not as many ladies came to the coffee group session as expected. Most of the ladies said they'd give the angels a try, but just as I started to show everyone what to do, a guest speaker arrived. She got her dates mixed up and thought she was supposed to come this week, but she was scheduled for next week. With everything so mixed up, some ladies didn't even make one. Those ladies who did figure it out were listening to the speaker at the same time they were making angels, so they didn't get as many done as if they had just been sitting there concentrating exclusively on the angels."

"I'm afraid to ask."

"I'd counted on the ladies' group doing over a hundred, but they only made fourteen; and I've got six in varying stages to finish up."

Trent squeezed his eyes shut. Even if he took a day off work, which he couldn't this time of year, he could never make up that kind of shortage. And time was running out.

"But that's not all. When I got home, a bunch of the beads were missing. I phoned Stephanie at the church, but she couldn't find them anywhere. A number of the ladies brought their preschool-age children, and I have a bad feeling that some of the young children thought the gold beads were pretty and took some home. Some of the white ones are missing, too. I have to count what's left, and then I have to go shopping again."

Trent checked his watch. "Maybe we could go together. I still have to get some garland and see if I can find anything else at a reasonable price to decorate the walls." To say nothing of needing to do the rest of his Christmas shopping. It was probably too late to do it online. If he left the rest of his shopping until after the banquet, that left him less than a week before Christmas to get it done. He thought he'd learned his lesson from last year not to let it go so late, but now he was finding himself in the same position. That it wasn't his fault this year wasn't going to make any difference.

A silence hung over the line. Trent waited, not so patiently, until Kim finally spoke.

"It sounds like you intend to pay for it. You don't have to. You're not even really on the decorating committee."

"I don't think it counts as a committee anymore, because you're now a committee of one. Besides, I already offered." If he didn't insist on paying, he knew that she would. He doubted she was going to ask Stephanie for the money. He didn't usually feel this way, but something inside him wanted to be gallant. Even though it was for the church and not directly for Kim, it was still important to her. "What time can I pick you up?"

Another pause hung on the line. "It doesn't matter. I'm at home now, making more angels."

"Then I'll pick you up at five thirty. We can run out, get what we need, then grab a couple of burgers on the way home and eat while we work."

He waited for her to say something, but she didn't.

Trent cleared his throat. "I think that's probably the most efficient way to get everything done the fastest."

"I think it's more efficient for one of us to stay home and the other to shop."

"I'm going to be the one stringing the garland, so I have to buy that, and I think you'd best buy the beads. I don't want to get the wrong thing. If the craft shop has garland, it will be a fast trip."

"Okay. I'll see you later."

Trent returned to his current project, but his thoughts kept wandering back to Kim.

He'd known her almost all his life, but he'd never really paid attention to her until the day she broke her arm while she was trying to build that ridiculous ramshackle tree house by herself. After she healed, he'd considered asking her out for a date, but his friends had laughed at him, telling him he would never have any fun going out with someone so religious. Actually, he'd always respected her for her faith, even before he became a Christian himself. She always did the right thing and never hurt anyone, except herself, and that was by accident. Most important, if he'd been more like her, sooner, then his whole life would have been different. But it was too late now. If the best he could do was take her shopping and sit and do crafts, then that was the way it had to be. As the saying went, he had made his own bed, and now he had to lie in it.

A day had never dragged on so long, until the time he pulled up in front of Kim's house. Just as he turned off the ignition, she ran out the door. He barely had time to open the door locks before she reached the door and slid inside the car.

"Let's go. I phoned ahead, and they have the beads put aside for me. The lady at the store said they also have lots of nice garland left, so this will be a quick trip."

Trent's mouth opened, but no sound came out. He hadn't wanted it to be a quick trip, even though he knew it should be.

Despite his earlier words, he also didn't want to rush, and he didn't want to get dinner from the drive-through. He wanted to go someplace they could sit down and talk without having a looming project distracting them, even though he knew that was wrong. That situation would be too close to a date, and he couldn't allow her to think such a thing was possible. Dating at their age meant that the possibility of marriage existed, and for him, that wasn't an option with Kim.

He cleared his throat. "I changed my mind. I want to go check out the mall. They have a better selection, and they might have some cheap decorations, too."

He pulled away from the curb and headed in the direction of the craft store. Even though she wasn't speaking, he could feel Kim looking at him.

"We don't have time for that. You're not taking this seriously, are you?" she asked in a voice so quiet she was almost whispering.

The hurt in her voice made his empty stomach clench painfully. "No, it's not that at all. It's just that. . ." His voice trailed off. He really didn't care about the mall, but once they were there, he thought he might be able to convince her to take some time off and go to a restaurant with him for dinner, even if it was just the family restaurant at the crowded mall. After the banquet was over, everything would be back to the way it was before, the way it had been for the last five years, which involved nothing more than exchanging a friendly wave over the backyard fence. The only other occasions he spent significant time with her occurred in the safety net of a group situation at the college and career events at church. For once, he wanted a taste of what he couldn't have, but that was wrong. "I suppose you're right. I'm sorry. I'm sure the garland at the craft store will be fine."

"The lady at the store told me she has the perfect thing, and she told me where to find it. We just have to hurry."

"Please don't worry so much. Even with this little setback, I'm sure we'll be able to make everything we need. I was thinking—you're doing some angels on your breaks at work. I can do the same."

"You'd do that? Don't you think you'll feel silly?"

Trent grinned, picturing in his mind the reactions he was bound to witness. "Nah. Actually, once I start, I know that initially I'll attract some attention. It's not often you see a man doing this kind of thing. But that's not a bad thing. I bet a few of the ladies would be more than happy to help me. We could even get quite a few extra done that way."

"What a great idea! Maybe I'll ask some of my friends at work if they could do one on their lunch break with me. At this point, every angel done is one more angel."

When they reached the small strip mall where the craft store was, Kim helped find a parking spot. As they walked toward the store, Trent noticed a number of men waiting in their cars, some with children but also a few alone.

Once he actually stepped inside the craft store, he discovered why. He'd never been inside a craft store in his life, and being inside, he felt even more out of place than he thought he would.

The first thing he saw was row upon row of flowers, lace, ribbon, frilly hearts, and other pretty things that most men wouldn't be caught dead with. He followed Kim to the left, where they passed a rack called "tools," which contained a variety of tiny little glue guns, many of them pink and other feminine colors, with glue sticks so small they would be used up in one press of the trigger if he were using his own glue gun in the garage. There were scissors of all shapes and sizes, little knives, racks and holders, and loops of wire.

There wasn't a hammer or a set of real pliers to be seen.

Kim turned into the next row. He followed her past countless skeins of thread of every shade of every color of the rainbow, and then some, along with little packages of cloth and a huge rack of pattern books. Those he could understand. His mother had done embroidery when he was a child.

When they reached the end of the aisle, he saw a display along the back wall of the store that contained everything from fabric to ribbon to plastic shapes, in obvious Christmas colors and patterns.

She turned to him. "They put the Christmas things in the back to make everyone walk through the entire store first, so hopefully they'll buy more than just what they came for."

"I suppose that's a common marketing ploy." He looked on the top shelf where there were, as promised, reels of garland. It looked a little different from the stuff he saw in the department store, but it was still garland.

"Those are really large spools. I've never seen it sold like this before."

"You buy it by the length. How much do you need?"

He pulled the envelope for his phone bill out of his back pocket, on which he'd written the dimensions of the room. "You won't believe this, but I calculated the exact amount I'd need, including the droops, just so I wouldn't buy too much. This is incredible. It will be cheaper to buy it this way than in precut packages." He put four of the spools in the buggy. "Where do we go now?"

"To the front. The beads are put aside for me. Let's go. The faster we get out of here, the sooner we can get back to my place and back to work."

# Chapter 6

**K**im measured some coffee into the filter and then the water while Trent unpacked the bag containing their fast-food supper.

She'd almost thought he was going to suggest they go out to a real restaurant, but he'd only said he wanted to go to the mall.

She had no difficulty in turning down that suggestion.

But if he would have asked to take her out for dinner, that offer would have been hard to turn down, regardless of how much work she had left to do. It would have been totally irresponsible, but she couldn't say for sure that she would have said no.

But he didn't do that. As she should have expected.

She couldn't show Trent how she felt about him— how she'd felt about him for years. All that mattered was that he didn't feel the same way, and to hope for anything to happen now, after so long, was foolishness. The trouble was that now, after being so close to him for these few days, the reasons she'd been so attracted to him were the same, only now he had maturity and his faith to add to the list. She loved him now more than ever, even more than the day so many years ago that she almost killed herself trying to get closer to him.

It wasn't sensible, but she couldn't change how she felt. She didn't know if it was better or worse that she had seen so much of him since Sunday, but she supposed this was better than not seeing him at all.

She turned around and forced herself to smile. "All we have to do is wait for it to finish brewing. Let's eat. I'm starved."

"Me, too."

They paused for a word of thanks, then began to eat.

Without hesitation, Trent reached for an already-cut piece of wire and began stringing beads to make another angel. "I think pretty soon I'm going to be seeing these things in my dreams."

"I'm already dreaming about them, except my dreams are becoming nightmares," Kim grumbled.

All Trent's movements stopped. "You shouldn't let this get to you so much. While these angels are nice to give away, it's not that important in the entire scheme of life. They're just decorations."

"I keep telling myself that," Kim mumbled as she slid the wire through the third layer of another angel body, "but this is really about a promise I made that I should be able to keep. I really had a month to make these, which would have been plenty of time. I should have realized there was something wrong when I was finished in less than a week."

"You made a mistake. It's not a big deal. We all make mistakes." Trent's voice lowered in pitch, so low she barely could make out his words. "Sometimes big ones," he muttered.

"What did you say? I barely heard you."

"Nothing," he mumbled. He pointed to the pile of lace clips without raising his head. "Can you pass me a wing?"

Kim wiped her fingers on a napkin and handed him one of the pieces, but when they both reached out at the same time, their fingers touched, nearly causing her to drop the lace. Instead of letting it go, she wrapped her fingers around his.

He froze under her touch but didn't pull away.

"What's wrong, Trent? You can tell me. We've known each other since forever. I like to think we're friends."

"It's nothing you or anyone can do anything about. What's done is done. It's not a big deal."

She waited for him to say more, but he didn't. His silence alone told her that contrary to his words, it was a big deal.

"Don't you want to talk about it?"

"No."

She waited, but he didn't continue. Indeed, his "no" really did mean no.

She thought for a few minutes, glancing up at him often as they worked together, trying to think of the best thing to say to get him to open up.

"Confession is good for the soul."

"I confessed already."

She waited, but he didn't elaborate.

As soon as the coffee was ready, she got up, poured

two mugs, prepared his the way she knew he liked it, and returned to the table. "It's okay. God forgives all our mistakes."

He didn't look up as he spoke but concentrated intently on stringing the gold beads for another halo. "That's true. I know God has forgiven me, but not everyone else has. Look, I really don't want to talk about this. Can we change the subject?"

Kim blinked. "I'm sorry."

This time he looked up and made eye contact. Her breath caught. She'd never seen such sadness and regret. His expression made her want to hug him and make it all better, but he'd made it very plain that there was nothing she could do. Even if there was, he wasn't going to allow her to do anything.

"Please don't be sorry. It's okay. I've come to terms with it. I've just had to make some choices, and life goes on. I was wondering. . . . This coffee is good, but you know what I'd really like? Have you got any hot chocolate?"

Kim rolled the chair back and stood, grateful for the blunt, if jarring, change of subject. "Yes, I do. I even have marshmallows. I can—"

The ringing of the phone cut off her words.

She answered to the sound of sniffling on the other end.

"Josie? What's wrong?"

Her best friend sniffled. "I'm so embarrassed. I hurt myself, and I have no one else to call. I slipped on the walkway and crashed backward into that old fence, and I have a sliver, and, uh, I can't sit down or it hurts. My medical plan at my new job doesn't kick in for another month, and, well, I don't have anyone else I can ask to pull it out. I can't see it properly, so I can't do it myself. Can you please come over?"

Kim squeezed her eyes shut.

"Please?" Josie sniffled for more effect.

Kim sighed. "Of course. I'll be right there."

"Thanks so much. I know you're busy, but the whole round-trip should take only an hour."

An hour. Three angels. But she couldn't leave her friend in pain.

"I'm on my way."

Kim hung up the phone, but she kept her hand on the receiver as she turned her head toward Trent. "I have to go. Josie needs me for something rather personal. It would probably be more efficient if you stayed here and kept working while I'm gone, if you don't mind. Just don't trash the place."

"But. . ." Slowly, his solemn expression broke into a grin. "That's pretty funny. Don't worry; I'll still be here, and I probably won't have moved except to make more hot chocolate."

Kim drove to Josie's home as fast as she could without getting a speeding ticket. Josie's red-rimmed eyes and the small spot of blood on her pants told Kim everything she needed to know. She knew how embarrassed her friend was, so she didn't say anything that didn't have to be said, including "bend over."

Once the splinter was removed, Josie's big hug and the fresh flood of tears told her she'd done the right thing by coming right away.

While Kim slipped her boots back on, Josie swiped her

face with the back of her hand. "I don't know what to say. You wouldn't believe how much that hurt. I didn't know what I would have done without you."

"It's okay. I know what it's like to need help when you're down. Do you remember when my tree house came crashing down with me in it?"

"Do I ever. Trent rushed you to the hospital. Do you still have that cast?"

"Yes." Only because Trent had been the first to sign it.

Josie grinned. "How is Trent anyway?"

Kim focused all her attention on the zipper of her boot, which had become stuck in her sock. "He's fine. In fact, I left him at my house to come here. That's why I have to get back quickly."

She stood and turned to leave, but Josie's hand on her arm stopped her. "Hold it right there. Details. I need details. You can't leave me hanging like that. What's he doing at your house?"

"It's not what you think. He's just helping me assemble the angels that we're giving to all the guests at the banquet at church Saturday night. While I'm on the subject, would you like to make some? I see you're not doing anything right now."

"Only because of, uh, what happened. I have to leave in ten minutes for Donna's house. We haven't finished the costumes yet. At least now I can sit to do some sewing. And then I have to stop at the supermarket on my way home. I'm glad it's open until midnight. I've got to make four dozen cookies for the banquet."

"I tried. I guess I'll see you Saturday."

Unfortunately, Josie didn't release her arm.

"Not so fast. Tell me more about Trent."

Kim almost told her friend that there was nothing to say, but there was something she wanted to ask.

"Josie, you've known Trent for a long time, too. I don't know what it is, but something is bothering him. He won't give me details, but it sounds like he's made some kind of error in judgment, and the guilt is crushing him."

"I don't know. I didn't really know him before he started coming to church three or four years ago. You've known him way longer than I have."

"I was just wondering if you'd heard anything."

"Sorry. Nada."

Kim finally disengaged her sock from the zipper in her boot without making a hole. "I have to go back now. I'll have to find out some other way."

"Just be careful. Guys can sometimes get funny about talking about problems and stuff like that."

Kim closed the door behind her.

She wanted to think that Trent was above that kind of thing, but she really didn't know. But the more she thought about it, the more she realized that while he certainly wasn't a recluse, he also didn't go out a lot, and she seldom saw him dating other women. Even if he didn't bring his dates to his home, the grapevine at church told her more than she wanted to know about his love life, or lack thereof.

All she knew was that something was wrong, and she wanted to do something to help him, even if it drove him further away from her.

She loved him that much.

# Chapter 7

Trent smiled the second he heard Kim's car pull into her driveway.

It sounded exactly the same as when he was at home listening for her, except it was slightly louder.

The motor cut, the car door slammed, and within ten seconds the front door opened.

He waited to hear, "Honey! I'm ho—ome!" but of course it never happened.

He squeezed his eyes shut. That only happened in his wildest dreams. This was very much reality.

Instead he heard, "I'm back. How many did you get done?"

"Nearly three. You weren't gone as long as you said you'd be."

"No. Traffic was really light. I think everyone is at a mall somewhere. I caught mostly green lights, and it didn't take very long to help Josie." Kim grinned. Something strange happened in Trent's stomach, only he knew he wasn't hungry. "She owes me big time for this."

Trent suspected that a lot of people owed her for a lot of favors, only Kim would never call on anyone to collect them. It simply wasn't in her nature to do so.

"I made fresh coffee while you were gone. Normally I'd say that I hoped it wouldn't keep you up, but in this case, the opposite is true."

"Smart man."

Trent felt his cheeks flush, which was ridiculous.

He cleared his throat. "We can't kill ourselves doing this, but we really are running out of time. While you were gone, I did some thinking. I don't have any other option but to take a bunch of stuff to work and see if any of the ladies, or even some of the other guys, will do some on their lunch breaks. Even if they don't finish one, that doesn't matter. Anything started is that much less that we have to do."

"I think that's a great idea. I'll do the same."

They worked in silence for a while, but Trent didn't want silence. Not that he wasn't comfortable without conversation, but he didn't want to waste this rare time of being alone with Kim, without anything on the agenda except for a common project for the mutual good of the church banquet.

"While you were on your way to Josie's, did you see that house on the corner of Maple Drive with all the Christmas lights? They had all the best-decorated houses in the area listed in the community paper last weekend."

"Yes. I saw it. It was spectacular. Actually, I'd love to take a drive around and see all the houses listed. Maybe even take some pictures. Would you like to come with me?"

He did want to, but he couldn't open a door that would be difficult to close; that's why, in the past, he hadn't done things like that. But being one in a crowd among the single young adults from the college and career group was a great safety barrier. "That would be great. I wonder if we could get Tyler to drive. He has a van that seats seven. I think it would be fun to go out for coffee and doughnuts afterward."

Kim's eyes narrowed, and she stared at him so intensely that he actually squirmed in his chair and dropped a bead.

He listened to it roll across the table, then bounce to the floor and continue on its way.

"I meant just you and me. Something to celebrate finishing this project together."

"Oh. I just thought the more the merrier."

She sighed, obviously not happy with his suggestion, but he knew she couldn't dispute his idea.

They chatted about the goings-on around town for the Christmas season until they were both yawning. The timer in his PDA went off, signaling the time they had agreed to quit for the night.

"Just take what you think you'll need for tomorrow and leave everything else on the table. There isn't much point in packing it all away. I'll be back at these again at breakfast time. Which is only a few hours away."

He nodded, stifling another yawn, and scooped enough supplies to do a dozen angels into a small plastic bag. "I know what you mean. I might do the same," he said as he began walking to the door.

He slipped his boots on without lacing them up, but before he could open the door, Kim reached out and touched his arm, preventing him from leaving.

"What you said earlier has really been bothering me. You sounded so sad. I feel bad, not knowing that something was wrong and letting you go through it alone. That doesn't make me a very good friend."

He looked down at her hand on his arm. Such a small, delicate hand, but some kind of inner strength radiated from her as she touched him, holding him in place. He couldn't move.

Something about the way she held him, gentle but strong, asking but not begging, firm but still giving him the choice, completely did him in. He couldn't believe how his voice shook as he spoke. All these years, he'd been stoic, holding his head up high, all by himself.

All by himself.

He didn't want to be all by himself anymore, but he gave himself no choice.

If the only way to make her see that was to tell her the truth, then that was what he had to do.

"A few years ago, I did something stupid and made a grave error in judgment. I got into some very serious trouble with the law. It was before I became a Christian, and I know God has forgiven me, but just because I'm right with God doesn't mean I'm right with the criminal justice system. I have a criminal record."

Her gasp stabbed him down to the depths of his soul, but it was nothing less than he deserved.

"Lots of people have criminal records. But I've known you almost all your life. You're not a criminal. You're a good man."

"I haven't killed anyone or done anything violent, but what I did was a felony."

"Wh—what did you do?"

Suddenly all the strength was zapped out of him. Trent sighed, leaned against the wall, and stared at the blank wall beside the door.

Anything was better than watching the shock and disappointment in Kim's face.

"It was before I became a Christian. I went to a party with some friends. There were drugs involved, and I knew it." He let out a short, humorless laugh. "I'm no angel now, and I certainly wasn't then. The cops busted the party. Russ had been charged before, and he said he would go to jail if he was caught again. He'd only just gotten married, and he didn't want his wife to know. When the cops came in, he jammed a bunch of stuff in my pockets, and I didn't know what it was. I should have known, because we'd all done a little cocaine at the party. But I really wasn't thinking clearly, for obvious reasons. He told me I'd get off with a slap on the wrist because it would be a first offense, so I agreed."

"It doesn't sound like that's what happened."

Memories of his arrest and the following court sessions flashed through his mind, as vivid as if they had happened yesterday. "We'd taken my car, and while the cops were inside arresting people, including me, they were also outside searching the cars. I don't know how it happened, but in addition to a rather large amount of cocaine that I had in my pockets, they found more in my car. I didn't know whose it was or how it got there. Of course they didn't believe me. I figure someone saw the cops coming and quickly put it in my lunch pail because I hadn't locked the car, and the lunch pail was sitting on the seat."

He almost laughed about the fact that instead of taking something *out* of an unlocked car, someone had put something worth a lot of money *into* his car. But it really wasn't funny at all. The end results would stay with him for the rest of his life.

"Naturally, my fingerprints were all over my lunch pail, and whoever did it was either pretty smart or very experienced. The only fingerprints on the lunch pail were mine. To make a long story short, things didn't go very well. I was a little stoned at the time, and I wasn't a stranger in the crowd where drugs were flowing freely. Compared to what could have happened, I guess Russ was right; but I ended up with a criminal record of having committed a felony of possession of narcotics, the amount exceeding what would be considered reasonable, as they say, for 'personal' use. I suppose I have to thank God that they didn't charge me for trafficking."

"Do you still see those people?"

"No. After that, they started avoiding me as much as I avoided them."

"Is that when you started to seek Jesus as your Savior?"

"No. I was actually pretty bitter about the whole thing. It was later, when you convinced me to start attending the college and career group at the church. Even though no one knew, no one asked about anything I'd done. Everyone simply accepted me as who I was for that day, and I knew God loved me the same way."

The unexpected touch of her other hand on his other arm made Trent flinch.

"I feel so awful for you."

"Don't. It's over now. I just have to live with all the restrictions. And not having to force anyone else into those same restrictions is part of it."

"I don't understand."

"You'll never know what it feels like having to say on job applications and credit requests that I have a felony on my record. I've been turned down for a lot, and people haven't even asked me about it. They just don't want to deal with me. That's the reason I'm upgrading at night school—so I can get into a good job that I can stay at for the rest of my life. It's been hard on my family, too. It's also put a lot of other restrictions on me. I can't even leave the country."

"Why not? They have to let you back in."

"It's not exactly that. I can certainly get a passport, so I can technically get *out*, but other countries that I would want to go to don't want to let a convicted felon *into* their country, especially since it's drug-related. I'm immediately under suspicion, whether I've done anything or not. I was an adult at the time, so it's part of my permanent record. It's just better to stay home."

"That's not such a bad thing."

Trent spun around so fast that both her hands dropped. Without thinking of what he was doing, he cupped Kim's face in his hands and stared intently at her, forcing her to understand his convictions.

"Maybe not for me personally; but when the day comes to get married, a couple should fly away on a great honeymoon to a far-off exotic land, and that wouldn't be possible with me. Being young and in love can make someone set aside goals and not feel restricted, but that won't last. I've always thought it would be great to travel someplace special with the one I love when the kids get old enough. But I won't be able to do that. I don't even want to think of what it would be like to tell a kid that their daddy had a felony conviction for possession of narcotics. Or what about wanting to travel after you retire? Would you be content to just stay home and look at the same four walls all your life?"

Kim's eyes widened, and she gulped. "When did we start talking about me?"

Trent had always thought about marrying Kim, from the day he took her to the hospital when they were both sixteen. Now, ten years later, he still thought about it—dreamed about it. But unlike the days of his youth, he now knew it could never happen. She deserved better than anything he had to offer.

He'd always thought about her. He'd also always thought about holding her close, staring into her eyes, just as he was doing now.

"Kim. . ." Her name tasted like honey as it rolled off his tongue.

She raised her hands and rested them on his waist.

Her soft touch was all it took. His eyes drifted shut, and he leaned down and kissed her, just like he'd always wanted to.

He expected her to flinch and push him away, and he would have accepted that. But she didn't. Her hands slid up under his jacket and around to his back, pulling him in closer as she kissed him right back, which made everything better. Or worse. His heart pounded, and everything he'd held back for the last ten years surged forward. Kissing Kim was everything he'd ever dreamed of. Even with the bulk of his jacket between them, she was still soft and warm and a perfect fit.

He yanked himself away and dragged his hand over his face.

"That shouldn't have happened. I think I'd better leave."

Doing exactly as he said, without giving her a chance to respond, he turned, walked out quickly, and shut the door behind him.

# Chapter 8

K im watched Trent as he toed off his boots, then walked into the kitchen carrying a plastic shopping bag. "I didn't get much help at lunchtime today," he said over his shoulder as he turned down the hallway. "Only two of the ladies wanted to try making an angel, and neither of them got one even half done. What about you?"

Even though the angels' production was coming to a critical point, Kim didn't want to talk about their progress or lack thereof.

She wanted to talk about what had happened last night, not about what didn't happen at lunchtime.

For ten long years, she'd been wondering how she would feel if Trent held her in his arms and kissed her.

Reality far exceeded her fantasies. Until he abruptly pulled away and bolted like a kid caught with his hand in the cookie jar.

All day long she'd been thinking about what he said. Actually, she'd thought of little else, including the angels.

She followed him into the kitchen. "I didn't have any real success either. Most everyone went shopping on their lunch break, so I was pretty much alone. Trent, what happened last night?"

At her question, he dropped a bag of beads on the floor. On impact, the bag burst and a hundred angel heads clattered and bounced and rolled helter-skelter. In an instant, Trent pushed the chair out of the way and lowered himself to his hands and knees and scrambled under the table to pick up the beads before they all escaped.

"I don't know," he mumbled, not raising his head. "Part of me wants to apologize; but part of me wants to do it again, and that's wrong."

Kim pulled a bowl out of the cupboard to put the beads into, lowered herself to her hands and knees, put the bowl between them, and also began to pick up the errant beads.

She spoke without actually looking at him. "As you can probably guess, I've been thinking a lot about last night, and you probably have been, too."

He grunted but otherwise didn't speak. Kim took it to be a confirmation of what she suspected.

"It's okay. I don't want to travel. I'm kind of afraid of heights anyway."

"Thanks for trying to make me feel better, but I'm really okay. I've dealt with it."

"It doesn't sound like it to me."

"I have. I've chosen to quit wallowing and get on with my life."

She wasn't so sure of that. Of course it was a positive step to attend night school, but she wasn't sure that was the answer. "But you're shutting yourself off from everything else—the stuff that's really important."

"I've chosen my path."

Kim had picked up all the beads in her area, but she remained on her hands and knees under the table with Trent, watching him as he gathered the last of what he could reach before moving and taking the bowl with him.

She didn't know if the travel restrictions were really so important to him. Many people with records traveled in foreign lands without incident. It was more likely that Trent had made his choices because of his other statement—one he'd only touched on briefly. He couldn't bear the thought that his future children would be disappointed in their father.

"You're forgiven by the only One who matters."

"I know that."

He shuffled away with the bowl to pick up the last of the beads that had rolled to the corner of the kitchen.

Kim's throat became tight. Instead of dwelling on past mistakes, she couldn't help loving the man who had lowered himself to the floor, literally, at least for the moment, to do something most men would never do. She knew most men didn't make beaded crafts, yet he'd swallowed his pride, even in front of his coworkers, to help when she needed it after making a mistake of her own.

She couldn't help loving him even more than she had before.

And now, after all these years of staying silent, he'd finally given her a sign that he felt something for her, too. Otherwise, he never would have kissed her, and especially not like he had.

It was time to stop waiting and do something. She could almost feel God pushing her to move forward.

She started to move in his direction, pushing herself up in order to sit on the floor beside him, rather than to be so far away, hunched over under the table. "Trent, I was thinking. . . . Would you like to—*ow!*"

The clatter of movement of the beads, scissors, and paraphernalia from atop the table echoed, and a sudden sharp pain made a bright light flash before Kim's eyes. The world spun, and her head felt strangely warm.

"Kim! Are you okay?"

Her eyes stung. She blinked repeatedly, both to clear her vision and to steel herself from the pain at the top of her head.

When she pressed her fingers to the sore spot, her hair was warm and sticky.

Her head swam even more. "No. I think I hurt myself."

Red dripped onto the floor.

Her stomach churned. "Correction. I *know* I hurt myself."

Trent scrambled and was beside her in seconds. His face paled, and he glanced at her head, then bent down to look up at the underside of the kitchen table. "You cut your head open on the metal bracket." He crawled more quickly than she'd ever seen anyone move when not on their feet, grabbed the towel she had hanging on the oven door, wadded it up, and pressed it to the wound, slowly at first, then increasing in pressure.

"I'm going to assume that since you've been using this to dry the dishes you eat from that it's clean. How bad does it hurt?"

"Strangely, not that bad," she said, telling the truth. It had hurt on impact, but now the pain had lessened to a dull throb.

"Head wounds bleed a lot faster and with more blood loss than anywhere else on the human body. We have to take you to the clinic for some stitches."

Her head swam even more. "How bad is it?"

"I can't tell; I'm not a doctor. All I know is that you're bleeding. Put your arm on me, and I'll help you stand."

When she was steady enough, Trent walked her to the door and helped her slip her coat and boots on, making sure to keep constant pressure on her head. "If you're ready, let's go."

All the way to the clinic, she couldn't look at him. All she could think of was how history was repeating itself, this instance so like the one ten years ago when he drove her to the hospital after she broke her arm.

Again, over Trent.

She spoke while still looking blankly out the car window, keeping the soggy towel pressed firmly to her head. She did notice that this time he wasn't speeding quite as much as ten years ago. He'd also become a much better driver. "It's not your fault, you know."

"I don't know about that. I'm beginning to wonder if this is a sign or just bad luck. It seems we've been down this path before."

"The only one to blame here is me for being so clumsy."

"Are you usually clumsy?"

"Well. . .I—"

"I didn't think so. I'm so sorry, Kim. I don't know what to say."

"I said it's not you; it's me," she said, still not turning her head to look at him. "I'm the one who should be sorry. It's not fair for you to have to run to my rescue when I do something stupid."

"Like we agreed not so long ago, everyone makes mistakes. Here we are. Let's go in and get you all fixed up."

# Chapter 9

Kim yawned, then winced at the pull of the stitches on her scalp. She raised her hand, but before she could touch it, she heard Trent's voice.

"Don't touch it! You've got to let it heal properly and do your best to keep it clean."

"You sound like my mother," Kim grumbled.

"Sometimes having your mother around to remind you of things isn't necessarily a bad thing."

"I suppose not. I think that's just an expression, really."

"By the way, how are your parents? Where are they now?"

Kim sighed. She'd hoped her parents would come home for Christmas, but it wasn't going to happen. "Last time I heard from them, they were in Florida and having a blast. I don't know how they can live like that."

"Lots of people travel around the country in a motor home after they retire."

"Yes, but for five years?"

"I bet they have some great stories to tell."

"That they do, and praise the Lord for e-mail and portable

computers. How are your parents doing?"

"They love their apartment. They said selling me the house and moving to a smaller place was the best decision they ever made."

Kim yawned again, and she sank into the couch. "I don't know what I'm going to do. I can barely keep my eyes open. Those painkillers really wiped me out. I can barely see, never mind make more angels."

"If you want to go to sleep, I can still make some."

She closed her eyes and sighed. "You'll never be able to catch up with the number we missed doing tonight. And besides, even if you did, we still won't have enough. I guess it's time to just give up and admit I've failed."

"No. It's not over until it's over."

"The banquet is less than two days away. Even if we didn't sleep, if all we did was go to work and make angels, we still don't have time to make enough."

"It's time to call in reinforcements. I'll think of something."

"There's no one. I think we've both asked everyone we know."

Trent shook his head. "There's got to be someone, somewhere we didn't think of."

"If you can think of someone, I'll be grateful to you for the rest of my life."

Despite the worry and the overwhelming cloud of pending doom, Kim's eyes fluttered shut, and she couldn't stop them. "I'm so wiped out," she muttered as she snuggled into the couch. "Maybe these painkillers were just the right thing, because I don't even care anymore."

"You'll care tomorrow. But tomorrow is another day, and we

both have to get up for work. Promise me you'll get yourself to bed safely, and I'll see myself out."

"Yeah. Sure."

Keeping the top of her head from touching anything, Kim buried her face into one of the cushions on the couch.

"Never mind. I'll see you tomorrow."

Instead of leaving, Trent stayed standing beside her. She heard beeping noises, then a gentle clunk on the coffee table.

"I've set the alarm on my wristwatch to wake you up in time to get ready for work in the morning. If you need me at any time, even in the middle of the night, just call. I can be here in under a minute."

"I know." And she knew he would.

Trent pulled the car to the side of the road and dialed Kim's office number on his cell phone.

"Trent? What took you so long? I've been waiting all day for you to call."

"I've been busy. I've got a solution—but we have to act fast."

"Pardon me?"

"I'm calling from my cell. Meet me at the craft store."

"What are you talking about?"

Trent barely kept from laughing. "I'm not going to tell you any more. It's a surprise."

"I don't like surprises."

"You're going to love this one. I'm already on the way. Bye."

He arrived at the craft store first. So as not to waste time, he found a parking spot and waited for Kim by the door.

He didn't wait long. In under three minutes, her car came whizzing into the parking lot. She'd obviously rushed, just as he'd requested, because when she found a spot and got out of the car, her coat wasn't fastened, and she was carrying her gloves and scarf instead of wearing them.

"This had better be good," she grumbled when she got within speaking range.

He tried to keep a straight face. "How's your head?"

She raised a shaky hand and brushed her fingertips along the wound. "It's very bruised feeling, but not bad. The worst thing is having to explain to everyone what happened. I wish they didn't have to shave so much of my hair."

"They really didn't shave that much; the nurse was very careful."

"I know. But it feels like a lot to me."

"It's not that bad. Really."

"Are you going to tell me what this is all about? I think you're stalling."

As usual, Trent was completely transparent. "Let's go in." He continued talking as they walked to the store entrance. "I called Josh, and he organized the youth group to have an emergency angel party. The kids are all out of school, so everyone managed to contact everyone else. In an hour, they're going to be meeting at the church, and we're having a late-night 'angel challenge,' the boys against the girls."

"Then what are we doing here? We've already got all the beads we need."

"I want to give prizes to the winning team, so I thought the most appropriate prize would be some kind of craft to make. I called the craft store to ask what kind of prize would be appropriate, and it seems the manager here has a nephew who has been going to our youth group. She's been so impressed by our youth group that she offered to donate a prize. So we're here to pick it up."

He was infinitely grateful that Kim had agreed to meet him there without question. Even though he'd been to the craft shop before, he didn't want to walk into such a place alone.

More than that, he needed to see her in private, to see how she was really doing, without an audience. Not that the craft store was all that private, but it was better than trying to find a minute alone in a building full of teens, whom they were supposed to be supervising.

The donated prize was a collection of small Christmas decoration kits, suitable for both male and female crafters and easy enough to be an enjoyable project even for someone who wasn't very skilled at making crafts.

Trent tucked the bag under his arm and walked Kim to her car.

"We've got to hurry. We should be there before everyone else because we have to set up the piles for the kids to grab from. Then we each have to lead our groups; you lead the girls, and I'll lead the boys. I figure the challenge will be over when the beads are gone and the last angel is made."

"What if there are different numbers in both groups?"

He shrugged his shoulders. "Then we'll have to figure out some kind of handicap system before we start to make it a fair fight."

Kim rubbed her hands together. "I remember doing stuff like this when I was in youth group. It was a lot of fun."

"I hope so. We're going to have to fuel the competition somehow, rather than make it look like we're just desperate for numbers."

Kim grinned up at him, and he knew the flag had been dropped.

"I think when the boys lose, you should have to mow my grass all summer."

"I think when the girls lose, you'll be mowing my grass all summer."

"Not likely. Is this a challenge?"

Trent grinned. "You're on. May the best man win."

Kim stuck her nose in the air, snorted, and opened her car door.

"No. May the best woman win. See you there."

# Chapter 10

N o, Tyler, you put the wire through like this."
Kim bit her bottom lip as she watched Trent out
of the corner of her eye. She should have given the
boys' group a bigger handicap.

But then, she really didn't like to mow the lawn.

She couldn't help smiling as she turned back to her own
group. "Great work, Melissa. Would you like another piece
of pizza?"

"I'm okay. These are fun to make. I think it's a great idea
to give one to everybody at the banquet tomorrow night."

Kim smiled. With thirty-two teens diligently working as
fast as they could, the angels would be finished in two hours.
At the end, all they had to do was move the tables from the
circles they now had set up into neat rows ready to be set for
the banquet, and the youth group could do whatever they
wanted to do for the rest of the evening.

Knowing that all the angels would now be done on time
allowed Kim to not only relax but actually enjoy herself.
With the challenge in place, both the boys' group and the

girls' group had taken it as their personal mission to win.

While she didn't really want to mow Trent's lawn, Kim didn't care who won. The purpose was to finish the angels in time for the banquet, and now, since they were going to meet that goal, there wouldn't be any losers, only winners.

She lowered her current angel-in-progress when Trent walked toward her.

"I hope your group isn't cheating," he said loudly enough for everyone to hear.

"It's impossible to cheat, Trent. All the girls are following the instructions exactly, as are the boys."

All heads lowered as everyone returned their concentration to their projects.

"I don't know about that," he said as he came close enough for only Kim to hear what he was saying. "I heard whisperings that if we lose, a few of them are going to volunteer to take my place mowing your lawn once or twice, just so they can be with you for an afternoon. It sounds like someone has a crush on you."

"I don't think so," she whispered. "It sounds like they have accepted that the girls are going to win, and they're trying to make themselves feel better, as if they lost on purpose."

"The boys are talking about doing something else in a few months like this, except making the challenge more guy-related."

"That would probably be fun. And maybe a payback time would be good. I don't know how I'll ever be able to pay the group back for this."

"Don't worry about it. They're having fun. Can't you see how some of the boys have infiltrated the girls' group, pretending they need more help than they really do?"

Kim giggled. "Yes. I did notice that."

"After we're done, I was thinking that we should head over to the Midnight Madness sale at the mall. I want to buy a can of that fake spray-on snow and put some on the tree before we put the angels on. I think that would look good. Also, then the tree won't look so bare when we're taking the angels off to give them away."

"That's a great idea. One of the girls suggested that I get a Christmas hat to wear tomorrow to cover my bald spot. I think I'm going to do that, and tonight sounds like a great time to buy a hat. There will probably be fewer people in the mall tonight than on Saturday."

"I agree." He jerked his head in the direction of the table they'd set up with the raw materials. "There aren't any more beads in the bins. We've come to the finish line."

Trent left her side and moved to the front of room. "We're down to the last ones, everybody!" he shouted. "Almost time for the countdown!"

All talking in the room stilled as the teens worked frantically to finish the angels they were working on. While the goal was to see which group could make more angels, they had agreed as part of the rules that when they were down to the last angels, whichever group finished first would get a bonus number for the number of angels the other group hadn't yet completed.

All the boys jumped to their feet. "We did it! We're done!"

A chorus of males grunting, "Whoo, whoo, whoo," filled the room.

"It doesn't matter!" Kim shouted to the girls' group. "We've done more. I know it."

They gathered around in two big circles.

"The boys did seventy-one," Trent said.

"Seventy-eight for the girls," replied Kim.

The girls cheered.

"Wait!" Trent called out. "We have to calculate the bonus points. The boys finished first."

Kim stood. "How many incomplete angels do we have on our side?"

Seven girls held up their angels-in-progress.

"That's seven points for the boys, so the winner is. . ."

The room fell completely silent.

"A tie," Kim croaked.

Both sides glared at each other.

Trent turned to Kim, lowering his voice so none of the teens would hear him. "I never considered the possibility of a tie."

Kim lowered her voice, also whispering. "Me neither. We needed an odd number of angels. It didn't even occur to me that the bonus points could even the score."

Silence loomed in the room.

"What about the prizes?" a male voice boomed from the back.

Trent retrieved the bag from under the table. "I don't know. Let's see how many we've got so we can figure out a way to divide them up."

He pulled out a bundle of three plastic bags tied together with a large ribbon and a red bow.

"There's a note. It says, 'In this season there are no losers, only winners. Enjoy! God bless you all, Rochelle.' And look at this." Trent lowered the note and untied the bundle. "There are three bags, each with a dozen kits." He grinned.

"We've got four more prizes than we have contestants. What a nice thing to do."

He gave one of the bags to Kim, and they handed out one to everyone. Immediately the teens began trading back and forth until everyone had exactly the kit they liked the best.

Kim also accepted a kit from Trent.

He winked at her. "I think we can each have one, too. After all, we were just as much in the contest as everyone else. I also think it would be nice to make something other than angels."

Kim grinned back. "I know what you mean. I think we should leave the last two for Stephanie and Pastor Mark."

Trent cleared his throat and raised his voice enough to be heard over all the chattering. "Okay, everyone! Let's get the tables back to where they belong, and then we'll start driving everyone home. Kim and I still have some shopping to do tonight."

"Shopping?" one of the boys piped up. "I still have a gift to buy. Can I come with you?"

"There's a big sale on tonight," a female voice joined in. "I'd like to go, too. I don't need a ride. My parents let me take the car. I just have to tell them I'm going to be late and where I'm going. They won't mind if I'm not alone."

"I've got a car, too," another of the boys called out.

Trent glanced around the room. "I can put five more in my car, and we can do three more in Kim's car. Josh can take four more. Who else brought their own car tonight?"

A few of the older youths raised their hands.

Kim forced herself to smile.

It was over. The angels were made, and she no longer had a reason for spending time alone with Trent. He'd made it more than clear that he had no desire for a relationship, especially with her.

Tonight was all she had left, and she wanted to spend the last of their time together alone with him. She wasn't ready to revert to the way things had been for the last ten years. One kiss had convinced her that things could be different. Trent just needed a little convincing to feel the same way. She only needed a little more time.

If they spent the remainder of this evening together, without any distractions other than shopping, she would have a better chance to convince him that his past record wasn't important—that they only had the future to look forward to. Regardless of what loomed in his past, a future together was better than a future apart.

Now that the pressure of making the angels was gone, this was the last time she would be with him, without the rest of the college and career group overseeing every move they made. At the mall they would be totally ignored no matter what they did, with everyone intent on their own business. Within the safe anonymity of the throng of holiday shoppers, Trent wouldn't be expecting her to pour out her heart until it was too late. Everything she ever needed to say to him she could say in the crowd at the mall. Being at the mall with him even forced them to stay together, regardless of his immediate reaction to what she said.

It was perfect. In the crowd of anonymous holiday shoppers, in effect, she would be holding him hostage.

But now it appeared the entire youth group was going to the Midnight Madness sale.

"Okay, everyone!" Trent called out. "We're ready. Let's go."

# Chapter 11

"Good-bye! Thanks for coming! And merry Christmas!"

Trent watched as Kim gave yet another couple from the church a big hug and sent them on their way.

The banquet had been a rousing success.

The drama group had put on a spectacular performance, and because of that, many people from the community who were not church members were staying behind to ask more questions.

The food was great, as Trent knew it would be. He couldn't remember the last time he ate so well, or so much.

And best of all, everyone loved the angel ornaments and were thrilled to be able to take one home.

As yet another family left, Trent scooted up the ladder, brought down another handful of angels, and gave them to Kim to give away.

*Kim.*

He watched her as she hugged someone else.

She wasn't hugging him.

Of course, that was by his own choosing.

Their time together at the mall played over and over again in his head. They hadn't been able to talk, at least not about anything too personal, but whenever they had been alone, as alone as one could be in the middle of a late-hours sale at the mall less than a week before Christmas, Kim had taken full advantage of every second.

He'd never allowed himself to consider her in a romantic way, at least not until recently, but when she had grabbed his hand, it was almost like coming home. Her hand was so small, yet with their fingers intertwined, the bond was so strong, all the pangs of loneliness left him so fast that he felt almost breathless. He could see the mischief twinkling in her eyes the second one of the teens caught them holding hands. He couldn't pull away without making it look like he was trying to hide.

She had him, and she knew it—except he hadn't wanted to get away.

She said they could be happy together. Was it possible she was right? He'd never felt anyone support him, no matter what he did, like Kim.

He couldn't help it. He loved her. But he didn't know if that was enough.

Trent reached up to pull the last set of Christmas angels off the tree.

His heart pounded when his fingers brushed Kim's as she took the angels out of his hand and gave them to the last guests to leave the room.

He looked up. All the angels were gone. Every last one of them. The tree was bare.

As bare as his heart.

All that remained were the remnants of the fake snow he'd sprayed on, and some of that was falling off.

Despite what he had tried to do, the tree now looked ragged and exposed.

Trent could relate to the tree. He'd exposed his heart and all his ugliness to Kim, but she accepted him anyway.

Yet as they went their separate ways when they left the mall, something about her was different. Her good-bye wasn't in the usual mood of "see you later." It was different, as if for the first time she really meant good-bye.

He didn't know if he could be the man she deserved, but he sensed that if he let her go now, he would lose her forever.

Trent turned away from the tree to see that Kim had already moved away. She'd returned to the table where they'd sat together for the duration of the festivities, and she was now putting on her coat, getting ready to leave.

If he was going to do it, now was the time.

Trent gathered his courage and hurried to her side.

"Kim. Wait. Don't go."

She looked up at him, her eyes big and wide. And sad. So sad it tore at his heart.

He fumbled to find the little velvet bag he'd tucked inside his pocket.

"You were the only one who didn't get an angel tonight."

She smiled weakly, and her voice sounded far too timid. "It's okay. I've seen enough angels to do me for a while, I think."

He pulled the bag out of his pocket and pressed it into her palm.

"I knew you wouldn't get one, so I got you this instead."

"You didn't have to do this," she said without looking inside the little pouch.

"But I wanted to. I saw it at the mall last night, and I bought it when you went into that store with Jeni. It's not much, but I thought you'd like it."

His heart pounded as she dumped his gift from the bag into her hand.

"It's a little angel. With a diamond on it. And it's a ring. . . ."

"Yes. But it's more than just a ring. It's a promise ring."

"A promise ring," she echoed hoarsely, in a voice little more than a whisper.

"Do you like it?" His heart pounded, waiting for her reply.

"Of course I like it. It's such a surprise; I don't know what to say. Why are you doing this?"

"When I bought it, I thought I'd give it to you for Christmas, but I can't wait that long. I had to give it to you now."

Her eyes became glassy, and she blinked a few times until they cleared. "I don't understand."

He reached forward and wrapped his hands around hers. "I've been thinking about what you said, and you were right. It's long past time for me to put the past aside and get on with my life. God has forgiven me, and that's all that matters. So I'm giving you this ring to start things off—to promise you that I'm going to try to be everything you need, first as a friend, and when the time is right, a husband."

Kim's eyes became glassy again, but this time, no amount of blinking stopped her tears from overflowing.

"Are you proposing to me?"

Trent gave her a lopsided smile. "Not with just a little promise ring. But when the time is here, I promise you that I'll do it right." He paused, plucked the ring from her shaking fingers, and slipped it on her finger. It was a little big, but the saleswoman had promised they could size it after Christmas.

When the ring was in place, he rubbed his thumb over her finger, as if he could seal it in place. "I love you, Kim. I do want to marry you, but I don't want to rush things just because we've known each other nearly our whole lives. So take this ring as my promise that for once in my life, I'm going to do something right. I want to court you properly, take you out on dates and stuff, and then when the time is right, I want to propose the way it should happen. Maybe on a beach at sunset in the summertime. Something really romantic."

Kim pulled her hands away and rested them on his waist. "I love you, too, and I don't have to do all that dating stuff. I'd marry you tomorrow, but if you want to wait awhile, I don't need a promise ring for that."

Trent reached down to her hand to touch the ring on her finger.

"Really?"

"Really." She smiled and raised herself up on her tiptoes, bringing her face close enough for him to kiss her. Except he didn't want to do that in the middle of the church, in front of the people who were now starting to clean up after the Christmas banquet.

She raised herself up even more. "But don't get me wrong. I still want the ring. It's gorgeous. And perfect."

Instead of kissing her lips like he wanted to, Trent grasped her hand, lifted it to his lips, and kissed the finger with the ring, his ring, on it. "Then I think I'd like a short engagement. Not that this is an engagement. I have a feeling the engagement will come soon. This is just a Christmas present."

Kim smiled, warming Trent from the inside out, like he'd never been warmed before.

"And with this Christmas present," she said softly, "this is the best Christmas ever."

# *Kim's Beaded Angel Ornament*

Materials: Gold beading wire; 21 medium round white pearl
  beads for body (suggested 5 mm); 1 large round white
  pearl bead for head (suggested 7 mm); 14 small white
  pearl beads for arms (suggested 3 mm); 20 small gold
  beads for halo (suggested 3 mm); 2½ inches (or longer for
  large beads) ribbon-style lace (1½ inches wide) for wings;
  6 inches thick gold thread for hanger
Size: 2¼ inches tall when complete, not including hanger
  thread
Skill level: Easy
Time: About 20 minutes

## INSTRUCTIONS

1. Cut a piece of beading wire about 18 inches long (if you
   use larger beads, you will need a longer piece of wire).

2. String 6 medium beads; push to the center.

3. Begin layering as follows: String 5 medium beads on
   one side of the wire; work opposite end of wire through
   newly added beads so that both strands of wire are going
   through the beads and coming out each end, layering the
   5 beads above the 6 beads of the first row.

4. Continue to layer beads in the same manner with 1 less

bead on each new row, until you have one bead at the top. Beads will form a triangle.

5. String 7 small beads for arms on one side.

6. Go around the 7th bead and reinsert the wire through the 6th bead and the remaining arm beads to "return" it, then through the single medium bead. You will end up with both wires sticking out the same side.

7. Repeat step 6 for the other arm using the wire on that side.

8. In like manner, add the large white bead (head)by threading the wires through each side.

9. String all 20 gold beads on one wire, and thread it through the head to make the halo. Do not pull, but leave it loose.

10. String the other wire in like manner from the other side so that you have 2 wires going through the circle of halo beads and back out the sides of the head. Now pull the wires tight.

11. Thread both of the wires through the single medium bead (top of body triangle) as you did previously; pull wires to the back of the angel and set aside.

12. Pinch the center of the lace piece and tie one end of the gold thread around it. Do the same with the other end of the gold thread, making a large empty loop to be used to hang the angel.

13. Use the wires to fasten the wings to the back of the angel; clip the wires.

## GAIL SATTLER

Gail Sattler lives on the West Coast with her husband, three sons, two dogs, five lizards, and countless fish, many of which have names. Gail loves to write tales of romance that can be complete only with God in their center. She has had many books published by Barbour Publishing and its Heartsong Presents line. Gail was voted the Favorite Heartsong Presents Author for three years in a row and is now in the Heartsong Presents Author Hall of Fame. Visit Gail's Web page at www.gailsattler.com.

# A Letter to Our Readers

Dear Readers:

In order that we might better contribute to your reading enjoyment, we would appreciate your taking a few minutes to respond to the following questions. When completed, please return to the following: Fiction Editor, Barbour Publishing, Inc., P.O. Box 719, Uhrichsville, OH 44683.

1. Did you enjoy reading *Angels for Christmas*?
   ❏ Very much—I would like to see more books like this.
   ❏ Moderately—I would have enjoyed it more if _____
   _____
   _____

2. What influenced your decision to purchase this book?
   (Check those that apply.)
   ❏ Cover          ❏ Back cover copy      ❏ Title        ❏ Price
   ❏ Friends        ❏ Publicity            ❏ Other

3. Which story was your favorite?
   ❏ *Strawberry Angel*          ❏ *Angel Charm*
   ❏ *Angel on the Doorstep*     ❏ *An Angel for Everyone*

4. Please check your age range:
   ❏ Under 18       ❏ 18–24        ❏ 25–34
   ❏ 35–45          ❏ 46–55        ❏ Over 55

5. How many hours per week do you read? _____

Name _____

Occupation _____

Address _____

City _____ State _____ Zip _____

E-mail _____